SOMEONE IS AIMING FOR YOU
FOR YOU
& OTHER ADVENTURES

J.D. COWAN

Thank you to L. Jagi Lamplighter, those in the PulpRev and Superversive movements, Kukuruyo, John & Diane Cowan, and Phyllis Pascas Goodwyn.

Someone is always aiming for you all.

CONTENTS

Preface

These stories were written between 2017 and 2019, containing both my earliest written short story, as well as some of my most recent.

The goal was to provide the reader with a world of magic and danger not far from our own. Here, both miracles and monsters exist, and both heroes and villains roam the streets after dark. Anything can, and does, happen.

So enjoy your trip into the world of Summerside! You never know just what lurks around the next bend.

And remember: Someone is always aiming for you.

SOMEONE IS AIMING FOR YOU

The Seeker moved at night, like always. The licensed government dogs had free reign of Summerside—and the world—during the day, but it was different after sunset. Night was for the Crusaders—vigilantes who had no one to answer to, except God and their own consciences.

Neon signs beamed across trash-strewn streets. The smell of stale cigarettes, and dew from an afternoon rain shower, kept the public away. It was rather quiet for two in the morning, especially for Summerside.

He traveled down the sidewalk toward Calloway Row. No one paid him any mind despite his dress. He wore a leather jacket and a black mask over his pale white face. His dark boots walked across the dilapidated sidewalk as he passed around pedestrians. With his towering height, and his wild black hair blowing in the breeze, he would have scared anyone who saw him. But no one could see him.

He wouldn't let them.

"*I'm in position, sir,*" Condor said through the earpiece. "*I've got DeLuca in my sights. He's in place. What next?*"

"Sit tight," The Seeker said. "I have to pry the info about the Inner Light out of him. Anyone who has a lifeline to a supplier of Demon Blood would have to know something."

"*I'd rather not think about it. But he has a lot of nerve, hiding out in Calloway Row, of all places.*"

"Why? That place has been abandoned since a wannabe hero with earth powers went on a rampage years back. Leveled the whole place. DeLuca's owned it ever since."

"*Oh, yes, that's true. But you know who it's named after. Colossus Calloway is one of the first vigilantes from before the government got into the game. He died on his feet fighting wave after wave of scumbags during a riot. Legends say he fought for two days straight.*"

The Seeker smirked. "Well, aren't you a

history buff."

"*No, I just hate what Summerside has turned into.*"

"Don't worry about it, Condor. That's why I'm here."

The night was unseasonably cool for a dead-end city like Summerside. The place had been known for insufferable humidity, and it didn't change much when the sun ceded to the moon. Despite the weather, the heat never reached The Seeker, even when he leaped across rooftops or walked these streets. There were hotter places than Summerside. He'd seen them up close.

His bright green eyes shone like beacons even under the lamp posts. If he hadn't been certain no one could see his real form, he might have worried.

But he didn't worry. The Seeker didn't worry about anything.

He passed a bus stop where an irritated couple waited for their late ride. They barely acknowledged his presence as he walked by.

The burly man—a middle-aged alcoholic with rancid breath—tipped his hat at the behemoth in the black mask.

"Ma'am," he said to The Seeker.

"Good day," The Seeker replied.

The man in the leather jacket kept moving. He didn't correct the drunk. He didn't need to. The Seeker could have chosen to appear as a cop or a child instead, but there were few things as inconspicuous as an old woman. His illusion power worked its magic. All was as it should be.

"*Sir,*" Condor said. "*I'm sure you can get into the hotel like this. You always do. But what about when everything goes to hell? I can't cover you through walls. We don't all have powers.*"

Cool wind knocked against the Seekers' jacket. He had crossed into the upper-east side. The bright signs of the nightlife gave away to boarded up abandoned buildings, and an eerie quiet. Calloway Row and the Star Castle Hotel were not far off.

"You do what you can, Condor. I have to do more. I made a promise." Visions of the dead filled his thoughts. They always did. "Some might consider my power is a curse."

"*That's your business, sir.*"

"Summerside is my business. The Inner Light, especially. And don't call me *sir.*" He tightened the gloves around his hands, and passed under the last functional street lamp. The hotel awaited a block away. "I hunt scum," The Seeker said. "And tonight, I'm here to kill a monster."

~

The magic launched through DeLuca faster than any needle could push it. His bloodshot eyes allowed him to see the empty hotel suite in a hard hue of red. Wet euphoria shot through his system. Underneath his fattened skin and twitching muscles beat the heart of a devil. Nothing did the trick like Demon's Blood.

"Might wanna ease up on that, sir," Newman said. "That stuff messes with your head. I heard it can make you hear voices. There are all kinds of rumors about that Magician crap."

DeLuca chuckled. "I've heard them. It can drown your soul, right? Clean your brain out. It's just a strong drink that costs a pretty penny, moron. I don't care if it's made of baby blood. This is strong. Delicious."

"Sorry, sir."

DeLuca sat in his chair, staring at the fluorescent lights he had installed a week ago. The desk was put in at the same time. Delightful fire burned behind his eyeballs. The artificial lights pounded in his skull.

Of course, he would put up with it all. He had to hide in this torn-up old hotel. It was the only way to escape what was aiming for him.

He glanced at the rotting white walls, torn up red carpet, and dusty floors, and sneered. Ronald DeLuca did not belong in this moldy museum to bad taste. The voice in his head agreed.

"Hey," he said. He felt his chin with the back of his hand. Drool had pooled there. He wiped it clean. DeLuca removed a can of hairspray from his desk drawer. He didn't need it to color his roots, but it felt pleasant. Only his men knew he hid it there. No one could know he needed it for such a simple and shallow reason. DeLuca sprayed his scalp, and his nerves settled. The familiar scent coated his greying mane.

Across the room, his two men in black suits stood guard at the door. Newman and Rollins had their hands by their sides. DeLuca's best men could always be trusted. But tonight was different. One of them was performing their job *too* well. Rollins had been staring at DeLuca strangely.

"Hey!" DeLuca repeated.

"Yes, sir?" Newman asked. He stroked his carefully-parted blond hair. His bull face was as ugly as ever, though not as frightening as it should be. He feared his employer too much. "Is there a problem?"

"What was it that note said?" DeLuca tittered to himself. It wasn't funny, but the blood found it hilarious. "*Someone is Aiming at You?* What is that supposed to mean?"

Newman wouldn't look at him. He kept glancing out the giant window at the other end of the ancient suite. The man wouldn't flinch when told to put a bullet in his broad's head but watching someone drink Demon's Blood was just too much. He really did believe those rumors about the junk. Newman had always been a moron.

DeLuca ran a finger over his numb teeth. "Stupid prank from a stupid wannabe hero. Stupid fool is gonna get his head blown clear off his shoulders. Threaten me? Who does he think he is?"

"He's an urban legend," Newman said. "Some vigilante who sends notes to his victims before he strikes. There's no evidence he even exists, only hearsay. No footage, no eye-witness testimony, just insane mooks on the stand spilling their soft guts to the jury."

For some reason, Rollins glanced at his employer again. He'd always been the quiet one since he joined up a few years back. Barrie Heights had drawn him, and many others, to DeLuca. That was when he showed how much power he had over Summerside and crushed those who tried to take his property. Strong men like Rollins always buckled in awe of leaders like DeLuca, but he had been staring far too much tonight. Like Newman, Demon's Blood probably made the idiot uncomfortable. DeLuca ignored him.

"Crusaders are nothing," DeLuca said, emphasizing every syllable. "What did I do, kill his mommy and make him swear revenge? I've seen it before. These vigilantes are all pathetic. They can't have what I have, so they find excuses to take it away from me."

Rollins chuckled under his breath as he should and glanced out the large window.

Newman laughed as well. "Right, sir. There are powered types that are already clowns for the government. These Crusaders are a special brand of pathetic. They never last long, either."

"I'll kill him." DeLuca's stomach twisted for a moment. He groaned. "I will . . ."

"You alright, Mr. DeLuca?" Newman asked.

Rollins stared again.

"Stop looking at me!" DeLuca shouted.

Newman flinched and glanced at Rollins. He turned back to his employer, perplexed. "But, he's not looking at you, sir."

Rollins turned from the window and glanced at DeLuca. "Is something wrong, sir?"

Sweat rolled into DeLuca's eyes. For a second he thought he saw Rollins' beefy frame and grey suit replaced by a teenage boy. The idiot boy smiled at DeLuca, a smirk he'd flashed so many times. The brat thought he knew the answers to every question.

DeLuca rubbed his eyelids and glanced away from his men. A headache began to rumble. He shut his eyes tight. It was the blood affecting his head. It had to be. That Magician said it would make him see strange things, but it was harmless. It was just a drink, after all.

When he opened his eyes, his son was gone again. The office was as it should be—abandoned and dilapidated. His men still stood by the door.

DeLuca breathed a sigh of relief. The dead stay dead.

Then the power went out.

~

Aldo Richards swore when the hallway lights flickered off. He already hated the abandoned Star Castle Hotel and that he had to waste his night patrolling it, but now he had to do it in the dark. What an annoying job. The enforcer straightened his tie, took out his small flashlight, and sighed. He could have been at the club by now.

It would have been less infuriating if Jameson Riggs wasn't taking a nap in the john. That moron was supposed to be patrolling with Aldo. Mr. DeLuca's paranoia over the Seeker since he first got that note days ago had only gotten worse. If he knew that Riggs was slacking, the big man would probably put two in the stooge's head himself.

"*Someone is Aiming at You,*" Aldo repeated under his breath.

Graffiti all over Summerside contained

that stupid slogan. Aldo didn't get why. It was the motto of a boogeyman invented by bored teenagers. Sure there were all sorts of people out there with powers, but it wasn't magic. Nothing unexplainable. Nobody had the powers this myth supposedly did. But people would always be a thorn in his side. They had a way of looking for a light in the darkest corners. People never failed to disappoint Aldo.

Old floorboards creaked under his careful footing. The third floor was just as disheveled as every other in the Star Castle Hotel. All the rooms had the same ugly green floral wallpaper—centuries out of date—and the same rotting dressers and beds covered with broken mattresses. At least, the power outage meant he didn't have to see them.

Mold and dust tickled his nose hairs. He stifled a sneeze and shook the filth from his dark blue suit. Riggs was taking too long.

He laughed to no one. "Guards all over this dump, and I'm worried about being alone." He raked his flashlight across the hall. Dusty tables and old paintings laid untouched and forgotten. The only light left shone from the window at the end of the hall. Cascading moonlight ran against the musty carpet. What a nice night to be stranded here.

"Yo, Aldo," Riggs said. "What's goin' on?" The moron hobbled down the hall, shuffling his belt around his waist. Riggs waved at Aldo with his free hand, as tubby and careless as always. The floorboards squealed under his weight.

Sometimes, it was hard to believe he was really an enforcer. He was the complete opposite of Aldo's hard worn leathery face and tall, mus-cular build. The rat-like face of Riggs squinted against the flashlight as he brushed his short brown hair back. For someone who slept on the can, the idiot looked way too happy. Riggs was always joking. Aldo never liked Riggs much.

"The power went out?" Riggs asked.

"Yeah." Aldo's attention went back to the window. He ran a thick fist across his sweaty brow. "Mr. DeLuca is probably having a spasm attack."

"Well, I can see why. Heard the rumors? The Butcher broke down on the stand, and the media wouldn't even report what he said. They say all this freak has to do is touch you, and he knows everything about you. He doesn't even need skin on skin contact. It's crazy. He can turn into anyone, too. He's like a monster."

Aldo shook his head. "Shut up, Riggs. That is not possible. You can only have one power. Whether it's Physical, Mental, Elemental, or Abnormal, there are only four types. And there are no powers like the ones this Seeker supposedly has. Either he's a Physical Type who can change who he looks like, or he's a Mental Type that can read thoughts. He can't do both."

"Maybe he works in a team with another freak."

"Then someone would have reported it by now. No camera footage, either. No, he just doesn't exist."

"Hey, Aldo," Riggs said, speaking slowly. "Why are you still looking out that window?"

Aldo flinched. He didn't realize he was still staring out into Summerside. The moon was in a perfect position. It reminded him of a bad night years ago. He tried to shake it off.

Riggs scratched his chin. "You look like you've seen a spook."

"Just thinking about old times," Aldo said. "Before Crusaders rose up and tried to ruin everything. Still, I'm surprised you even bothered coming back. I can barely see anything."

"Why did Mr. DeLuca ask us to come out to this relic, anyway? He's not scared of anyone."

Aldo shrugged, finally pulling himself from the window. "The rumors say this guy has only been around for a few years, and he only moves at night. He comes and goes like a fever dream and messes with your head. That's bad for business. If he exists, he doesn't need to punch through metal doors to be a threat to Mr. DeLuca."

"Crusaders are mostly rumors."

"The only description anyone has given has been of a figure with hard bright green eyes. They only got that? Can't say I buy it. I also heard kids in the playground say that he poses with one arm out pretending to shoot his victim. Give me a break."

"Sure," Riggs said, "but then, who sent the note? No one knows how deep Mr. DeLuca is into this Demon Blood mess. You think the sender of the note is just some pretender?"

"Everyone is a pretender, friend. It was just a prank. And *if* he shows up, he's dead. We have enough wannabe heroes working during the day. Night is our time. Crusaders need to learn that."

Wind slammed against the window glass.

Aldo swore and dragged his flashlight over it.

Riggs sighed and stared at the floor.

"You're alright," Aldo said. "Get a grip on yourself."

"Neither of us is alright." Riggs slowly shook his head. "Especially not tonight."

"Of course, we are. Mr. DeLuca wants us to do one thing. All we have to do is squash a bug."

"Sorry to hear that, Aldo." Riggs rubbed his knuckles together, and chuckled. He glanced up at Aldo, his blue eyes beady and abnormally large. "You're in so deep you just can't see it."

"What?"

The right hook smashed against Aldo's cheek. His brain somersaulted. A left knocked him backwards. Riggs had lost his mind. Aldo went for his gun, but Riggs clasped Aldo's right hand. His grip was a vice. Then, Aldo was off the ground, and the ceiling became the floor. He crashed down onto the hard floorboards.

He tried to get up, but a kick struck him in the gut. The shoes were like concrete. Aldo rolled over, breathless and coughing.

"But then," Riggs said, his voice echoing in Aldo's head, "if you were smart, you wouldn't be in this line of work at all. Riggs has nothing on your filthy soul."

Aldo tried to yell, but his throat got stuck in coughs.

"Did you know he used to pour sugar in gas tanks when he was a boy? That habit never really died. But compared to you? Riggs is just low level. A wannabe tough."

Aldo's blood froze. He spotted Riggs' eyes again. They were no longer blue. Bright green daggers stared down at him. For an instant, he thought he saw a pale white face with wild black hair, but it quickly blurred into the darkness of the old hotel. Despite his throbbing skull, Aldo wasn't seeing double. This man was not Riggs.

The green eyes spoke to him. "Adrian Jones died during a full moon like tonight, didn't he?"

"Shut up," Aldo said. His heart jumped. Nobody should have known about their connection.

"Your soul is dirty, Aldo Richards."

"Wait! Stop!" The lump rose in Aldo's throat. "Who are you?"

"Someone will be with you soon," the green-eyed man said. "Sit tight."

The figure shaped like Riggs fled down the hall. Aldo struggled to get up after him. But he had a more pressing concern. There was someone else in front of Aldo now. The figure faded into the world like the ghost of a forgotten dream. Aldo's legs shook, and he lost his balance.

A dead man stood in the center of the hall. Aldo knew this middle-aged man in a clean, olive-colored suit. He had his hands folded behind his back and smiled pleasantly at Aldo.

"No!" Aldo screamed. He crawled backwards on his elbows. The window frame banged against the back of his head. Moonlight fell against the phantom. "What kind of joke is this, you freak?" Aldo couldn't look away from the dead man. "What did you do to me? I know you don't know about him! Riggs? Where are you? Don't leave me here!"

"You are alone," the dead man said.

Fear dripped down Aldo's neck. Goose-flesh spread all over. Dead men don't talk.

"Do you recognize the bullet hole over my left eyebrow?" The dead man pointed to the exact location. A thin stream of blood dripped down.

Aldo's teeth chattered. The dead man slowly stepped toward him. The old floorboards did not creak.

"My son drinks a lot these days. He still thinks about me all the time. He's a lot like you. How much do you drink to forget your lousy aim, Aldo?"

There was no malice in the dead man's smile. It had to be an illusion, but it didn't make sense. Nobody knew about this man's connection to Aldo. Mr. DeLuca didn't even know.

"Leave me alone," Aldo squeaked. "Nobody can pin it to me! They can't!"

The dead man's brown eyes held an impenetrable sadness. It hid a truth that Aldo could not make out. This was real. It wasn't an illusion.

Aldo went for his gun, slapping against his jacket, but it was gone. His legs shook once more. Adrian Jones continued forward. The truth crashed in on Aldo: he was going to die.

"The Seeker took that from you. He knows your kind. But he didn't call me here. No, not specifically. He can't even see me. But you can, Aldo."

"Stay away!"

"Hold still," the dead man said. "I'm going to show you something. It won't be so bad. Do you want to see what lies in the shadows of this world?"

The moonlight shone over the dead man, just as it did the night he was killed by Aldo. It had been past midnight then as well. A pink neon sign had hovered over the bar during that humid night. The shots were fired, and Aldo had hit his mark. Eventually. There were no witnesses. It was a night that never went away.

Now it was back again.

The dead man's hand touched Aldo's shoulder. A chill colder than death launched through his bloodstream, and the rising scream was choked out of him.

~

Those who heard rumors of The Seeker believed one of two things. He was either a man out for revenge or a criminal knocking off competition. None of them would think to reference Lenora, a town leveled by those such as the Inner Light. In this world where humanity had come back from the brink of extinction when powers had appeared, it was easy to forget threats beyond them. The comforts of a civilized world mean that much can be forgotten out of convenience. Voices screamed in the victims' nightmares—memories of those who lay dying. The Seeker had seen them. No one else could see what lay in the dark corners: but he could.

The Seeker had a gift, and he would use it.

Condor had warned him earlier from the earpiece. *"Sir, are you sure about this?"*

"Don't call me *sir*, Condor. DeLuca's men at the docks told me everything about the layout. Numbers mean little to me. All I have to do is touch them once. You know that."

"I do. But do you think DeLuca knows about magic?"

"The fat fool knows something, I'm certain. Stand by for further directions, Condor."

"Alright, moving into position. Got a few more floors to go. Burn it up when you need help."

"That is the plan." The Seeker slunk up the stairs. The seventh floor had the most guards. He'd memorized the rotation thanks to Aldo Richards. He had been told where everyone would be, and now that knowledge was The Seeker's. DeLuca was still up on the target floor.

The Seeker changed his appearance into Aldo Richards, and took out the first guard he saw. It was easy. He dragged the poor sap into the bathroom and let the stall door meet his skull a few times. Of course, he didn't feel bad about it. This creep, Carlo Peck, was worse than either Aldo or Riggs He left the heap on the toilet to sleep it off.

The Star Castle Hotel was like any of the old hotels in Summerside. Every floor was built exactly the same, with the same garish rotting furniture, and the same awful green and white floral wallpaper: a reminder of brighter days. Years ago, a bomber took out most of Calloway Row which left it abandoned. Everything there had been left to decay.

He kept his eye on the halls. The roving guards were about as predictable as the ugly décor.

The Seeker had it mapped out in his head. The next guard in the rotation, Mitchell, would be taking a smoke in the sixth room on the left. It was a guarantee. Everyone knew his habits.

This was the easiest part of the job and the most fun.

The Seeker moved into the room and closed the door behind him. He crossed the torn up floor into the bathroom. Mitchell stared into the mirror with a lighter to his face and a cigarette dangling from his mouth, checking his teeth. He jumped when he spotted the intruder.

Despite himself, The Seeker smiled.

"Carlo?" Mitchell said. "What the hell are you doing here?"

"Are you aware that Carlo is sleeping with your wife, Mitch? Aldo, Riggs, and the guys down the hall already know."

"I don't—"

The Seeker leaped across the room. His fist dashed against the scumbag's nose. Mitch's skull launched backwards with the rest of him. The back of his head shattered the mirror. Memories rushed into The Seeker's mind as he threw a few more jabs. Mitchell fell limp to the dirty tiles.

The Seeker saw everything. Six years ago, Mitchell broke a teenager's fingers for scratching the paint on his convertible. A messy scene. He shattered the slim kid's jaw and a few bones before leaving him in an alley. That was tame compared to what he did later that night.

It made The Seeker's job easier when he saw visions like that.

Mitchell struggled to rise to his knees. "Rotten bastard. You're who the boss wants."

The Seeker kicked him in the gut. Mitchell

dropped, and his attacker brought his boot on top of his head. The scum went out like a streetlight in the west end.

"I guess you didn't know what your woman was like," The Seeker said, kneeling beside Mitchell. He transformed into the creep, and his voice morphed with his appearance. "But I don't think it's gonna work out. You're both screwed up. No counseling session is going to help you."

The Seeker breathed deep. His next play would be sticky, but he'd done it many times before. Thankfully, Mitchell remained unmoving beside the toilet.

He leaned out into the hall. Now to pass the buck.

"He's here! He's here!" The Seeker shouted in his new voice. He shut the bathroom door behind him, sealing the unconscious Mitchell inside.

Calls bellowed down the dark hall. A flood of footsteps hurried toward him. The four guards on the east side of the seventh floor crowded the doorway. Flashlights shone across his face.

"What are you babbling about, Mitchell?"

"The guy who sent Mr. DeLuca the note!"

the fake said. "He's in there. He tried to take me down, but I got him first. You won't believe it—he can transform into other people!"

The false Mitchell led them inside. The real Mitchell remained unconscious on his stomach, still beside the toilet. The others all gasped as they crowded around the lump.

"I gotta tell Ray, Dominic, and Eli, about this," fake Mitchell said. "Me and Eli had a bet, and I intend to collect on this."

"Wait," the one with the overbite said. "How do we know you're not the fake?"

"Because the fake couldn't have known about the bet." The Seeker rolled his eyes. "Work with me, Reynolds. We had a silent bet, right, Stevie? Only the three of us."

The one on the right nodded. "It's true. Fake couldn't have known that."

The Seeker patted Stevie's upper arm, deliberately shouldered past Reynolds, and brushed the final two by the door. No one objected to his exit.

"Keep him here," fake Mitchell said. "I'm gonna go get the others, and we'll take him to Mr. DeLuca. He's gonna wanna see this freak personally."

They were all tagged and didn't know it. Once his touch worked its magic, it only took a few moments. He made three steps down the hall and shifted into a run. Then it happened.

"Who the hell?" Reynolds yelled.

Screams and gunshots erupted from the room. The chaos had begun.

The remaining three guards on the floor met The Seeker in the middle of the hall. He feigned a shortness of breath and fell to one knee. The trio arrived at his side, asking all sorts of clueless questions. He let them help him up.

"The freak who sent the note is here!" fake Mitchell said.

"Is that what's going on?" Eli asked. He scratched an old knife wound on his cheek.

"You guys can handle him, right? I gotta go tell Mr. DeLuca he's here."

"Right," Eli replied. They all nodded to each other. "We got this."

They all ran off, oblivious as to what would hit them in mere moments. The Seeker couldn't feel bad. They were even worse than Mitchell.

"Someone will be with you shortly," The Seeker whispered.

Then he heard the screeching.

"No!" Eli screamed down the hall. Shouts and gunshots followed his own.

The Seeker kept moving.

At the end of the hall, more men came running down the stairs. He told them the same story he gave the others and made sure to tag them all. They wouldn't see it coming.

Soon enough, the seventh floor was filled with anguished cries and madness. It was always the same with this power. The Seeker left them to it.

He had a job to finish.

~

The Seeker was spotted in the building. DeLuca cursed as he drank the last of his flask of Demon Blood. The noxious stink of burnt wood choked him as he forced it down, and the rough sandpaper texture made it more difficult; but the buzz arrived instantaneously. He lived for this. DeLuca threw the empty canister to the floor. Not enough! The Magician could always make him more, for a price, but not if this Seeker got to him first.

Newman and Rollins stood by the locked door in the dark of the suite. Newman stared at his phone, while Rollins continued watching the window. DeLuca was ready to kill them himself.

His chest tightening, DeLuca shot up from his rotting desk. "How is he not dead?"

Newman dropped the phone into his pocket. His face fell, refusing to look at his boss.

"Well?" DeLuca asked.

"Ph-phones are down, sir."

"The power, the phones . . . the maggot cut all communications." A tickle in his throat caused DeLuca to laugh. "Amusing. Very clever."

"Sir?"

DeLuca wiped drool from his chin. He sprayed his hair. The chemicals calmed his rage. "The last message you got was from the first floor, correct?"

"Yes, Thomas told us the others were acting insane. Like they were seeing ghosts or ghouls. Then the phones cut out."

"Just like the rumors. It looks like this Seeker wants a piece of me after all."

Rollins grimaced. He went for his pistol at the mention of The Seeker's name. The man could be the model of a good employee. His brown eyes blazed. DeLuca couldn't stifle a proud grin.

"Cool it, Rollins," DeLuca said. "We've still got aces up our sleeves. The Crusader won't be able to get into this room without coming through that door behind you. It doesn't matter how sneaky he is. If anyone comes through there, we just blow them away. Easy."

"He's just one guy, Mr. DeLuca," Newman interrupted. "He won't make it this far."

"You idiot." DeLuca rubbed his temples. "You don't know anything about this Seeker, do you?"

"Rumors. I assumed that's all they were."

"You would. If you weren't quick with a trigger, your idiocy would have killed you years ago. Did you hear about what happened to Paulo Rand and his men? One went comatose, another ran out into the streets screaming and shooting at shadows, and the third beat his own pals into traction. Paulo himself jumped out a sixth story window. Moron's lucky he's still alive."

"Paulo Rand," Newman mumbled. "That sounds familiar."

"It should. He's the mook who broke down on the stand screaming about the angel of death whispering in his ear. Crazy as a cockroach. Right now, he's at a high class bed and breakfast where rubber rooms are mandatory."

A red sheen broke the shade of the room. The color split into DeLuca's head. He ran to the window and pushed the curtains open, letting in a crimson moon. He couldn't escape the vision of blood. What was this feeling? For some reason, he laughed.

"Sir," Rollins said. "If the stories are real, that Seeker should be here soon."

Newman scratched his carefully-combed hair. "Don't bother him with that, Rollins."

DeLuca crossed the room and sat on his desk. He faced the window; he couldn't look anywhere else. Tickles not unlike wriggling bugs shimmied through his bones. The blood was still working its magic.

"Sir?" Rollins asked.

The world was on fire. The Demon's Blood played tricks with his head, but it amused him to no end. Delicious. None of this was real.

"Keep alert, idiots. We've got a real devil on the way."

"Are you ready to meet eternity, Mr. DeLuca?"

DeLuca smiled and turned around. It was what he was waiting for. Death was already here.

The gun fired. His head jerked backwards with the impact. Crimson red overtook the world, and a murky void enveloped him.

~

DeLuca's forehead burned like hot coals. He blinked his eyes open and felt around his suit. Everything was where it should be. He touched the bloodied old carpet below his stiff fingers.

On the floor near the door lay Newman. He'd been shot twice and left to bleed out.

Across from the twitching body stood Rollins, firearm in hand. He had just unlocked the door to the hall and was swinging it open when DeLuca sat up.

"Very impressive," DeLuca said. His vision blurred and reddened. "You were quicker on the draw than Newman."

Rollins jumped, turned, and pointed his weapon at DeLuca once more. His eyes were as wide as his square jaw.

"What's wrong?" DeLuca asked. "Have you seen a ghost?"

"I shot you."

"In the head!" DeLuca climbed up slowly. His muscles ached. He wiped off the stream of blood dripping down his forehead with his thumb and licked it clean. Delicious. "It's odd that I'm not dead, isn't it?"

"You don't have any powers. I know you don't."

"No, I don't. You've done your research. You must have been waiting a long time for your chance. Though I'm not sure what you hate me for. Don't really care, either. I am thirsty." A blinding heat cut through DeLuca's thoughts. "Aren't you going to shoot me again?"

"I've been waiting too long," Rollins said, shaking his head. "I picked this exact moment. You were distracted, meeting with the Inner Light, worrying about that myth, and constantly looking over your shoulder. I just needed to earn your trust. I waited for someone like this psycho to show up and scare you into hiding like the rat you are."

"And you still couldn't kill me."

Rollins fired two more shots into DeLuca's chest. His former superior did not fall. DeLuca whistled at his numb wounds. Rollins turned and ran for the door.

"Slow down, friend!" DeLuca shouted. The squat man dashed the full length of the room toward Rollins. It felt like taking two steps. DeLuca clung onto the back of his attacker's neck. Rollins froze at the touch. DeLuca only needed one hand to hold him still. He lifted him off the ground. Rollins struggled, but it was futile.

DeLuca laughed. "I didn't say you could leave."

He flung Rollins back into the room. The large man crashed into DeLuca's desk, smashing pieces of wood off the impact area. The hairspray can rolled past DeLuca to the door. That was fine with DeLuca: he didn't need that junk any longer.

Rollins wheezed and slumped back against the desk.

DeLuca kneeled before his victim. "You're still my employee, Rollins. Show some respect when you speak to a superior, yeah?" DeLuca shoved Rollins. He only meant to pin the big man back against the desk, but the traitor cried out as flesh parted. Blood poured onto DeLuca's arm like an overfilled barrel of wine. His limb had jabbed into Rollins' stomach.

The large man yelled.

"Oh, I'm sorry," DeLuca said. Saliva dripped from his mouth. He wanted to laugh and laugh some more. For some reason, he found everything funny now. Everything, except his reddening, overheated skin. Imaginary snakes squirmed through his veins, and his organs were cooking on an invisible grill. But he couldn't stop smiling. His bones and skin stretched and sharpened like some demonic multi-tool. The Demon's Blood was part of him now.

His victim struggled against DeLuca's iron grip, but nothing could break free from him now.

"Demon's Blood is amazing, isn't it? The Inner Light is spectacular. So glad I got in with these freaks! Hey, so much for those rumors, huh, Newman? Oh, right. He's dead."

Rollins spat blood.

"I'll have to get in contact with the Magician again," DeLuca said. "This junk gets more potent every time I use it. Amazing. I never thought it was this strong! The rumors said nothing about this. It's only blood, after all! If I keep this up, I could be a god."

"Not even close," someone said.

DeLuca turned to meet a boot to his face. Cartilage snapped. It knocked him off Rollins and towards the center of the floor. Boards creaked as he landed.

His vision cleared as he got up. A figure stood before him. It was a pale-faced man in a leather jacket and black mask, standing at well over six feet. He held a lighter in one hand, and DeLuca's hairspray can in the other. The Seeker's eyes were an odd green color.

A thousand voices screamed at once in DeLuca's head. "Seeker!"

"Here's a preview of where you're going next," The Seeker said. He lit the lighter and sprayed the can.

The resulting blowtorch burned into DeLuca. Screams choked in his throat. His body pulled in a million different directions. The voices didn't like it. They all wanted blood, and they would have it.

Curtains and carpets were set ablaze, as was the furniture and desk. The entire room burned. The fire clung to DeLuca. Eventually, the can ran out, and The Seeker tossed it aside. He pocketed the lighter and raised his fists to DeLuca.

As he burned, DeLuca lunged for The Seeker. His right arm stretched like burnt rubber, skin blackened and smoking. The Seeker caught his deformed arm and twisted it. He spun around the god. Momentarily, DeLuca thought he saw two green circles staring back at him in the fire. The Seeker bent the limb as he spun sideways and brought his elbow down on DeLuca's arm. Bone shattered, and DeLuca screamed.

He didn't scream because it hurt. DeLuca didn't feel anything at all. He screamed because every voice in his head told him he should. They ricocheted through his brain, bouncing up against his thoughts. He fell to one knee, and his arm hung limply at his side. This was not the treatment a god deserved!

DeLuca looked up at The Seeker. But he wasn't The Seeker anymore. "This is . . ."

In the wannabe hero's place was a young boy, no older than sixteen. He had rusty blonde hair, bright blue eyes, and a suit as black as DeLuca's right arm. The boy smiled.

"Get out of here!" DeLuca yelled. "You aren't real!"

The boy raised a handgun and fired four times into DeLuca's chest. DeLuca stumbled back despite the lack of pain. More flames licked against him from the burning room. He couldn't die.

The boy morphed once again. This time he became a middle-aged man in a grey suit. DeLuca's heart seized momentarily.

"You killed that boy," DeLuca's father said. "He had a conscience. He told the cops about the women and the contacts. Jeffrey was spoiled but not evil. He couldn't stand the pacts and the bids for power. The Demon's Blood scared him. The Inner Light terrified him. So you put a bounty on him to Summerside's worst and looked the other way. Your own son, Ronald! Despicable. What makes you such a coward? Is it because your kind is so powerless in a world where people can walk through walls as easily as they can walk into your head?"

Blinding heat spiked in DeLuca's skull. His thoughts numbed, stiffened. "Shut up!"

"Do you know why I'm here?"

"Seeker," DeLuca's voice spoke on its own. "You waste your time. You will not find the Inner Light here. The Demon's Blood has been drained."

"This is why I'm here, DeLuca. You can barely talk anymore, can you?"

Anger built from DeLuca's confusion.

"Shut up!"

"Those same two words, huh?"

He charged The Seeker, ignoring the fake's visage. His broken right arm twisted forward, the enemy ducked, and the limb slammed into the opposite wall, crunching in the impact. Drywall cracked and spilled out. The Seeker sidestepped, unaware of what was coming.

DeLuca brought up his left arm up in a sweeping motion with blinding speed. His blackened appendage crashed into the enemy's right side. The Seeker flew sideways through the fire and bashed into the right side of the room, indenting the wall.

The Seeker hit the burning carpet on all fours. He coughed and wiped his mouth clean. Once more, DeLuca saw a man with a pale white face, leather jacket, untamed black hair, and green eyes staring back at him. No more tricks! The Seeker fled across the room.

Angry joy took control of DeLuca. The vigilante was scared! DeLuca's arms shot forward again and again, striking into the burning walls and breaking it. The Seeker jumped, slid, and tumbled to escape him. The gnat slipped through. He reached the window at the back of the room.

The realization that he was facing a god surely panicked him. There was no escape now.

"You are out of your league!" DeLuca shouted. His blood chilled and his thoughts dulled. "Mortals are nothing to gods!"

The Seeker stopped at the giant window, his back to the blinding night behind the glass. "I can't stay away. I've seen what your Magician is capable of. I know what the Inner Light is. Do you know what happened to Lenora?"

"That old town? One of you powered freaks went wild and leveled it with enough earthquakes to cave the planet in. That's why the government tries to keep you on a short leash."

"No. That's what they were told. I was there. It was one of those Magicians, the Inner Light, who did it. Just like the man who gave you that Demon's Blood you've been slurping like a parched horse. They grow because of people like you. You invited something into your home that you never should have."

DeLuca wobbled toward The Seeker, his insides oddly hollow. "So what? Is this an appeal to my sense of mercy?"

"I'm afraid I'm too late for you, DeLuca." He pointed a finger at the god. "Your soul is dirtier than anyone in this building, but it looks like I won't need to lift another finger to stop you. It's over. I just needed to waste time."

"Stop your babbling and say what you mean!"

"You're dead."

"What?" A pit grew in his stomach and died out instantly.

Green eyes pierced the flames between DeLuca and The Seeker. "You were drunk on Demon's Blood when Rollins shot and killed you. It clung to your dying body to keep you alive and feed off you. It's the only thing keeping you alive. And it's running out."

DeLuca glanced at his fingers. He could barely move them. His eyes refused to look where he wanted. Breaths came tighter and tighter. His bones contracted, and his head thumped endlessly inside his skull. The screaming in his brain grew unbearable.

"Shut up!" He only had a small bit of energy left. It would give him what he needed—the Demon's Blood always did before. He would use it to slice this interloper apart. "I'll give you the quiet death dear old Dad never got!"

Glass shattered over The Seeker's head.

Whipping wind cut through the blazing flames. The bullet struck dead center into DeLuca's chest. His heart burned. Vibrations ran across his stiffened body, and his march ceased. The god fell backwards into the burning carpet.

Blood spurted from his mouth. He couldn't rise.

"You dug your own grave," The Seeker said. Bright green eyes stared down at DeLuca through the flames. He stood over DeLuca like the specter of death.

From the corner of the fire, DeLuca spotted Rollins. The big fool was cringing by the door to the hallway, holding his guts in. The Seeker ignored DeLuca and approached the moron on the other side of the blaze. He didn't look back. Did they forget they had a new god?

DeLuca tried to shout after the Crusader, but his voice was choked shut. The fire leaped from the carpets and walls onto his melting flesh. It tore through his blackened skin as his senses dulled and died. Pain returned worse than ever before.

"Someone will be with you soon, DeLuca."

He lost The Seeker in the fire. Two figures stood over him looking down at his crumpled body. His son and father were dressed as immaculately as ever. Then, countless other dead men and women joined them. He knew them all. They stared down at his burning body.

And they were getting closer.

Screams of strangers overtook his voice. They pitched higher and higher into the darkness, until he found his voice among them.

Then he fell limp under the cascading inferno.

~

The Seeker stepped through the flames towards Rollins. The wounded gangster still had his gun at his side and showed no intention of surrender. He grimaced at the vigilante and then turned and ran down the hallway.

"Wait!"

"Stay back, freak!"

The Seeker pursued through the smoky hall. Rollins fired two shots back and kept running.

Both gunshots missed The Seeker, striking the ceiling and the left side of the hall. Rollins wasn't aiming in his panic. The big man threw open the doors to the stair, and disappeared into the dark.

The Seeker kept pursuit, his weapon still drawn. A thin stream of blood led down the stairs. Echoing footsteps bounced floors below.

Sparks sprayed in the gap between the railing and the stairs. Shots rang off the steps. The Seeker returned fire and kept moving. He was closing the gap between them. There were only a few more floors before ground level.

"Why are you running?" The Seeker asked.

"You wanted DeLuca, and you got him." Rollins struggled for breaths. "I saw what you did up there, and you aren't doing it to me. It's over. You won. Just go away!"

More shots clanged against steps. The Seeker continued after his prey.

Rollins shouldered open the emergency exit. It swung shut just as his pursuer reached the bottom floor.

The Seeker pushed it open and was smacked in the face with the cold air of the night.

Across the alleyway, he spotted a large dumpster. The Seeker peered around the door-frame and found Rollins running down the right side of the alley. The vigilante went for the dumpster, sliding behind it. The big man limped forward, his pace slowing.

Sirens went off in the distance. There wasn't much time left.

Rollins loped and dropped his firearm in his rush. He tipped over and leaned against the brick. Papers and other loose trash blew past him. Finally, Rollins slid to the pavement with his back to the wall. He sat on the dirty ground, his arms and legs spread, unmoving. An old newspaper flew by his face in the breeze. The big man's head tilted back.

The Seeker kept Aldo's handgun trained on Rollins and sidled up to the downed thug.

"You got me," Rollins rasped. He pulled his suit jacket open. There were no weapons. However, red stained his shirt. Rollins sighed and let his hands fell limply back to his side. "Two in the head, please. The faster, the better."

The Seeker knelt down, his weapon still trained on his prey. "That's not why I'm here."

Rollins spat blood on the concrete. "Don't act like you're some kind of hero. I saw what you did to DeLuca. I've heard the rumors. You're a monster. If you had any sense in that broken brain, you'd turn that piece on yourself."

"DeLuca and your whole gang got into business with the Inner Light. He drank down Demon's Blood like a greedy pig. He deserved the end he got."

"And what about me?"

"What about you, Rollins? You have heard about Lenora? That was what your boss was trafficking in. You deal with the Inner Light, and this is what you get."

"Lenora? That was nothing. DeLuca has been in that game for years. *Had* been. You heard about the Barrie Heights district? That was fifteen years ago. He razed it himself to provoke a gang war to cash in on reconstruction. The government spent months cleaning that fight up, but it didn't stop the whole place from going to hell. A lot of good men and women died. Families."

The Seeker scratched the top of his wild black hair. He knew about Barrie Heights. It wasn't because of the Inner Light that the whole place became a warzone, but they almost certainly capitalized on it just like DeLuca. Free blood, flesh, and bone, are a villain's stock in trade.

"I know what DeLuca's done," the green-eyed Crusader said. "But what about you? How clean is your soul, Rollins? What was your boss to you?"

"He was a cockroach." Terror momentarily flashed across Rollins' face. "I pretended for a long time. I waited, watched, and picked my moments. I did what I was told. It took everything I had left to become one of them. I was there when they put two in the skull of DeLuca's kid. I joined in when Newman and Aldo and the others made bets on which of the Aldine brothers would survive drowning the longest. I saw the Demon's Blood rot DeLuca's mind. I had to play the part. I watched, and I waited for the right moment. Now it's done. Now there's nothing left."

"And you waited for me to threaten DeLuca to make your play."

Rollins sunk back. His eyes grew glassy. "It doesn't matter. It's over now. He killed them. They're gone, and now so is he."

"Let me see for myself."

Rollins shrugged, and groaned. "I don't care what you do. I'm done. If you want to turn my head into goo like you did DeLuca, it makes no difference."

"I can't see what you will see," The Seeker said. "So, I don't know what this will do to your mind. But it might save you."

"I knew you were mental," Rollins said, laughing and wheezing. "All Crusaders are, from what I've heard. But what are you even talking about? I'm not walking out of here."

The Seeker shook his head. "I have three powers. One I was born with, one I was given, and one that resulted from their combination. My touch is the first one."

"And?"

"I can read you. Hold still."

The Seeker placed his left hand on Rollins' forehead. The Crusader's power kicked in, and Rollins flinched.

Memories weaved from a lush tapestry spiraled out before The Seeker. Birthdays, picnics, funerals, weddings, fights, celebrations, and tragedies—all became one. The life of a man became a string in the twine ball of humanity. People, places, and seasons, swirled in a vortex, spinning into a vivid dream. It became real. The tidal wave crashed against his mind and soul.

The Seeker removed his hand and let out a deep breath. He saw it all. The information he needed was in there, but that wasn't what mattered right now. He stood up and let his weapon fall to his side.

"I mentioned Lenora because I was there, Tim." He ignored Rollins's twitch. "I saw people die. Good people. The government covered it up and buried the bodies and forgot about it. They went on with their stupid, meaningless jobs. But I didn't forget. I still hunt. Every single night. I won't let anything like Lenora, or Barrie Heights, happen again. This is who I am. You still have time to become what you were always meant to be, before you let yourself rot away. I will leave you with that chance. Now, just sit there and wait. I don't know if you'll see Christine, or little Lorraine, but you'll see somebody. They always show up. That's my third power."

Wind blew trash across the empty alley. Sirens drew closer. The Seeker turned back down the alley. He had to get moving.

"What are you talking about?" Rollins called after him.

"Someone will be with you soon enough. Don't worry, they can't hurt you."

"Who are you?"

The Seeker did not turn back. "Your last chance."

As The Seeker reached the end of the alley, the lights flicked back on. Calloway Row had its power back. Condor yelled in his ear about one thing or another, but The Seeker was already planning ahead. This job was over, and it was time to move on.

He heard Rollins talking far behind him now. For the first time that night, there was no terror. Perhaps, they were wrong about his power being a curse. He grinned.

The Seeker looked up to the large graffiti sprayed on the wall halfway up the nearby building. It said "*Someone is Aiming at You*" in stylized red letters. He laughed to himself, wondering if the kid who wrote it knew just what he was talking about. Summerside was in for a rude awakening.

"Yes, Condor, I hear you. It was a good shot. And stop calling me *sir*. I'll meet you at the rendezvous point in fifteen minutes. You'll never guess what's next."

ENDLESS NIGHTS IN VILLAIN CITY

~20 Years Ago~

I have always hated the sun, but it was particularly harsh on the day I abandoned it. In a world of light, I lived for the dark, and the day was particularly bright at the time I fell upon the Truth.

Bystanders, children and adults, elderly and adolescents, of all shapes and sizes crowded the crime scene. They waited by the police barriers as the criminals were taken down. The fools didn't understand anything. Cries broke through the heavy humidity of the late summer afternoon.

These bystanders were cheering as the pair of government dogs, one with fire breath and one with no clear power I could understand, walked out of the apartment complex dragging the perpetrator out in handcuffs with them. A pathetic attempt at a robbery concluded in this embarrassment. The entire event lasted twenty minutes, and then the wannabe freedom fighter ended up caught. Villains like this were a useless bunch and gave better ones a bad name.

As the so-called heroes loaded their captive into the police van, the crowd went wild. Their shouts bore into my brain like a migraine. I receded from the gaggle into the shade of the nearby alleys as my rage began to overtake me. Sweat stuck my shirt against my skin and left me tasting my emotions with the sour stench of the trash. Shadows fell across the alley as I fell further into the shade and into the dark corners.

Since first coming to Summerside years previous, I'd been met with only disappointment. This was supposed to be the chaos capital of the world. Summerside was a frontier of unlimited possibilities in a world of powers. Villains were everywhere, and they owned it all. It was the worst city and, therefore, the best.

This event had once more shown that myth to be a lie.

"Horace Abalone," the man said.

This lout had emerged from the shadows of the alley before me. I forced a fake smile as he bowed.

The black-robed speaker was a stringy piece of work. He clashed against the red brick of the alleys and the dark violet of the dumpsters. His words massaged my thoughts, which took me far away from the streets of Summerside and my rage. His golden eyes glimmered like his smile, and they were all I could make of his shaded face under the hood. Somehow, I trusted him.

"You have been seeking," he continued.

"And I've found nothing," I replied. "No one will wake up from their sleepwalk to address the real injustices. I suspect you are nothing but another huckster looking to sell charms or hallucigens to soothe the troubled nerves of sub-versives. Is that it? The racket around here is booming. You scum will do anything to avoid af-fixing real change in order to line your pockets."

He laughed and nodded his head at the as-sertion. The shadow under his hood did not break even as he chuckled. "I see you are also disappointed with this supposed city of villains."

"No one will admit the truth. They all lie to themselves. They cannot admit that all things fall. It is in their nature for them to fail. We are mistakes, every one of us."

"There is truth in you." The robed man rubbed his thumb on my forehead. "I can offer you what you seek for a very easy price."

I swatted his hand away. "I'm not interested in another Summerside scheme."

"This is no scheme. I am offering you what you have always wanted. You were not born with powers, were you?"

"No," I said. I reached my palm to my head. Chalk-like dust had been rubbed into my skin. It itched like mad, leading my nails to rake across my flesh.

"There is power in you," he continued, "whether you were born with one as silly as fire in your lungs, or the stubbornness of a bull, or nothing at all. The light inside is far greater than those mere fireflies. I am part of an order that offers truth to those who seek it and to those who wish to take part in the next step forward."

"What have you done to me?"

Suddenly, as soon as it arrived the itching subsided. I was fine once more.

"I have marked you," he said. "It will fade after a full day unless you partake in the ceremony. We have been watching you, Mr. Abalone. You have what we seek, and we have what you want. We are joined."

"I join nothing. I'm not a sheep."

"We are all individuals here, Mr. Abalone. You have come to this town as many do: to seek riches and fame amidst the chaos of the villain city. You have been disappointed after failures calling themselves free men allow themselves to be arrested by self-appointed guardians of justice. I know you've been waiting for the right moment. This is your time. Your procrastination is stealing what little time you have left. Do you wish to only sit and watch as the great war unfolds?"

His words slapped my pride. I had no answer for this insanity, but I wanted one. I wanted it to be true.

My nails pierced the inside of my palms. I was very adept at keeping my feelings separate from the task at hand but watching yet more imbeciles cheer fools who had robbed men of their freedom pushed me too far. News reports had all been the same: focused on criminals foiled, and the status quo maintained. And we were meant to be grateful for it. At that moment, my fists whitened under the pressure.

This man spoke to me at a higher level—I felt it in the air. My sixth sense whispered into my ear like the wind misting through the alley. He wasn't a huckster. The glimmer in his golden eyes shone as one who knew as I did.

I cleared my throat. "What is it you want?"

"All I ask is that you allow me an object of yours. Then you are free to do as you will."

"What object?"

"It is not your life, your lifesavings, or your freedom. Do you need more than that?"

I paused for a moment. There was nothing else I had. Women came and went; I had money in the bank, and a fairly decent job in an insurance firm. I had taken the day off, but I wasn't missed. My superior was a scum sucker, anyway. I had nothing to lose in this deal.

"If you can give me what I am missing, I will give you what you want. I want a place where the night never ends."

"Marvelous," he said with a curled lip. From the folds of his robes he handed me a flask. I almost shrank from the large gashes on his wide fingers. "All you need do is drink. We will meet after sunset, and then the final step begins."

I sniffed at the open flask. The smell was not rancid or even all too strong, but a sweet scent that pleased the senses. I tasted sugar on my tongue. The liquid was thick like mud, but it slid down smooth. For a moment, I saw red and wondered if I had been poisoned.

But I had stars in my eyes and saw the possibility before me. I momentarily believed everything I learned from him. My dream was in sight. It was only a drink—a formality. A delicious formality.

This drink was far better than anything I had ever put to my lips before. The buzz of alcohol, the energy of caffeine, and the sweetness of wine combined as one perfect drink beyond taste. I guzzled it down in seconds and asked for more. The robed man chuckled.

"You can have all of the Demon's Blood you could ever want later tonight."

Without warning, I fell against the wall, queasy and dizzy with vomit at my lips. The sunlight peaking over the steep buildings burned as I fell behind the dumpster. My insides twisted and turned with every gag I made. An indescribable force swirled inside of me.

Crouched by the dumpster, my thoughts were ablaze with the rest of my bones. The sun hurt to step into and my concentration fought against me. But I could focus my burning thoughts on nothing to escape the pain. The cloaked man disappeared into the alley, leaving me to my agony.

My thoughts drifted to old memories.

The last woman I had been with was Angelica Simonson, and that was years ago. I do not even remember the last human being I had anything to do with since I threw her away. Loyal and thoughtful, she had always been where I needed her but remained much too nice and stupid. I had to let her go when she started talking about unsavory things like marrying and moving in together. Disgusting. Human beings always made me sick.

My family had long since been forgotten to the mists. I no longer remember any of them, though it had been years since I thought of them even in passing. The world moves on.

That was when I realized that I was right all along. The world offered me nothing, so I gave it nothing in return. I was doing the right thing. I was the man to set it all back in order.

I did not regret my choice to drink from that flask. Blood boiled and ached with flaring bones and muscles twitching underneath it all, and yet it would pass. I would get through this. I would grow and reach new heights.

What replaced this pain was a craving for more. Newfound strength built inside, a mountain of promise and hope that I had not ever felt in my life since coming to Summerside. This was what I was waiting for. The robed man had saved me.

"You are still alive, Mr. Abalone."

There my savior stood above me. When did he return? I did not notice. Night had fallen at some point, with cold moonlight replacing the burning sun. I did not reply to his words. I could not.

"I take it this means you wish to join us. I will give you your initiation. Please stand."

"The . . . sun," I whispered. "It hurts."

"The sun is gone, Mr. Abalone. That is the moon."

I had already forgotten the time. Muted pale light splashed down over the tops of the alley with me being none the wiser. My eyes adjusted and welcomed it.

I stood as my headache subsided.

Before I could take a breath of the night air, a weight crashed into my ribcage. It took a moment for me to notice the robed man now standing before me. His hand was sticking into my chest. Blood dribbled down my lips.

"Now we shall see if the rune does its work," he said.

A fire erupted inside of my bones before it was consumed by a frost that chilled my entire being. The cold caused my lungs to cease, and my limbs to convulse. He removed his claw-like fingers, and I dropped down. My skull struck the bottom of the alley with a crack.

Even as I bled out, I could not stop smiling. It wasn't because that Demon's Blood was still coursing through my veins and giving me untold pleasure. It wasn't because I was glad to finally have it all end—no, it was just the opposite. I understood it all—I wasn't dying.

I was being reborn.

Warmth left the back of my skull as the chill embraced me and cradled my essence into its bosom. The sickening call of silence whispered to me before my mind gave in to the pleasure and shut down.

It was time for me to show this villain city how it was meant to be done.

~

I didn't remember entering the apartment, but I did remember pulling the door off its hinges and forcing my way through the threshold. My head struck the doorframe, and I had to wedge my awkward size to get inside. I couldn't understand why. I had never been particularly tall.

Mixtures of blood red and harsh white light streaks filled my wavy vision. Slowly, the world focused, but my sixth sense guided me to where I wanted to go—where I *needed* to go.

My ears were not as fortunate as the rest of me.

Nearby screams bore into my brain. My sensitive hearing made it excruciating. I lashed out at the source, and my fingers struck warm flesh. A voice gargled as I removed my nails from it. A corpse toppled to my feet.

Then I understood what was wrong with me.

I stood abnormally tall, my back hunched, and my fingers extended like knives. My skin had turned black like the bottom of a well, and my frame moved lightly despite the gigantic size. The world was like a child's dollhouse to me.

The realization made me laugh, a cackle darker than the apartment I was in. I had no inkling as to where I had been led, but it didn't matter. I had become what I was supposed to be.

A woman screamed.

My head snapped toward the source. The female was yelling into a phone about her dead husband. Not knowing what she meant, I licked my fingers. The blood soothed my nerves.

The moon shaded her in shadow, her back in the corner of the living room beside the shattered electronics and the torn couch. She clutched the phone while staring up at me.

"Did I kill him?" I asked. My guttural voice sounded deeper than it should have. "It happened so quick."

Her mouth fell open. "Horace?"

I tiled my head and thought on it. "In a way."

She did not get to reply. I leaped upon Angelica and followed my urges. Blood flew loose. The resulting screams soothed me just as much as the earlier ones.

A sweet scented smell interrupted my enjoyment. Another human.

My bulky body slunk easily through the hall like a wolf to prey. So much strength, so much intensity. I had all I wanted in that moment.

A tiny crib in the room distracted me. I went for the light switch but instinctively pulled away at the last moment. My fear puzzled me, but I soon forgot it. There was enough light thanks to the moon shining through the blowing curtains.

The silent child was wrapped in a blanket. Somehow, this baby had remained asleep through the carnage, with only the heavy Summerside wind and sirens on the air to pierce the quiet. This was good. The voice drifting through my thoughts told me so. This creature wasn't much more than a morsel, so I could easily snatch it up.

But there was a better use for this one.

They could use this thing. Children were useful. Not yet hollowed out and dead like me or my ilk, or as stupid and cynical as teenagers, or as far gone as the elderly: these had promise. This thing would make a fine gift for the ones who gave me what I had. I owed them.

Ambulances screamed outside, and I moved. I grabbed the glorified fetus, making careful to keep it unharmed in the blanket and shielded it as I slammed through the window to the outside fire escape. My hardened flesh sprouted tiny lacerations, but nothing I couldn't handle. Glass sprayed everywhere, and the baby started to cry despite not even being hurt. This city was full of whiners.

Heavy humid air beat against me as I scampered up the fire escape. Brick and metal tore around me as I fought my way up. My hunger gave me power. I leaped to the roof and bounded onward slicing through the wind with extreme velocity. Nothing could catch me now.

That was when I realized I was naked, a mass of purple skin and bulging veins and tightened muscles. I could be mistaken for a walking lump of exposed nerves. It was a beautiful and raw sight.

The city streets lay stories below as I soared to the next roof across the street. I landed with a heavy weight, concrete crunching under my bare violet feet. A clear path of escape in my mind led me to where I was ordered to go. I could never imagine being so invincible before!

A force stabbed into me. A knife sunk into my chest. It twisted and turned, bringing me to my knees.

"Where do you think you're going, villain?"

I glanced across my oversized shoulder. A man dressed in black from head to toe with heavy boots, dark gloves, and a matching mask over his eyes waited across from me on the rooftop. A dozen knives floated around him in a satellite circle.

"Hero," I rumbled out.

The blade did not even hurt. I effortlessly tossed it to the ground, blood leaking loose. A simple knife trick was not enough to bring me down.

"A Metal Elemental Type," I said. "This is not a good match for you."

"Drop the child," the hero replied.

"The weak should kneel before their betters."

"What are you?" The man was tall and handsome underneath his black mask with blue eyes and dirty blond hair perched atop. The sort that the news would love and the rumors go for. How I wanted to rip him to bits. "What is your power?"

"This isn't a power. It's a gift. And I will tear down your whole world to prove it to you."

"You won't get another warning, villain. On your stomach, arms spread."

I pounced. Three of the knives plunged into my chest as I crashed down on the hero. He groaned and then screamed as I sank my jagged teeth into his shoulder. A force prevented me from closing my large jaw down for a full bite, but I still felt supple skin and delicious life force leaking into my taste buds. Just like those nothings in the apartment, he would die.

The blood tasted so good I barely even felt the other knives sinking into my back. I hardly noticed them twisting.

My jaw stung and stiffened. The metal man had jabbed one of his blades into my purple cheek. His reddened knuckles held the knife forward which prevented me from clamping down further. The hero pushed back with his blades, forcing me to retreat. How could a simple man do that? But I was actually being pulled back from the inside. Sharp sensations stabbed inside my violet skin. Sparks of crimson blood flashed across my vision and something I faintly remembered as pain pulsed in my bones.

I floated upward without a say in it. The knives lifted me an inch off the ground.

The child fell from my grip, and the hero dove forward and caught it. He held his bloody shoulder with his free hand and the baby with his other. The hard stare he gave me as the baby cried gave me pleasant shivers.

"You're not a transformer," he said. "You're no animal, at least not one I've ever seen. You're not even bleeding blood. What are you?"

The blades burrowed further into my flesh. I was being torn asunder exquisitely.

"I am the first of many," my voice said for me. "Do what you will. You have won very little tonight."

"Talking big? You're just another villain like all the rest. You think you're any different than the last ten psychos I stopped? You're just uglier."

I threw myself forward. My flesh tore free of the restraints, and my feet slapped against the roof, knocking up rubble. I sprinted toward the hero, my heart in my throat. I was just another villain? Hardly. I was much more. I would tear him up. The hero crouched down defensively and held the baby tight. He had already given up. What a fool! I had won. Two bites for two morsels!

It hurt. I cried out at the sudden pain in my bones. Limbs pulled apart and severed in every direction as my pleasure died. My momentum continued my remains forward, and both my head and left arm flew over the edge of the building. The hero silently watched my remains fall to the street below. Even the pain inside me had numbed to nothing.

The heavy weight of my remains struck the pavement. My detached arm melted away into the road ahead of my face like so much ice in the desert. I didn't understand. I had lost?

"*Is this all you are worth?*" The robed man spoke into my head. "*I thought you were going to change everything, Mr. Abalone?*"

"You have underestimated me. I am not finished."

"*Do what you will. There are other subjects to change this world for the better. You are just another failure.*"

"I am not finished. The night never ends. He was not right!"

My head melted into the pavement as the police cars drew closer. The hero looked down on me from the building, and I whispered a curse under my breath. His words rang in my head as I went over my loss. How could I be just another villain? I was so much more than that. I would change this city of chaos!

And yet within mere minutes I was no

more.

~

My journey only started there.

My glorious body had died, but my spirit remained. I slid through darkened alleys and along the shade of buildings and inside sewers away from the sun of Summerside. I made my home in the dark train tunnels where I sat and waited in the shade. The shadows held me close.

The lights and sounds of the trains sometimes stung as they blew by my essence, but the quiet and the years allowed me what I needed. Quiet. This was the world I wanted. This was the place where the moonlight spoke like knives flashing in the night—violent and real. This was where the memory of the false world faded and where the future was as unending as the night where I belonged. My villain city would someday be made reality.

For now, I wait. One day, I will be whole again, and the failures shall join me as we howl to the mighty god of oblivion under the moon. It is the nature of all things to fall. Eventually, the light will also fail. It must.

I still think of that accursed hero, and his words to me as he ripped my life from my gifted frame. I was just another villain? Perhaps. But this is my city. Eventually, I will reclaim it.

No, I have not failed. As I have already said: the night never ends.

Under Suspicion in Summerside

~The Present~

1.

The footsteps of the two hired hands echoed down the wide and barren corridors of the underground passageway. Flatline ran ahead as his protégée lagged behind, crucial seconds behind schedule. Sparks popped off Flatline's muscles.

"Slow down!" Concrete said. "We don't all have speed powers."

Flatline cocked his head. "I have electric powers—not speed powers. My muscles and endorphins might be supercharged, but it's not far off from what you can do. Stick to your workout schedule."

"Are you kidding? My name is *Concrete*, not *Marathon*. My body just solidifies. It has nothing to do with my stamina. No amount of training is going to make me as fast as you." He huffed. "Where is the incident anyway?"

"Corner of 23rd and Mobius at the Royal Troop Bank. Hostages: over a dozen, maybe two. Four confirmed perpetrators. One or two might be Metal Elementals. We're going in through the sewer. Ready for a real mission?"

Two months had passed since Flatline finished training him and yet going out on the field remained awkward. Summerside was a hotbed for low level crime, which typically meant purse-snatchers and assaults. The police called free-lancers like them in when the heat was too high. And when it came to Flatline, the furnace was always on full blast.

"Why did they call us?" Concrete asked. "We usually get passed over."

"We're the closest, and the bigger names are indisposed. Who cares about that, anyway? I'm going in first, and you follow after. The bank is made of stone so that the more common Elementals don't have an easy time walking in. You phase through to the second floor for possible hostages and get them out. They probably don't have men up there, though spotters say they caught two suspects sneaking upstairs. I'll deal with the perps on the main floor."

"My power would be the better choice if they're armed."

"You're not ready to take on four of these guys at once. For now, just cover my back." Flatline flashed a triumphant smile. He sure loved that grin of his.

"Got it." Flatline would see how much he'd learned in training. Concrete was no mere teenager. "Do we have any names?"

"One of them is called Bullet Face, and he's just as crazy as he sounds. Former hired enforcer for Sunset Red before they were slaughtered by rival syndicates. He escaped from maximum security five months ago, and he's not too happy about what left him there."

"Sunset Red was big time. Why's he robbing banks?"

Flatline moved faster down the echoing tunnels. His tone turned dour. "Why indeed."

2.

Julia fell through the open door of the bank manager's office. Polished and carved stone walls reinforced the damp humidity inside with only a large oak desk in the center to remind her that this was a modern building. She caught the odor of an old pine air freshener when the door clicked behind her. The criminal pushed her to the floor, and she backed into the desk.

Filing cabinets and poorly watered plants surrounded the length of the room. In this age where those with powers ran rampant, it made sense to vary the building materials to keep those types from breaking in. The manager must have been proud of this work. Unfortunately, he was downstairs with the rest of the hostages, and no plan was foolproof.

Bullet Face loomed over her, metal spheres floating from his palm like a magic trick.

"You're Julia Winters, one of the worst pains in Summerside. You write under the pseudonym *Wicked Town* about the crazier rumors of good 'ol Sewerside."

"I never gave you my name. You've mistaken me for someone else." She stood up and straightened her crumpled blouse. Thin clouds of dust burst from her skirt. Sirens screeched outside matching her pounding heartbeat. Sieg would be okay—she had to believe that. For now she needed to keep it cool. Julia ran a hand through her long dark hair and leaned against her slender hip. "Look, whoever you are, just think about this rationally. The police are coming. Turn yourself in and don't make it worse."

"The Big Man has been keeping tabs on outsiders. Too many foxes getting into our hen-houses these days. You've been making it worse. They put me in charge of icing you, and what better way than during a heist. Nice of you to take the bait of an interview. Sad to say that was me you were talking to on the phone. Too bad it has to come to this. Gorgeous women with amber eyes are kind of my thing. But I can't let the Big Man down."

"Your boss is a psychotic who creates explosive orbs from his skin. I saw him yelling at the prisoners downstairs before you dragged me here. The Exploding Man is just a thief."

The criminal laughed. "Now, we both know we're not talking about him. The man just wants pocket change. Robbing digital banks became so much easier thanks to all the Mental Type hackers out there. Why else do you think the government went so hard in with print? We're in their heads. My kind changed the world. You, however? You're just another bystander."

She'd heard rumors about this punk, Bullet Face. He looked the part of a minion, wearing a patched up leather jacket with spikes over his hoodie, dyed purple hair, and a few too many nose rings. But that was a façade. He wasn't just a punk. This man could not be trusted.

"Robbing banks is silly these days, no?" she asked. "Summerside may be the pits, but the cops still come fast. Not to mention, they've got tougher guys than you on their side."

Bullet Face laughed. He laughed like he was oblivious to the sirens outside or that robbing banks was near impossible these days. Even in a den of rats like Summerside, crime was not so easy to get away with during the day. His horse face grew a smile.

"We don't live in that era anymore, babe. People hate these *Crusaders*, for good reason." He ran a hand through his purple hair. "We're a long way from when they were untouchable saviors even a few years ago. This is the Trash Age, ruled by people like me. As a media lackey, you're supposed to do your job and show those failures as what they are—government funded tools or deluded vigilantes looking for a place to die. I've seen your pathetic articles."

He leaned in close. The punk rolled tiny

metal balls in his free hand, his rotten breath piercing her nostrils. She closed her eyes and felt the hair on her neck stand up. Because she came to this city, she was going to die. It had already destroyed Sieg, and now it was her turn.

"What is your end game, woman?"

Ice cold water chilled her blood. She let out a shaking breath.

But then she remembered. There was a reason she came to this dead city in the first place.

"The Seeker," she said, opening her eyes. Her breath steadied. "He isn't a government controlled puppet or one of you creeps. He's real, too. You've seen that graffiti everywhere."

Bullet Face guffawed, spittle spraying from his chipped teeth. "The Seeker is an urban legend. There isn't anybody out there after dark keeping you safe. It makes kids happy to have their fairy tales. Grown-ups know better. You're even shaking right now, you stupid git."

"*Someone is Aiming at You,*" she said. The phrase that had been tagged in graffiti all over Summerside became a slogan. It was the motto The Seeker sent his soon-to-be victims. "Can you say what happened to the Butcher, Grunge, or Patterson? You can't explain that away."

"The pressure got to them, or they were paid off to act crazy. Believe what you want. It doesn't change reality."

The spiked metal bracelet clanked around his wrist. His clothes shook violently with all the metal pins lining it. In his hand, the metal spheres melted together like hot liquid. The loose bracelets and metal covering his skin rattled in time with his breaths.

He winked. "Watch this."

With a wave of his hand, the metal bracelet straightened into the shape of a dagger. It merged with the spheres and extended out an extra inch with its added mass. He threw has hand forward, and the metal flew past Julia's head, splitting desk wood in two. The sunlight stabbing through the gaudy window shades glinted off the makeshift blade.

"Decay is the rule," he said. "There's nothing after me. This is my time."

A tall figure stepped out of the shadows. She gasped as it swooped in towards them.

Bullet Face's head snapped back when the punch struck his nose. He lurched backwards against a potted plant. The intruding figure stepped between Julia and him.

This strange intruder was a teenage boy no older than seventeen. He wore dark boots to match his uniform and black mask and small helmet. He thrusted out a badge before slipping it back in a pouch. This boy had been hired as an enforcer by the police.

"Speaking of being in the wrong place at the wrong time," Bullet Face said, massaging his cheek.

The boy's skin looked colored like grey rock or possibly brick or concrete. He must have phased through the walls to get in the office with them. An Elemental Type. It wasn't The Seeker, but Julia wouldn't complain.

He literally cracked his knuckles. "I don't mean to interrupt, but that speech was a bit too much. Especially from a trash pile who hits women. I had a hard time keeping quiet."

A mad glint flashed across Bullet Face's grin. "What's your name, you stooge?"

"Concrete is what they call me," the boy said. "Do me a solid and come quietly. That way I won't have to break your arms and legs."

"A kid?" The villain laughed, his metal accessories rattling against his shabby clothes. "The government is hiring kids to do their dirty work now? All you've done is proven my point."

"Not exactly. I work with a firm who partakes in contracts with whoever pays. We pick and choose jobs. But it's not like anyone worth his salt would turn this one down."

The metal piercings and bracelets on Bullet Face twisted into jagged edges matching his jacket spikes and the metal bits on his boots. They all pointed out as like heat-seeking porcupine quills toward the boy. The cold sweat on Julia's spine returned.

"See?" Bullet Face said. He laughed, gesturing to her with his wiry fingers. Rings rattled against him. "This is what your heroes are: kids with no sense and heads full of stupid dreams. Want to see what he'll look like when I'm done carving him up?"

"You're gonna cut me?" the kid asked, legitimately surprised. "Give it a try."

Bullet Face and Concrete collided in the center of the office. Stone and metal clashed. Julia hoped that this boy knew what he was doing.

3.

Sieg flinched, and the hostages murmured when

the lights went off in the bank. The three criminals that had spread out among the sixteen hostages were the only ones who didn't react. They must have expected this.

Every hostage, including Sieg, was tied with a cord of some sort, provided by the criminal named Wire. As long as he stuck around, the bonds would be impossible to break. Even though Sieg had the appearance an overweight, balding, middle-aged man and no one gave him much thought, he still planned escape. Wire's power made that difficult.

The bank's interior was a cramped affair with a long counter on the west side of the room, chairs in the middle waiting area, and a row of square offices on the east end with stairs at the rear to the second floor—where Bullet Face took Julia.

Sieg thought up a plan to get up those stairs. Outnumbered and outgunned, he would be slaughtered. Now that the power had been shut off, the police would arrive soon with their hired enforcers. He felt dirty just thinking about it.

"I hope they aren't idiots," he whispered to himself.

The gangliest thug glanced his way. Sieg

recognized him as Pulse Pound, an Abnormal Type criminal. Normally, he worked alone but not today.

The punk stomped over to him. Twinkling sparkles of static flecked across his black clothing. The group of prisoners sitting around Sieg looked to their shoes instead of them.

"Shut it, fatty," Pulse Pound said. The thin man pointed a flashing finger at Sieg. "You think you're safe because cops are on their way?"

The Exploding Man laughed from his position leaning against the counter. The bald man was fat enough to give Sieg a run for his money, with a protruding bulbous gut and arms and legs flapping with loose skin under his suit jacket. "Don't worry, Pulse Pound. A few government stooges should give us some excitement. Nothing more fun than blowing away arrogant snots."

"I hope you're right, man. I like it when they fight back." Pulse Pound stepped around Sieg and winded around the crowd towards the counter. "Long as we get what we came for."

The longer Sieg waited the more Julia was likely to be hurt. He needed to get up those stairs. As he thought up a plan, a meaty hand had clasped his shoulder.

The Exploding Man crouched beside him and smiled pleasantly.

Sieg froze. "We all know you're not here for money."

The Exploding Man placed his right hand on his own left forearm and dug his nails in deep. Without so much as flinching, the villain pulled back to remove a strip of skin like ripping fabric and rolled it in a ball with one hand. Skin bubbled on his open wound to reveal new flesh replacing the gouged piece.

"How would you know what we're here for, hmm?" The large man rubbed the ball against Sieg's cheek. It stunk of sweat and grease, churning his stomach. The ball hissed as if releasing air. The young women beside him gasped. "Easy, ladies."

Sieg grimaced. "Playing a bit loose with those, aren't you?"

"Don't worry; this isn't enough to kill you. It'll probably smart, though. Not that I would know: the explosions don't hurt me."

Abnormal Types were the worst. "Where did Bullet Face take my friend?"

"What do you think of Crusaders?" Heat escaped the orb as the villain gently caressed it.

"Why do you care what I think?"

"I don't. I just want to know what your last thoughts will be when they fail to save you."

Sieg glanced at the other two toughs. Wire was a fairly weak Abnormal Type who could lift and contort long lengthy objects like ropes, chains, and wires. Pulse Pound fired plasma energy from his fingertips, and Bullet Face upstairs could use metal itself as a weapon. The Exploding Man had his skin. The four of them together made quite the crew.

Wire left the counter for the vault, and Pulse Pound kept watch at the entrance blocked and reinforced by torn chrome gathered from the cars out front. They thought they were safe.

A flash of electricity crackled from behind the counter. The hostages turned in unison, and the Exploding Man bounded towards the action.

Wire flew across the counter, sparks tumbling from his clothes. He crashed down in the center of the floor beside Sieg and the hostages. The Abnormal Type laid unconscious, his eyes rolled back and his tongue out. Muscles convulsed like a stun gun hit.

The metal chain dropped loose around Sieg's wrists, and the crowd shifted at their newfound freedom. Before any of them could move, the source of the electricity emerged from the back room and leaned against the counter.

Sparks rolled off of his dark, government issued uniform and mask. A sharp face and a strong jaw smiled through the blackened room. "Sorry, I took so long, but it's always easier to take down a pack of criminals when one is stupid enough to get a bolt of electricity to the back."

Sieg knew this man both from Julia's research and his own knowledge of Summerside. This was Flatline, a freelance enforcer who had a reputation as being wild. The man twitching on the floor certainly agreed. The police hired a real firecracker for this one.

"They sent you to negotiate?" Pulse Pound asked. Light hummed around his gloves.

Flatline chuckled. "I don't negotiate with your kind."

The Exploding Man tossed a sphere. The skin hissed as it spun through the air. Flatline, without even a pause, fired a bolt of electricity at it.

"Don't!" Sieg shouted.

At the same moment, Flatline yelled: "Get down!"

The hostages all sunk to the floor.

The ball burst into a small wildfire and wave of smoke. Stone fell from the ceiling. Drops of water rained down on the carpet. The sprinkler system had gone off.

Electricity sprayed from Flatline's black boots as he ran through the smoke plume. His speed had increased tremendously in an instant. Pulse Pound was still coughing and waving the smoke away from his face when Flatline appeared before him. The masked man threw a right cross covered in volts. The stunned enemy cried out, and the sprinkler water shocked him further.

The hostages fled toward the exit, and Sieg remained alone watching the pair tussling.

Flatline's electric fists relentlessly crashed onward with extra sparks spraying out around him due to the water. Pulse Pound flailed back, uselessly flashing fist beams into the walls. A stray shot struck the ceiling, shattering light fixtures. Glass rained down on them. Flatline kicked the villain's head, sending out an arc of sparks with it. Finally, Pulse Pound was downed.

The fire alarm rang, and the dust cleared in the spray. The hostages pried their way out the entrance door through the broken metal.

But there was someone missing! The Exploding Man had slipped out.

"Are you okay, sir?" Flatline asked. He pointed Sieg toward the emergency exit.

"My friend is upstairs," Sieg said. "Can you help her?"

"Don't worry; I've got a guy up there. Did anyone see where the big man went?"

"Through the office behind you!" an elderly man called to Flatline.

"On it," Flatline said. "Head out the front with the others, please."

Sieg grunted. "I should trust you? You could have electrocuted us or blown the ceiling!"

"If I was a rookie, maybe. My control is too good for hitting civilians, and blown ceilings are a dime a dozen in Summerside. Now, where did the elderly gentleman say they went?"

Flatline fled toward the office and checked the floor leaving Sieg behind. Behind him, the shouts of police officers sounded. This robbery was over.

Sieg slipped from the crowd toward the stairs. No one noticed him through the mayhem.

A tremendous rumbling caused plaster to fall from the walls. An explosion had rumbled from below. Sieg stumbled on the steps and leaned on the cold stone wall. If the moron they sent upstairs was anything like Flatline, they were all in trouble.

"Why did they have to be idiots?"

4.

"Something wrong?" Bullet Face asked. His pierced lips split into a smile. "You alright?"

Concrete took a step back, and the woman sidled up behind him. His stone knuckles cracked, his hands ached. The two opponents only had one exchange of blows with each other, but it was enough to know where this would be going. A new tact was needed.

"Miss," Concrete whispered to the woman. "Stay behind me."

"What a chivalrous display!" The villain ground his teeth together. "I am going to enjoy slashing you both apart."

"What about the people downstairs?" she whispered from behind Concrete. "I have a friend who is still there."

"Rest assured. There's someone dealing with it. I give him ten seconds."

"Until what?"

The floor rumbled and threw picture frames and stone chips from the office wall. An explosion had gone off below. Both the woman and the villain stumbled, but Concrete had already steadied himself.

"Until that!" he shouted.

Concrete's fists hardened to jagged stone, and he swung them at the enemy. Bullet Face roared with each strike against him. An uppercut sent him backwards.

The villain crashed through the office door and knocked into the opposite side of the hallway. Stone splinters sprinkled onto his wincing body. Ambulances whirred outside.

"You could be a bit more subtle, Flatline," Concrete whispered.

The woman cocked her head. "What?"

Concrete ignored her and followed his enemy into the hall. "Move back, miss," he said.

"Look!" She pointed to Concrete's side and shouted.

His solid frame shook, and numbness trembled inside his ribs. Through his shirt, a metal knife sat jabbed into his stone skin. Bullet Face laughed and pumped his fist from his position crouched on the floor. His toss had hit the mark, and Concrete's sloppiness allowed it to happen. Blood would have gushed out the wound if his skin and organs had been normal tissue.

Bullet Face grinned through his bloody teeth. "Got you, nitwit."

Somehow an invisible force lifted Concrete off the floor. His gut cracked and tore under the knife's pressure. The blade in him would be a killer if he didn't pry it out quick. Elementals only needed to touch their compatible element and, depending on how strong the power is, could do most anything they want with it. Unfortunately, Bullet Face was not a weak elemental.

The villain leaned back against the wall. "Now, let's see if you can fly."

Bullet Face waved his hand, and Concrete soared upwards. The ceiling crunched with his weight. Concrete winced and was thrown sideways. He battered against the sides of the halls with each toss. The place surface fractured and crumbled under his weight.

Options had dwindled. He had no way to fight back. Though he might not win, at least the hostage needed to make it out. Concrete yelled to the woman. "Get downstairs!"

She paused for a second before accepting his advice and running for it. Bullet Face couldn't do much else, and the stairs were wide open.

A metal chain slithered across the floor, sprang and wrapped around her ankles. She landed elbows first on the carpet. The chain dragged her along the floor toward Bullet Face.

The villain's concentration caught in two places was enough for Concrete to pry the knife free of his ribs. Without focus, Bullet Face's hold had loosened just like most powers. The knife clattered to the carpet, and Concrete landed on his knees.

He bounded forward, and his stone fist cracked into the side of the metal man's nose. Bullet Face spun backwards.

Rubbing his nose, Bullet Face's beady eyes narrowed on the teenager. Red blood from his nostrils matched his flushed cheeks. He outstretched his hand, and the knife flew from the floor back to his palm like a magnet. Without a further wasted movement, he attacked.

The knife slashed at Concrete. The boy reeled, and his shirt sliced open.

"It's one thing to get thrown around like a ragdoll," Concrete said. "It's another to get embarrassed in front of beautiful women, too."

"What?" the criminal said.

The woman pried the chain from her leg and shook her head. "Kids."

"And how does it feel to get killed in front of a beautiful woman?" Bullet Face asked, blood streaming down his lips.

"There are worse ways to die," the boy said.

Concrete pooled thoughts into his side wound, steadying his breaths. In this form, most blades wouldn't go through him, but Flatline had taught him that Metal Elemental Types were not the same as normal punks in a knife fight. Their weapons could be made sharper and thinner and could split through rock. Bullet Face was also no amateur.

Pushing his power into his wound, wet concrete slid along Concrete's hardened skin like sweat and into the opening. A cool sensation slid between his ribs, and the skin crackled and hardened.

Bullet Face growled. "You think you're invincible, don't you, boy?"

The truth was that he didn't. Healing wounds took way too much energy. He wouldn't last two more minutes if he had to do this again. Concrete form was hard enough to maintain in a fight without that worry. But Concrete did have a bark to match his bite.

"I think you're done, stretch," he said. "Like I said before—you can't cut me. But kudos for trying. Think you can scratch my back next?"

Concrete ducked the wide knife swing. He bear-hugged the gangly thug and squeezed tight, lifting him up and locking Bullet Face's arms at his sides. Concrete pressed him close.

"Are you crazy, junior?" He thrashed in Concrete's hold, metal scraping against hardened skin. He couldn't get an angle to cut the kid. "I don't have to move my arms to split you."

Instead of answering, Concrete head-butted his opponent's skull. Concrete on bone. The villain spat blood and shouted. The knife fell to the carpet, and he weaved in his enemy's grip. Concrete head-butted again and again. The resulting cracks could be heard blocks away.

The villain gargled, and his eyes rolled back. He fell limp, and Concrete dropped him unconscious to the carpet.

Back down the hall, the woman still struggled with prying the chain from her leg. Concrete easily snapped it in two.

"It wasn't a very cool victory, but a win is a win," he said, rubbing his solid skull. He winced, running his hands around the chipped concrete. Even if it didn't physically damage him, he still felt every hit. He concentrated his remaining power on healing. "Are you okay, Miss?"

The floor trembled again, and the woman fell. Light fixtures plummeted from the ceiling. He grabbed her arm and brought her close. She looked up at him, perplexed.

The sprinkler system flashed on, and the pair shielded their eyes from the dousing.

He shook his soaked head. "Well, that ruined the mood. You okay?"

"I'm fine," she said, scrambling to remain steady. "I didn't expect an enforcer."

"You're welcome. I hope you're not hurt." He snapped his fingers. "Oh, one second."

He brought Bullet Face's hands behind his back. Slipping the special plastic handcuffs around the villain's wrists, Concrete read him his rights. His first solo collar without Flatline.

"I don't think he can hear you," she interrupted.

"It's the rules, Miss. I don't make them,

just enforce them." He pressed the limp Bullet Face against the broken wall. "What is your name, if you don't mind me asking?"

"Julia Winters. Thanks for what you did. Who are you?"

"My official moniker is Concrete. You've probably never heard of me."

An explosion rang from several blocks away. A plume of smoke wafted between the cramped buildings outside the window. It could only be Flatline.

"I have to get moving," Concrete said.

"A friend of mine is still in the bank with all those people."

"Hear those sirens? Cops are already inside. He's safe. I need to find my superior. He was the one who sent me here to begin with."

"Does your superior usually blow things up?"

"No, that was the Exploding Man. But he probably caused it. Flatline is good at his job, but he likes pushing buttons."

Another small quake shook the building. Concrete peered out the hallway window. More smoke slipped into the sky streets away. It was a chase.

"Flatline," Julia mumbled. "I know that name."

"You do? He's not popular or anything. How much do you know about hired enforcers?"

"Look me up online sometime. You might be surprised."

"Hey!" a man yelled.

At the end of the hall, a fat, balding man stumbled up the steps. He had a bad crumpled suit on, but for a man his size, he ran surprisingly fast.

Concrete reached a hand forward to stop him, but the big man swooped around him and went right for Julia with an impressive weave.

"Are you alright?" the newcomer asked the girl.

"I am." She shot Concrete a knowing glance and then turned back to her friend. "But what about you? What are you doing here?"

"The crook got away." He pointed a finger at Concrete. "Flatline's already gone after him through the sewers. You need to follow him. I'll make sure the cops pick up this scumbag."

Shouts of police cried from the stairway behind them. This guy was telling the truth.

"Are we famous?" Concrete asked. "It's

like everyone knows who we are."

The teenager ran to the office he first entered by and opened the window. Cops milled the back lot overlooking smoking sewer lids. Flatline was long gone.

"There's a lot of blown pavement, but where is the Exploding Man planning on going?"

"He's heading for the Sun Gardens," the fat man said. "You can cut him off if you head south and cut through the mall."

"How do you know where he's going?"

"He trusted me a bit too much. But you need to know something about his power."

"I know about it," Concrete said. "Flatline says he peels skin off and uses it as explosives. Abnormal Type."

"What you *don't* know is that it goes off when comes in full contact with any substance except one. Skin. I didn't get to tell your boss that before he took off into the sewers."

"Well, I'll let him know." Concrete waved to Julia. "Next time, be careful who you keep company with, Miss. Online anonymity is a blessing. This isn't the type of thing good-looking women should get tangled up with."

The large man blinked. "What's he talking

about?"

"He's crazy, never mind him."

"Right." The fat man laughed. "A lot of that going around."

Concrete ran and nimbly jumped through the open window of the bank. He dropped like a stone. The cops shouted from their barricades as he fell.

He tucked his limbs in, landing in the parking lot. Pavement fissured around Concrete as he crouched knee deep in the road. He winked at the dumbfounded officers, and dove into the pavement, his body merging with the rock.

Diving straight into the road from the building would have been too risky. Flatline always cautioned him from jumping at too high a height. Too deep and he would land in the sewer and might possibly break something. Plus, that slop just doesn't come off even after six showers. Concrete pushed through the road like a professional swimmer.

He resurfaced beyond the police barricade a block away. Tire marks lead out from behind the building from an empty lot. They used a getaway car. The fat man was right; they were heading north.

A cop car barreled down the alley to his left. Trash cans tumbled like pinballs. Their sirens went mad as they barreled in his direction. Despite braking, the car spun out at him, tearing up pavement.

Concrete sunk into the road, like a frog into a lake. The vehicle swerved over him and skidded to a stop against a dumpster. More vehicles screeched to a stop beside the first one. The officers shouted to each other, confused as to what had occurred. Concrete pushed onward.

Without another wasted moment, he swam toward the Sun Gardens.

5.

Flatline had finally caught up with the villain in the sewers but could do nothing. The Exploding Man screamed obscenities at thin air and began tossing skin bombs left and right with no rhyme or reason. Sewage and stone sprayed, and pipes burst with the impact; but the criminal hardly noticed. He aimlessly trudged onward as if unaware he was being pursued.

The tunnels shook making the sewage stink even worse, and the structure crumbled slightly above him. Flatline cautiously followed in silence. He wouldn't risk a scuffle and more destruction. Thankfully, the noise let him approach stealthily.

The Exploding Man climbed up to a side street for air a few blocks later. A small car with a man in the driver's seat pulled into the empty lot. The villain hopped inside just as Flatline reached the surface. The Exploder threw small orbs of flesh out the vehicle's windows, destroying pavement, while civilians swerved through the roads to avoid the chaos. Flatline shielded his eyes from stray rubble blown in his direction. He had only one way to pursue.

Electricity surged in his body. Flatline climbed the nearby fire escape to the rooftops; his jumps charged with each leg push and hop. The getaway car plowed onward as he leaped up the steps.

Flatline hopped from rooftop to rooftop. Down below the chaos raged on. Metal and rock exploded around his prey, and the passing cars spun to avoid it. Electricity leaped in arcs from Flatline as he bounded across buildings in pursuit.

Inside his body, he built an electric-like force. What this strange white energy did was supercharge his muscles like a battery, enhancing the strength of his adrenal glands and organs, and supplying him with endurance close to that of a Physical Type superhuman. That came at a cost; however, it was not one he could worry about now.

"Looks like he's heading for the bridge up north," Flatline mumbled. It was times like this that he wished he could wear a com unit or phone without frying the thing. He couldn't contact anyone from here.

The scrappy getaway car turned hard at an intersection, narrowly avoiding a one-way street and collision. The driver swerved through oncoming traffic and caused the vehicles and oncoming cop cars to swerve out of the way. Horns screeched. At the following intersection, the escapee made a sharp left. The getaway vehicle lifted on two wheels, tremendously decreasing speed.

"That's my cue," Flatline said.

He aimed his jump and leaped from the rooftop.

His black uniform and boots kicked up static as he plummeted, and the wind rustled by.

The vehicle clanked back down on the

road at the same moment Flatline landed on it. He split the roof and slammed into the passenger seat. Sparks from his body lashed out and shattered the window beside him, and the driver flinched. Civilians screamed outside as the car rocketed forward.

"What was that?" the driver shouted, shielding his face from the volts.

The car wobbled all over the road. Light posts crunched and clattered around them. The driver swore and straightened the wheel. He went for the piece in his long jacket.

Flatline didn't bother looking over when he punched the driver. Electricity hopped from his right hand and shattered the driver's sunglasses. The punk fell against the wheel, and the gas.

The car tore onward, and Flatline steadied himself.

He reached for the wheel and jammed it to the left. The car whined, and tires screeched. Flatline directed it to the side of the road, jumping the curb. He made sure to avoid stray civilians, leading the wheel toward a lamppost.

The Exploding Man fell over in his seat behind them. He mumbled crazily to himself.

The car crashed against the streetlight, and the post groaned. It tipped over and smashed against the hood. Steam sprayed out the engine through the busted hood. Flatline kicked open the passenger door and jumped away from the old jalopy. The muffler wheezed and broke loose.

All around him screaming civilians scattered and sprinted in different directions.

Flatline put space between himself, and the crashed car. He charged volts in his right arm.

The driver lazily pushed open the door and dropped into the busted road beside the car, unconscious. At least, that was one less problem to worry about.

But one of them still remained inside the vehicle.

"Come on out," Flatline said. "Unless you want to fry in there. I've got the juice for it."

"Now, I know you." The exploder leaned out of the now destroyed roof and folded his bruised arms. Covered in sweat, his fingers twitched at skin. His unfocused eyes had glazed over. "You were a Crusader when you were a teenager. You were pretty famous in the underground for a while. So what is a big time hero like you doing in this pit? Summerside is for our kind.

Vanessa and Walter here tell me all the time."

The villain nodded to his left and right, apparently unaware that no one was actually there. Somehow, he'd totally lost his mind.

"You have five seconds to get out of the car."

"Roscoe blew himself up trying to hold off one of you Crusaders. Why waste your time being a government puppet? We could own Sewerside and build an empire."

Flatline raised his left hand and pointed a forefinger up into the air. "One."

"Weren't you part of some hero group years back?"

Flatline raised a second finger. "Two."

"You were! A group of Crusaders down in Oxford. Lead by that Comet hero wannabe, the man who would create some golden age. Now, he was a legend. Lewis was scared out of his mind over that one. Poor Lewis fell off a roof, though. That was a messy scene."

"Three."

"What happened to that group, anyway? I kept hearing about how these great new Crusaders were going to create some *Golden Utopia* and revive the world. Never happened. They're all dead like Roscoe and Lewis, huh?"

"Four."

"Poor vigilantes." The villain chuckled. "So many failures gave up hope the day your hero died. His whole quest was a waste, and we should all be glad. Sewerside is grateful."

"Five."

"They're all dead now. Right, Walter? Hey, Vanessa? See? They even agree with me!"

Electricity leaped from Flatline's boots as he dashed in.

The Exploding Man threw his orbs toward the hero. Pavement burst but none hit Flatline. There were just too slow.

Flatline bounded over the first explosion. His spread of volts blew the second ball out of the air. The third landed short, sending shards of stone out, but the fourth smacked the road beside him. He had no time to fully dodge the impact, so he leaped forward.

Blown road crashed into his back like shrapnel and brought Flatline to one knee. He grimaced and held back a whine. Blinding pain surged through him like his electricity did.

A bright smile dawned on the villain's fat face. His fingers plunged into the lethal flesh—

then the vehicle shook, and the sidewalk rumbled underneath them. The villain waved back and forth, pulling himself out onto the roof of the car. The vehicle whined as it was lifted.

"What's going on?" the exploder cried.

Flatline sighed. "My fun is over."

The car groaned and flipped over. It landed on the passenger side. The Exploding Man leaped off, landing on his back in a roll, passing the unconscious driver. Under the broken pile of metal and windshield emerged a teenager with grey skin. Concrete dusted off his stone hands.

"Good to see you, Flatline. I'm glad you didn't get blown to bits."

"That's just what a supervisor likes to hear from his underling."

"*Underling* is not the right word. We're not criminals."

"Don't be pedantic," Flatline said, waving dismissively. "Did you clean things up?"

"Yes. No injured civilians. I also learned a neat trick from one of the hostages."

Concrete let his stone form fall away bringing back his Caucasian skin. He slid off his gloves and put them in the pouch on his belt before approaching the agitated villain. Flatline called after him, unable to rise from his crouch, but the boy ignored his calls.

For some reason, the Exploding Man swore at Concrete. The villain flung a ball of skin directly at the boy's face. Concrete raised his hands, not realizing it wouldn't do him any good.

"Stupid kid," Flatline said. He rushed forward, expecting an explosion.

But none arrived. Flatline slid to a stop beside his underling.

Concrete showed him the skin orb in his bare hand without looking at him. The dumb grin on his face was enough to bring Flatline's blood pressure up.

"What was that, Concrete?" It took everything he had to avoid punching the kid.

"This," Concrete said, holding the sphere over his head. He stepped directly in front of the exploder. "It doesn't detonate on contact with epidermis, does it? That's why you never aim directly at people with exposed skin. You always go for the floor or the wall beside them."

The Exploding Man flinched. He reached for more skin on his gut.

Concrete's free hand solidified, and he brought it down on the villain's skull. The Exploding Man's eyes rolled back in his head, and he fell unconscious. Concrete placed the orb against the villain's bruised cheek, and it absorbed into him like water drops into a puddle. The Exploding Man slept on in his crumpled lump.

"How did you know that would work?" Flatline asked.

"Like I said, I got a tip from one of the hostages. Not sure how he figured it out. Probably this guy's blabbering mouth. How are you doing?"

"Better." He slapped Concrete on the back. "For a kid, you sure have a mean left."

"Don't call me that." The kid rubbed his back. "You did most of the work. But I have a suggestion. Maybe stick closer to the rules next time and not run off without back up. This is why they don't call us in. What are you hiding behind your back, anyway?"

The police cars skidded to a stop behind them. Officers surrounded the fallen criminal. But Concrete didn't look away from his supervisor.

"Hey," Flatline said, keeping his injured back out of view. "When you're dealing with an exploding man, your first priority is not getting anyone blown up. Nobody was hurt here. I call that a win. Good job, kid. You're on your way."

6.

"I can already see the headlines tomorrow," Julia said. "*Blockhead Kid and Reckless Idiot Save Hostages from Gang of Thieves*. Not like I would write anything that hacky."

Sieg didn't reply.

The pair strolled under the setting sun, the apartment building a block away. After hours of questioning, the cops had finally let them go. Streetlights flickered on, and the humidity choked the city again. Another long night was on the way. But her old friend still said nothing.

"Sieg?"

He sighed, scratching his chin. "This is why I stay away from places like banks. This kind of thing happens all the time in Summerside. You'd know that if you lived here as long as I have. Why did you even come to this city, Julia? It's a cemetery. If you want to know what the rest of the world will look like in a few years, look no further than what you saw today."

"There's nothing left of Lenora, either. Doesn't mean I want that to happen here."

He grumbled. "You didn't answer my question."

She didn't get it. Nothing about him added up. Sieg was an energetic boy when they were kids, but when Lenora fell, so did he. Julia left with relatives, got an education, and some sense of a normal life. But Sieg disappeared, and when she found him, he had become an entirely different person. This man walking beside her had completely given up on everything.

"Why'd I come?" She mused it over a moment. "Because I want to find the truth. Bullet Face knew my real identity. If it wasn't for those two I'd be dead. I'm getting close, Sieg. The villains, the gangs, and the mob, they're all deep into it. If I could just find The Seeker, I could finally reach the truth."

"The Seeker is a bedtime story for kids." He rolled his deep blue eyes and grunted. "Just be thankful those two were there to save you. All these cities will be just like Lenora one day."

Finally, they reached the building. Sieg had been gifted the place from his uncle's will years back. It was well-maintained, despite plumbing issues and the outside regularly being stained by graffiti. But he always kept it clean. For someone who had given up, Sieg still tried at certain things. The two of them lived there in separate apartments; but it often felt like they were different worlds, and his was imploding. She wouldn't let him escape hers so easily.

"No," Julia said, walking up the concrete steps to the foyer. "I don't think you really believe that. But, that aside, tell me how you knew how the Exploding Man's power worked?"

"Because I've seen it before," he said, bitterly. "There are no secrets in Summerside."

~

After finally dropping Julia off in her apartment, Sieg made his way to his. She always asked too many uncomfortable questions. It was no wonder she made enemies so easily.

But she didn't know about Sieg despite what she believed. He was a whole new man from the boy she knew.

Mrs. Thompson met him in the hall to ask about her plumbing. She had a plump figure, a hawk nose, and greying short hair, and the nasal pitch in her tone never failed to stand his neck hairs up. However, he told her he would get to it tomorrow. Finally, she left, to catch her bus.

She didn't ask about the bank. She probably didn't hear about it yet. It would be all over the news in the morning. The Adams twins in 403 would probably pester him about it, though. Boys were like that.

Sieg locked the apartment door behind him. The day was finally over. He breathed a sigh of relief that he no longer had to be *that* person anymore.

He dropped his power of illusion. The image of an overweight, balding man with blue eyes fell away. He became a well-built man with wild black hair again. He removed his blue contacts to reveal piercing green eyes.

He wasn't that boy Julia grew up with in Lenora. She couldn't know about his ability to touch and learn about his target, just as she couldn't see through his illusion. The Exploding Man made the mistake of activating The Seeker's hidden power. Within seconds, the villain was visited by ghosts of the past just as that Flatline punk arrived on the scene.

But none of them knew the truth. None knew that Sieg actually was The Seeker—he was the Summerside myth.

Fading sunlight streaked orange through the blinds into the cramped living room. In the locked closet by his bed sat his weights, written notes, and black mask and leather jacket with the rest of his night garb. The time to bring them out was near. The moon grew close.

"The Exploding Man," he mumbled. The criminal wasn't connected to bigger fish, so there wasn't any real info to parse through from his fat head. "Just another cog in the machine. Those two interlopers, however . . ."

In the villain's mind sat a story about a teenager with electricity powers who fought alongside a man named Comet a few times in Oxford. The Seeker soon recognized the boy in the memories as a certain other Elemental Type he had met hours ago. The Comet was long gone now, but Flatline—and now Concrete, were still here. The Seeker couldn't hide his smile as his power revisited the story once again before it faded with the stolen memories. He wrote down the relevant information, and got ready for the night ahead.

He thought about what Julia had said about those two enforcers. She might have had a point. "Summerside isn't dead, Julia? Perhaps this is the start of something big, after all."

KNIVES IN THE NIGHT

The shotgun muzzle pressed violently against Walker's temple. The click made his eyes slid open in response. He had fallen asleep on the balcony. Not good. A two day lack of sleep was no excuse for a sloppy mistake. But this was the reality of the situation.

He slowly raised his hands and tasted the humid night air when he sucked in his breath.

"What are you doing up here?" a voice said from behind the barrel.

Rain beat down hard against the old brick apartment building. He was still on the sixth floor, across from the Neon Beetle bar. He was so close to *them*. There had to be a way to explain this without arousing suspicion.

"I apologize," Walker said. He glanced up past the wide brim of his leather hat. An old man with greying ruffled hair, the face of a Doberman, and hard coal eyes stared down at him. Beside him stood a young woman Walker could barely make out in the downpour. "I fell asleep on your balcony trying to get out of the rain. This is just a misunderstanding."

That wasn't entirely a lie. This area of Summerside had a curfew; experimental drones flew above on the hour to scan the streets and roofs for heat signatures to enforce it. If he could have found a better place to hide, Walker would have taken it. Sleeping against cold brick, cracked pavement, and dilapidated balconies, wreaked havoc on the shoulders and neck. Your body gets used to the rough feel, but you never get accustomed to the cold.

"It's not my balcony," the old timer said.

"The shotgun says otherwise."

"What is with your eyes, anyway? What kind of odd power do you have? Purple eyes aren't natural even for Mental Types."

Walker narrowed his brow. "It's not an ability that'll do any good right now."

"Shana, what do you want me to do with him?"

"I wonder," she said.

The girl had a slim figure, an ocean of blue

in her eyes, and long strands of flowing dark hair that fell past her small shoulders. She wore a simple black skirt and matching sweater and leggings to match her Celtic facial features. A knowing smile accentuated her form perfectly.

It had been a while since he'd dealt with a woman of her caliber. He would have tipped his hat if it wasn't likely to be blown clear off his shoulders with the rest of his head. Not to mention it would have made him look pathetic, but friendly folks were less likely to end up with a buck shot to the skull. He didn't make it this far in the city by being nice, and he wasn't going to start now.

"Good evening, little miss. Don't mind me. Just a vagrant passing through."

"I don't recognize him," Shana said. "He's not one of the Bulldogs. Doesn't have the right colors, and this is rather high up . . . besides, who wears a trench coat and leather hat these days?"

Walker raised an eyebrow, and, instantly, felt the shotgun press tighter against his skull. He held in a breath. "You're lucky that I don't have metal elemental powers, old timer."

"Of course, you don't," he said. "Don't have the right glint in your eyes. Not crazy enough."

"You sound certain, mack."

"If you did," the old man continued, "then you already would have turned my gun inside out and sent it through my spleen, lungs, and heart. I've seen them do it to stupider folks than me. Elemental Types are crazy that way. You're not one of them."

Walker let out a small grin. "You got me there. I don't have those kinds of abilities. I'm just a guy trying to get out of the rain for a few minutes. Haven't slept in a few days. Summerside isn't the most hospitable city," he glanced at the shotgun, "as one can clearly see."

"Now, now," the girl interrupted. "He's just a homeless drifter, Mr. Desmond. We don't need to resort to violence. Let's just have a nice talk inside."

"Check his coat," the old man said.

Shana leaned over and went for Walker's pockets. A scent of lilies and hair spray swam against the dank city odor. Her thin lips muttered to no one as her small hands opened his coat. A pit grew in his gut. There were few things left in this world of crooks that weren't ugly beyond repair, and some things should always remain sacred. He grumbled. Women should stay away from blood. But, thanks to the old man, he couldn't stop her from looking.

The girl recoiled when she spotted the throwing knives. She ran a hand over them, and he couldn't help but look away. For the first time in a dog's age, Walker felt the sting of shame.

The old man pushed the gun harder. "What's he got?"

Instead of answering, she watched Walker's fuchsia-colored eyes. Her fear settled down to a vague stare that he couldn't puzzle out. Did she figure him out?

Heat ran through him like a good drink. He didn't like being flustered. Could she have had powers? He would have certainly asked at a more opportune time. Maybe a situation where he wasn't certain to lose his tongue with his cerebral cortex in the ensuing buckshot.

Without speaking, she closed his coat and stood back up.

"Is he dangerous?" the old man asked.

"He's good," Shana said. "He might be able to deal with our problem."

"You didn't answer my question."

Walker finally eyeballed the old man. He

had ruffled grey hair plastered on top of his leathery skin and wore old track pants and a wrinkled long-sleeved red shirt. Despite how frail he looked on the outside, there was a spark that told of tougher material. The old man was the type to always keep his word. He was right not to trust Walker, though not for the reasons he assumed.

"Enough, Mr. Desmond," she said. "No one in the building has any powers, and we're not going to find anyone after curfew. He can do it. We need someone before they come back."

Desmond dropped the shotgun to his side. He sighed. "You think you can trust a bum who fell asleep on your balcony to take on the Bulldogs? Where's your head, girl? He could be related to them."

"No. He's not one of them. I'm sure. And he's definitely got a good power. Check his eyes. Mental Types, the really potent ones, have different colored eyes. They're usually red, so his must be something rare. And since Mental Types are pretty rare themselves, he's our jackpot. Don't forget that the Bulldogs have a Mental Type, too."

"And what makes you think I'll be helping, lady?" Walker stood, stretching his back. The other two flinched at his towering height. He stood around six foot and eight, a foot over the girl and a bit less for the old man. "I just told you that I'm only passing through. I wasn't lying."

She watched him for a few additional seconds and then patted his arm. "I've got a deal for you. Come on in out of the rain, and we'll talk business. We might be able to help each other out. Also, I apologize for the shotgun. Mr. Desmond can be a bit intense."

Walker raised an eyebrow. A deal? She couldn't know about the Inner Light.

"Well," he said. "I'm not one to turn down a beautiful woman, so you have me against the ropes."

"That's the spirit," she said, with a chirp.

Desmond groaned.

The two of them exited into the apartment. Walker watched after them, rotating his shoulder to get the dampness out. He straightened the grey shirt under his coat and readjusted the belt on his black pants. Falling asleep was such an amateurish mistake. He was lucky they were gullible enough—at least, the girl was. He glanced down at the bar across the street. He could taste victory. The Inner Light was just in reach.

For a moment, he thought he saw a black

mist streaming across the roof of the bar. He blinked, and it was gone. The downpour continued unabated, and the bar looked normal once more. He rubbed his eyes. Lack of sleep could screw with you something fierce.

He put it out of his mind. Business first, then he could continue the real job.

The inside of the apartment could only be described as awful. Desmond and Shana sat on an old ripped-up couch on the right side of the room. The front door out to the building's halls lay across from his position by the balcony door. A hall beside the couch led to the bath and bedrooms and on the opposite awaited a small kitchen. The small and decrepit space suited this neighborhood. The living room was far too cramped, the drywall chipping, and it stunk of the musty rain. On the cracking walls hung framed pictures of three young girls in the arms of a mother and father. Between the kitchen and the couch was an ancient television that played an old western. The place looked about as comfortable to live in as the balcony was to sleep on. Walker began to think she'd taken this apartment for the same reason he fell asleep on the balcony—the view.

Desmond nodded at him. "Your name, son?"

"Walker," he answered.

"First or last?"

"Last."

"Where are you from?"

"The void."

"What? Is that another name for the sanitarium?"

"He doesn't need to tell us all that, Mr. Desmond."

"What can I help you with?" Walker asked. "Keep in mind that there are things I won't do no matter how much you're offering. I have my own problems to worry about."

"I don't have much to offer." The young woman closed her eyes and put a finger to her temple as if in thought. "I can give you a free shower, change of clothes, and a meal. It's not much, but from the looks of you, that might be enough. Everybody needs to get cleaned up once in a blue moon, right?"

"Your hair isn't naturally black, is it?"

She brushed her hair and shrugged. "Do we have a deal?"

He caught her glancing at his coat. The

throwing knives were something a normal person would be scared of. Two weren't even metal, but a special artificial plastic that he had custom made. They were to deal with Metal Elemental Type punks easier. But she couldn't know any of that. She knew nothing of the void or his mission.

"Depends," he said, addressing her offer.

She tilted her head and pressed her thin lips together. "Depends?"

"I'll need to know two things. What does the full job entail, and what are your powers?"

Desmond growled. Shana patted his shoulder, and he looked to the floor instead. Her rosy cheeks parted in a pitiful smile.

"You got me," she said. "Is that why you chose this balcony?"

"No. I saw your eyes sparkle when you touched one of the knives. That wasn't the look of a woman scared for her life. You saw something."

"He has knives?" Desmond exclaimed. "For crying out loud, Shana!"

"It's fine! You know what I can do, Mr. Desmond." She put a hand up, still watching Walker. "I can see the perspective of any object I touch at every point in time at once. It's an Abnormal Type ability, and it doesn't always work. I have to concentrate, or I'll either not remember anything or accidentally block out my own memories. It's very difficult to use and terribly inconvenient. I don't want to know what will happen if it goes really wrong."

"And what did you see?" Cold sweat ran up Walker's spine.

"Bloodshed, agony, and despair." Her breaths stiffened, and her nails dug into her knees through her skirt. "Dark nights. Bloodstained alleys. Cultists screaming for their lives."

"Cultists?" Desmond wondered aloud. "You don't mean gang members?"

She shook her head. "I don't know who you are, Mr. Walker. I don't know what your powers are. But I saw you. I know what you do. You might not trust me, but I can trust you."

Anger flared in Walker, but he held it in check. A series of rookie mistakes had brought her too close. And he was so very close to reaching *them*—the ones he'd been seeking.

"If you don't tell me what the job is in ten seconds, I'm leaving. I don't play well with shrinks or pity parties."

"The Bulldogs," she said. "They keep

breaking into our building. They're looking for a girl, apparently. One of them has been appearing in different tenants' homes over the last few days. No one knows how he's getting in. I need you to chase them out. This neighborhood has enough problems without these hoods making it worse."

Walker laughed. "Hate to break it to you, miss, but I'm no hero. I'm not a mercenary, either. Whatever problems this festering wound of a city has is none of my concern. I have one job, and nothing is going to stop me from carrying it out. Sorry. There are worse things in this city than simple street crime. What makes you think I should help?"

She put up her hands. "Powered folk can be hired to deal with a lot of requests, but they cost money unless there's a disaster of some kind. Working with the government will do that. They only operate during the day, too. Police can't be trusted when it comes to gangs. Especially around here. With the ties the Bulldogs have, nothing will probably ever be done to stop them unless we think outside the box. You're outside the box, Walker."

"What about Crusaders?" Walker asked.

"Vigilantes?" Desmond barked. "You're

not serious. Even if we could find one of them, how do you suppose we convince them to help? The cops want to roast them all over a tall grease fire. They'd be easy targets if they did small jobs."

Walker let out a low laugh and removed the leather cowboy hat from his head. He pounded the water from it on his thigh. A beautiful woman had him wrapped around her finger, and there was little he could do about it. Sickening. He couldn't just walk away now—Alma would never forgive him, and he would never forgive himself. He threw the hat back on, and let out a deep breath. That was right: Alma was still waiting for him.

"I'll do it. My clothes could use a good cleaning, and a meal does sound good." Walker looked the pair over. "And you do owe me an explanation, lady."

She looked at him askew. "About what?"

"About why you're hunting the Inner Light."

"I-I," Shana said, with a stutter. She glanced over at Desmond who couldn't have been more lost. "How do you know these things, Walker?"

"Your eyes again. When you mentioned

cultists, you flinched. You know who I mean. Why else would you live in a rat hole like this? That is why I'm agreeing to do this stupid job. If you know anything about the Inner Light, you will tell me when this is all over. Got it?"

She nodded. Desmond glanced between the two of them, still confused.

Walker held back a laugh. If this suspicious woman was working for the Inner Light, then he was falling into a mousetrap designed to break his spine when he went for the cheese. But Summerside was already a snake pit even without its magic problem, and he already had no intention of walking out of this alive. But he had no choice but to keep moving forward. There were no leads aside from the one before him.

"Just please be quick about it, Mr. Walker."

He glanced at the girl's thin downcast face. His blood boiled, but there was nothing he could do to help her. All he could do was what he was good at.

And that's what he would do.

"Right, lady," he said. "I'll get to work. Just have a hot meal ready for my return."

"One thing." Her cheeks reddened. "I really want to know what your first name is."

"Don't push it."

"Come on, I bet it's good." Her bright eyes lit up. "It wouldn't be good if you weren't hiding it."

"No offense, but no one needs to know. It's better to forget about me when I'm gone." As he thought about what he would to the Inner Light when he finally reached them, his resolve only strengthened. "Trust me; it's better for all involved."

~

Walker strode the apartment halls with his knuckles tightened by his side. He had plastered his black war paint around his eyes to darken his otherwise pale face, but he didn't feel amped up. Irritation ruled him. The Inner Light was close by. All he had to do was catch one of those pigs and make it squeal. There were few things Walker enjoyed more than making hooligans cry.

But first, he had to get through this mess. A man never breaks a promise with a woman if he can help it. The Neon Beetle Bar would still be standing in the morning—unless he got there first, that is.

Shana's voice crackled through his earpiece. *"Where are you?"*

"Patrolling," he said. "You didn't need to give me one of these. It's not like I can't find this guy on my own. I do this sort of thing all the time."

"Yes, yes, you look very capable." She sighed. *"You didn't have a phone. I only want to be able to contact you if something comes up. Is that alright with you, tough guy?"*

"Just don't get in my way."

"Tell me you first name, and I'll shut up."

Instead of grimacing, a smile slowly slid across his lips. He fought it away quickly.

"What's the deal with the knives?"

"There was a man with metal powers a long time ago who used them. Now that's a story. You can say that he inspired my weapon choice. Anyway, let me get to work."

Few people walked the halls after midnight. He spotted a handful of teenagers roughhousing and going on about some football game and a pair of middle-aged women chattering and carrying laundry baskets. Walker glided around them easily.

It wasn't as if they could see him.

Invisibility was a true gift of a power. Not only did they not see him—he could swiftly avoid them, too. There was a hidden world to Summerside that none of these people saw. With black war paint around his eyes and knives under his coat, he was ready for it.

They had no idea what was out there in the rain.

"*I got a call from Mr. Desmond*," Shana said. "*There's a disturbance on the fourth floor.*"

Walker made a beeline for the stairs. "Roger."

As soon as he reached the fourth floor, he heard a ruckus. Ear-splitting screams pierced the yellow-stained white hallway. A small crowd milled about, blandly staring at an apartment door. Walker brushed passed them towards the source. Another scream broke their chatter.

Walker kicked the door in. Splinters burst from where his boot landed. The knob slammed against the drywall with the rest of the door.

"Did you see that?" someone in the crowd said.

"That door just flew open!"

Some punk laughed. "Dude, there's a Crusader in the building!"

"You don't know that. Maybe it's some psycho with sick brain powers."

A young woman stood on the other side of the threshold, staring at the dented wall. Her platinum hair was ruffled and unkempt as if she had just awoken and her old wrinkled shirt and blue pajama bottoms reinforced this impression. Yet another frightened woman he had to deal with. Walker was beginning to dislike this place.

Despite her panic, she ran through the opening. Walker sidestepped, and let her pass.

"What happened?" an older woman asked.

"One o-of the B-Bulldogs," the woman said, still breathing hard. "He's in the kitchen. I woke up when I heard someone going through my cabinets. I froze when I saw him there."

A teenage boy looked on in awe. "Did you knock open that door?"

"No," she replied. "I didn't."

"Then what happened?" an old man in sweats asked.

"*What was that sound?*" Shana said in Walker's ear.

"Quiet," Walker whispered.

The apartment was exactly like Shana's

shabby place except with different tacky furniture. They were most likely all more or less like this. Not a good neighborhood.

He crossed into the kitchen. There a gangly man wearing a ripped blue jacket and dark green hair leaned against the counter. It didn't look like he had pals. The dumb-looking punk had dark circles under his eyes, a square face, and an under bite. He held a sandwich from his mouth.

"What are you doing out there?" the scumbag said. "I just wanted a snack, yeah? No need to get your panties twisted and knock the damn door down. This job isn't all fun and games for me either. You're not even who I'm looking for."

He rolled his eyes, and Walker stood in front of him. The stink wafting from the loser's mouth was matched only by the odor on his unwashed body. The kid mindlessly took a bite of his sandwich, unaware of the invisible man before him.

Walker spoke softly. "How did you get in here?"

The punk froze. He glanced around the kitchen. Bits of salami fell from his teeth. "Who was that?"

"You have powers, don't you?"

"I do, ghost man." The goon nodded and produced a switchblade from his pocket. He waved it around in front of him, still oblivious to the invisible Walker. He spun the weapon in his hand, and the blade slipped through his fingers like they were made of air. "But what about you? Do you bleed?"

A smile spread across Walker's lips. He leaned forward and became visible two inches from the punk's face. The scum screamed and swiped his knife. Walker brushed the left hand sideways, grabbed the wrist, and twisted. The blade tumbled to the laminate floor, and the punk yelped. Walker lurched over him.

The punk stuttered. "Holy Mother of G—"

Walker squeezed his right hand tight around the punk's throat. Choking gasps followed.

"You're a Physical Type, huh?" Walker asked. The punk rapidly nodded, struggling for air. "You can phase through objects. That's how you got in here."

"Yes!" he squeaked out.

"But not if you can't concentrate." Walker

spun around and slammed the punk into the fridge door. Magnets bounced off, and the appliance shook. He twisted the punk's arm behind his back. "Two questions before I make your arm extra flexible. What are you here for? What do you know about the Inner Light?"

"Inner Light? What are you talking about?"

Walker sighed. The liars never ceased to be tiring. He dragged the idiot by the arm out of the kitchen, approached the living room coffee table, and slammed the punk's face down on it. Pens and scraps of used paper dove outward with the impact.

"Are you going to answer my questions," Walker whispered, "or be put in traction? I'm good with either, but lying isn't going to help you out of this."

"Alright, alright!" The punk scrambled against the table. "I'm here to find a girl. The boss wants a girl with red hair and a small scar on her elbow. That's all I know. Just let me go, yeah?"

"I asked a second question."

"I don't know what that means! What is the Inner Light?"

A small voice told Walker to squeeze

harder. That voice had some agreeable ideas.

"You work for a gang like the Bulldogs, and you don't know the Inner Light?"

"They Crusaders or something?"

"Crusaders! They're the furthest thing from it." Bitterness twisted in Walker as he whispered. "They're calling up things they shouldn't be. They destroy lives, places, and families. Sacrifices. Kidnapping. Murder. They're like the Aztecs except with worse fashion and are a lot meaner. Now, tell me what you know."

"You made that up! Something's wrong with you, man. You're the one who should be locked up. You're crazy!"

"That's not an answer." Walker slipped his free hand into his coat and felt a blade. "But probably true."

"Walker!" Shana yelled from behind him. "Stop!"

A crowd of people beyond the doorway milled about behind him. Shana stood in front of the pack. That look of fear—the wide eyes, the tight lips. He cursed to himself. She watched his hand fall away from his coat and let out a relieved breath.

In that moment, he finally realized what he

was about to do. This was just some dumb kid, after all. Why was he considering ending him? Lack of sleep played hell on the senses. But that was just an excuse. Walker knew what he was doing.

He looked away from her. "I'm just doing my job, lady."

"Yes, you caught him. You don't need to do anything else. He's defenseless."

"Where's Desmond?" he asked her.

"I don't know. Probably still upstairs."

"Do you think he'd be any gentler than me?"

"He wouldn't be doing what you almost did. This wasn't part of the job, Walker. You know that. I only wanted you to catch him. What is the deal?"

He slammed the punk's face down again. The table shook. Walker's rage gained a second wind. "Because I have another job to do."

"What about that girl in the picture you carry around?"

He glanced at her, mouth agape. Her cheeks reddened. This was even worse than aggravating. She lied. It wasn't his knives she touched before—it was the picture he hid inside his inner coat pocket: the picture of Alma. What was she butting in for? The past is the past, and yet everyone always dug for it like an old corpse. No wonder he strayed from people. They could never keep to themselves.

She put her hands out. "Do you think *she* would want this?"

"And what, exactly, can *you* tell me about *her*? It's just a photo. You have no idea what these people did, what they are *still* doing. You have no idea why I'm here. I told you I'm no hero, no Crusader; I have only one job, one reason for existing. This is it."

Without warning, the punk elbowed Walker in the chest and loosened his grip. The kid bent down and phased through the floor.

Walker swore. He pulled down his leather hat and ran for the balcony. "That's why I was hurting him!"

Walker threw open the balcony door and leaped over the railing. Rain doused him to the bone in an instant, chill cooling his rage. He kept his right hand on the railing and slid it along a vertical bar on the balcony as he fell. Momentum carried him downwards. He gripped the metal bottom of the balcony and twisted, swinging back toward the building. His inertia guided him.

He landed easily on the lower balcony. The light was on in the apartment before him and allowed him to see the inside. The punk was still there. Walker charged through the door.

The punk knelt in the center of the room. He was still regaining his breath when he spotted the man chasing him. Walker cracked the thug's jaw. The enemy spun with the strike, hit the opposite wall face first, and then tumbled down. A nearby lampstand wobbled with the landing. The punk didn't get up.

"Not enough time to phase through that one," Walker said.

He spotted movement out of the corner of his eye. He put a hand in his coat and turned and met the young couple sitting on the couch. They were in their early twenties—the man wearing slacks and a light sweater, and the woman in a plain skirt and green top. It looked like a date. They stared at him and the downed punk with open mouths.

"Sorry about that." Walker tipped his hat and forced a smile. "Didn't mean to ruin your night. Just forget I was here. You didn't see anything."

~

Walker rubbed the lingering slumber from his eyes. This was going to be a long night.

Shana was a righteous pain. Women could be pests, but she took it to a new level. She followed him as he carried the unconscious gang member down to the basement door chatting away. Part of the crowd also followed them down there, mumbling amongst each other, but at least they didn't get in his way. When he finally reached his destination, he found that the door was locked.

"Anyone have the keys to this place?" Walker asked.

A young boy in blue pajamas answered, "Mr. Desmond does."

"Someone go and get him."

Desmond soon showed up, surly as expected. He didn't bat an eye at the unconscious punk on Walker's shoulder and walked right past him. Keys in hand, he unlocked the door and let the stench of wet paper waft out of the basement.

"Just don't leave a mess," Desmond said.

Walker made sure no one followed, turned on the light, and shut the door behind him. He descended the stairs, placed his victim on the cement floor, cleared a space in the center of the room of stray boxes, screws, and tools, and got to work. There were a few low beams on the ceiling and enough of an open area for what he needed to do.

Walker grimaced. This part wasn't going to be fun.

He fished a fistful of screws and nails from the utility closet, dumped them in his coat pocket, and grabbed more. His pockets filled, he moved on.

Thankfully, the superintendent kept things tidy. Walker procured a good size rope hanging from the wall and pushed out some heavy wooden crates from the corner. These would support a solid amount of weight. He threw the rope over the beams.

It didn't take long before the thug was dangling from the floor. His arms tied behind his back, the rope wrapped around the beams, and the heavy crates piled on the frayed ends kept him hanging in midair. Walker tied a blindfold around the prisoner's eyes and readied his conscience for what he was about to do.

"Is this necessary?" Shana asked.

Walker glanced over his shoulder. What a pain. "About as necessary as you changing your hair color. You shouldn't be here."

He removed the nails and screws out of his coat pockets and sprinkled them under the dangling punk, spreading them out evenly. A bad fall would mean problems for his prisoner.

"This should break any lingering illusions of me being a hero," he said.

"We only want to know why the Bulldogs are doing this." The strain in her voice grated. Guilt trips never failed to annoy. "What *are* you planning on doing, Walker?"

"If that's all you want, then just call the cops. This punk isn't going anywhere. But I know you're looking for something else." She jumped when he suddenly turned. She looked away at his stare. "You're an Abnormal Type. Mental Types like me are rare and a high commodity, but Abnormal Types blend in so easy with normal people because their powers are so simple to hide. I doubt anyone here even knows you have those abilities other than the old man, and you probably told him. So why are you here? It's not the Bulldogs you want, but the man behind the curtain. You want the Inner Light, and that's what I'm trying to get, so you must know what they're like. What exactly are you expecting here? I don't fight with my hands behind my back."

She kept her attention to the opposite wall. "I don't even know if they're real. They're the only lead I have among many similar ones. The Eye of the Serpent, Deathband, and Last Countdown are other rumors with nothing to substantiate them. They could just as easily be real. Why do you think the Inner Light is the culprit?"

"I've seen their victims. Criminals think they're top dogs in this city. Police think people like me are the only obstacle in the way of a utopia. They're both blind. There are darker forces in this city—and I'm going to dig them up for all to see. Now, get out of my way."

Walker made sure the blindfold and ropes were tight as possible on the punk. It didn't matter if the girl wouldn't supply him with information. Doing things on his own was how he worked, but he wouldn't be doing it much longer. The Inner Light was so close he could taste it.

He slapped the punk's cheeks. "Time to wake up, sweetie. Breakfast is getting cold."

No reaction.

Walker tapped him three more times.

The punk moaned. "Huh? What?"

"Your Papa ran off this morning, and your Mama's passed out on the couch." Walker tried to hold back a smile but failed. "Who do you think it is? Wake up, halfwit!"

The thug's lip trembled. "Who? Why can't I see anything?"

"Don't try phasing through the ropes. You're hanging above a large stack of sharp instruments. Unless you want to lose some weight, stay still. These suckers aren't fun to pull out." Walker kicked some nails across the cold cement to make sure the punk heard them. "You get it yet? It's not worth the trouble."

"You again," the prisoner said. He gritted his teeth. "Who are you?"

"I'm in charge here, not you. Losers don't dictate terms. Tell me your name."

The punk bit his lip. "Brandon, man."

"Now that's the name of a kid who can't take a punch." Walker knocked his hat against his leg to shake out the remaining water and plopped it back on his head. "Alright, *Brandon*, time for truth. Who runs the Bulldogs? And I'm not talking about the Mouth."

"The Mouth answers to no one, man. I'm here to scout. The Mouth wanted to find a girl because he wants one. There's no big secret." His throat gulped. "Just give me the name of the red-haired girl. I'll go tell him, alright? I won't come back. Come on, man."

Walker punched Brandon's solar plexus. Shana gasped and the thug wheezed. The thump echoed through the concrete basement.

"This isn't a joke, you colossal waste of skin cells!" Walker roared. "I took out the Piranhas, the Westside Killers, and the Rokudenashi Bombers. They all said the Mouth was in on it, that he's getting information from some new player—a dark man that answers to no one. A man wearing black robes with a power darker than his red eyes. Tell me what you know, Brandon. I'm trying to keep cool here. You don't realize what you idiots are getting into!"

Walker struck him again. The punk choked out a breath.

Shana let out a squeak, and Walker turned back to her.

"Would you get out, already?" he roared.

"I don't know," the punk said. "The Mouth never told me anything. He yells orders in our head like a megaphone, but he never gives us all the details. I've never even heard him talk! I only joined a few weeks ago, man. I really don't know!"

Walker let silence set in. He rubbed the bridge of his nose, gathering thoughts.

"Come on, man," Brandon whispered. "I won't come back. Just, like, give me something for the Mouth. I just don't want him to kill me, yeah?"

Walker cracked his knuckles and took a step forward.

Shana flew to the dangling punk, stepping between the two. Before Walker could say anything, she laid a hand on Brandon's jacket.

After a moment, she let go.

"He's not lying," she said, turning back to Walker. She winced as if a bad thought stabbed into her mind. For a moment she paled, then straightened up. "His jacket was given to him four weeks ago. But there's an odd presence staining the material. The only thing I can make out is the distinct picture of a big bald man with a scar over his left eye. He hangs out in the basement of the Neon Beetle."

"As good a lead as any," Walker said. That

had to be the Mouth.

Walker moved toward the stairs.

"Hang around for a while, Brandon. You're not going to want to see what happens next."

"Wait a second!" Brandon exclaimed. His teeth chattered. "I was just having a little fun, man. I wasn't gonna hurt anyone. Mouth is just looking for a girlfriend, right? Right?"

Shana ran up behind Walker. "What are planning to do?"

"Go get Desmond," he whispered. "Tell him to watch the halfwit. We can't have him warning the Bulldogs."

"Warning them about what?"

He grunted. She didn't know when to stop pushing, and he didn't know if he could stomach it much longer. But it didn't matter now—not with Death Itself in his crosshairs. He began to turn away when she grabbed the edge of his coat sleeve.

"I dyed my hair for a reason," she said. "I need to find the Inner Light—if that's what they're called—before they find me. I don't know how much time I have. They've taken someone close to me, and no one knows who did it. There are no leads."

"One of the girls in that picture in your apartment. Your sister, I take it."

"The Bulldogs must have learned I was here. I made sure to dye my hair and cover my arms to not stand out, but that didn't stop them from sending people like this into the building. If you know who they're working for, you have to tell me! I need to find her."

"Why did they take her?"

"She has a power. Why else?" She sighed. "I was this close to finding out just who the Bulldogs were contacting. I don't know what to do if they're going to keep sending their men in here to look for me. Someone is going to get hurt. All I want is to get her back."

"You will. We're so close now. The silver lining behind this storm front is that I met you, and you gave me the Inner Light on a platter. This is working out perfectly."

"Hey!" Brandon shouted. "I hear whispering. Come on. I wasn't going to hurt anyone."

"Shut up and wait," Walker said.

"Just tell me why I didn't see you enter the apartment. Were you invisible?"

"Yes."

"But I should have seen you at least a little! We have the same power type, yeah? We're both Physical Types. We should be able to cancel each other out on some level."

"I don't turn invisible," Walker said. He climbed the stairs back to the apartment hall. Shana fell silent behind him. "I just make everyone think that I do."

~

Thick drops dashed against Walker's coat and hopped from his hat. Rainfall smashed against the city around him as he crossed the street. The weather was not in his favor. His illusion power would keep him hidden from man, but nature knew the truth. The downpour soaked him mercilessly.

It would be some time before the next drone made a scan. He already did the math. It would be an estimated half hour before it returned and bathed the streets in an infrared glow searching for illegal bodies. The piece of junk would be able to scan him, too. It was as hard to hide from machine as it was from nature—they didn't have minds to fool.

The Neon Beetle's old sign flashed hard bright pink against the drenched brick. Even for this end of town it was quite the dive. In the old days, bars would be forbidden from being too close to residences, but this was a new era—an era of rebuilding. These drones were put out just for that reason despite protests from the populace. Someone needed to cover up the more unsavory parts of Summerside from the rest of the world.

Outside the Neon Beetle, two Bulldogs chatted underneath the rain gutter. One had a cigarette dangling from his lip and the stocky one wore an old cap on his round head.

"Crowded room tonight," the smoker said.

The other shrugged. "It *is* Brandon's last chance. Mouth says if he doesn't get back in the next hour then he's going in himself. Kid's wasted enough time."

"We shoulda just done that in the first place. Relying on our pet freak was a waste of time. It's not like any cops are gonna care if we bother some girl."

"Mouth wanted this done low key. Don't know why. It's just a girl. He's had plenty."

"Might be we're getting her for someone else." He took a hard drag. "Someone who doesn't want to be caught."

The stocky one laughed. "Mouth doesn't work for anyone."

"Probably not. But I don't know why else we're doing this. Doesn't make a whole lotta sense any way ya slice it. Like you said, it's just a girl."

"Just do your job, fool. The Mouth wants it, we get it. Not exactly quantum physics."

The cigarette man shrugged. "Right."

Walker blew past them towards the entrance. They didn't so much as glance in the invisible man's direction. The thick wood of the front door looked ripped from a fancy country inn. It contained a very elaborate floral pattern painted on which made it feel out of place, but there were no better options for restaurants and bars these days. There were men who could take apart metal like a skilled surgeon. The mismatched doors existed for the same reason Walker carried special knives. Those that controlled plants or greenery tended to stray from the city, for obvious reasons, so thick wood made for a better protector than metal or stone.

He slid the door shut behind him but his cautiousness was wasted. The bar blasted ancient

Blues Rock music from an ancient era and the boisterous chatter of twenty rowdy men unafraid of the dangerous night outside matched the music. Cannons could have gone off, and no one would have noticed. They wore dark blue shirts and jackets and sat around the tables yelling amongst each other.

Handcrafted wood archways propped up a large room littered with stained tables and large booths lined around the perimeter. The bar at the far left wall held bottles lined against wall-length mirrors between each hand-carved arching pillar. A lone bartender stood separated from the crowd in the room's center with one punk receiving drinks. The bar was otherwise empty. The unmistakable scent of turpentine mixed with the odor alcohol made it stink something fierce.

Walker slowly stepped through the madding crowd. It wasn't as if any would notice him, but he wouldn't take the chance. One slipup would be enough, and Walker would be done.

The man at the bar had more over-descriptive tribal tattoos than muscle. He spun from a barstool sloshing a mug around and met Walker face-on. Walker held his breath and ducked under the large man's long arms, sliding between two empty bar stools. The oversized man kept on toward his target table where three others awaited him. One disaster averted.

Being invisible was handy in public, but it was considerably less useful in crowded areas. He had to keep his eyes everywhere.

Walker leaned against the counter next to the bartender. The middle-aged man with a leathery face vigorously polished a mug. He had his back to the crowd and sang the tune *Tore Down* to himself. Walker tapped the slim man on the shoulder.

"Where's the Mouth hanging?" Walker yelled over the noise.

"Hmm?" The bartender scanned the empty seats around him, and shrugged. "Damn louts. Now I'm hearing things."

"Where is he, ragman?"

The bartender sighed but didn't turn this time. He continued cleaning his glass. "You know he's downstairs. Stop playing hide and seek. Some of us have jobs to do."

"What's this water on the floor?" someone asked.

Walker froze and searched over his shoulder. A scrappy-looking, fresh-faced punk wobbled over to the bar. As he approached, Walker slid sideways, his fingers wriggling for a throwing knife. The punk skidded on the water puddle and steadied himself on a stool. The bartender spun around to meet the newcomer.

"Are you still playing games, Rich?" the bartender asked.

"Games?" The kid's voice slurred. "What are you talking about? There's water all over the floor. You cleaning again?"

"Keep talking, and there'll be blood on the floor with it. I'll say it again—shut up."

"Whatever!"

The kid slunk into the stool, and the bartender went back to his cleaning.

Walker held back a breath and removed his fingers from his coat. He stepped away from the bar with his nerves threatening to fail on him.

But something was still off. Eyes were on him—he could feel them. Pin pricks jabbed at his neck and spine. The air itself grew thick and balmy. A dark presence drew close.

"*Abyss!*"

He spun around.

A shadow like an ephemeral cloak spun across the floor over his small puddles of water.

The figure dissipated under a table where four punks were shouting about a missed field goal in some football game.

Walker rubbed his eyes. Was he imagining it or were the shadows moving again? It couldn't just be lack of sleep. Coincidences didn't exist.

The basement door lay on the opposite wall from the place he entered from. None of the loud patrons gave it much attention; they were all busy drinking and telling irrelevant stories to each other. Walker slipped through the heavy door, letting it gently shut behind him.

He'd scoped this area out from the balcony before he fell asleep like an amateur. No matter how much he looked he couldn't find a way in through the back or the sides. The emergency exits had armed guards and were locked tight, and he was fairly certain they were cemented over from the inside. This was his best chance to find the big man.

Cement steps lead him into the damp basement. The creeping frost chilled even through his wet coat. At the bottom, a thin hallway with thick wood nailed against the walls and doors led onward. The hall twisted to an archway where a lone lightbulb hung in a small solitary room. The windows were all boarded over to block out the outside world which left that bulb as the only light source. There was no other way in—or out.

A poker table had been set up in the middle of the room. Six figures sat playing a game underneath the lone light. They were all deep in thought over their game, sitting in quiet. Behind the table were a closed utility closet and a resting wooden chair like the rest of the occupied seats awaited him. Walker circled the sextet and observed their game.

The biggest one had a shaved head and wore a heavy leather jacket. He had his back to the entranceway. Walker didn't have to see his face to know that had to be the Mouth. The fat sack could afford to have his back turned since he would know if anyone was coming with his power. Mental Types could be cocky like that— Walker had too much experience with them.

All wore blue jackets except the Mouth. The other players included two greasy men with shabby jeans and old shirts sitting on either side of the bigger one. Their rough faces were covered in almost as much sweat as fat. On the opposite side of the table, three younger guys, maybe in their late teens or early twenties, played silently. One held a card up his jacket sleeve. Apparently the Mouth could project thoughts and not read them or else this guy would be dead.

Walker rounded on the closet. Only one of the punks carried a firearm—the rest held knives or brass knuckles. That meant this could be done quickly and quietly.

"Who, Boss?" the man behind Walker asked. "What are you talking about? Nobody came downstairs. It's only us in here."

Hairs on Walker's arms stood tall. Had he been seen?

The speaker frowned. "What are talking about, Boss?"

Walker grabbed the empty chair by the closet door. He spun around slammed it over the head of the speaker. The legs broke off with the impact. The man choked and fell sideways. Walker caught him by the collar of his shirt and whipped the weakened man backwards. His head crashed into the closet door. Pieces of wood darted across the cement floor. The players at the table jumped.

The big bald man's eyes blazed in the direction of Walker. Only a Mental Type could have possibly seen him. The Mouth pointed directly at Walker, but his men only expressed puzzlement.

"I don't see anyone," one of the young men said.

The fat one with the blue baseball cap began to breathe hard. "Boss, there's no one here. I don't know what you're saying."

Walker did not hear whatever they were hearing, only muffled thoughts in the back of his mind. It was quite clear what was happening. The Mouth could barely see Walker but his stooges could not see anything; Walker couldn't hear whatever the villain was projecting. Their powers clashed against each other.

That was almost a problem. But the lesser men were still easy prey.

An old fashioned handgun lay in the inside pocket of the downed man. Walker filched it. He checked and found it loaded and ready to go. Walker fired once into the table. The men all leaped from their chairs. A shot plunged into one of the greasy men's kneecaps. The tubby man screeched to the cold floor. But the gun already clicked empty. Walker tossed it.

Shouts filled the room. The remaining

three thugs ran for the exit.

But Walker was faster. He blinked into existence in front of the doorway. The built kid in the black cap cursed. Walked bashed a fist to his throat. Walker vanished again as the body fell listlessly to the floor.

The fat man with the beard stepped backwards. "What was that?"

The Mouth slammed his thick hand on the table. Poker chips sprayed all over. He pointed directly at Walker again.

"I don't know what you're talking about," the bearded lackey said. "But I'm out of here!"

The remaining two punks barreled toward the entranceway, head first. Walker bashed their skulls together. They stumbled back, and he took hold of their jacket collars. He struck their heads against the stone wall and the impact made a satisfying crack. The pair slumped over.

Meanwhile, the man shot in his knee continued screaming. Walker stomped down and sent him into dreamland.

Only the Mouth was left standing. Walker let his invisibility fall since hiding was a waste of concentration. The Mouth's beady black eyes locked on to Walker's war painted ones.

"Is the Mouth your real name?" Walker asked.

The big man swung his arm up. The poker table flipped over onto the bodies of his men and chips and cards darted everywhere.

"I'm guessing your power is to mentally project your voice into other people's heads." Walker tapped his own temple. "Thing is, I can barely hear a thing! You know what that means. We're both Mental Types. We mess with people's heads but not each other's."

The Mouth growled and dug his nails into his bowling ball fists. Veins popped through his reddening, scarred face. His voice cracked as he attempted to speak.

Walker stifled a laugh. "Can't talk? I'm going to make this quick. So listen up, you walking mound of irony. The Inner Light. Name your contact."

"So you're *The Abyss That Speaks*," the Mouth croaked. "I've heard rumors about you. But you're just a man, no monster."

"I caught Brandon sneaking into the apartment. Too bad that the girl is already gone."

"I knew I shouldn't have trusted this to a kid."

"He's not in this as deep as we are," Walker said. "We know what's out there. Now tell me about your friends."

A big toothy grin fell over the Mouth's namesake. "You need to work for it, punk."

Walker followed the thug's glance to the empty hallway out of the room. Reinforcements would certainly be on the way soon.

"If you've heard of me then you know my reputation, Mouth. Smart thing to do would be to just tell me what I want to know."

The Mouth rasped out a laugh. "Whether or not you get what you want, you ain't leaving here alive."

Walker's violet eyes shone through black war paint. "Was never planning on it."

Within a single motion, the Mouth slipped on brass knuckles and sprang forward. His speed betrayed his size as he nimbly shot across the room. Sweat poured from his boulder-sized head. It was hard to tell if he was more nervous of Walker or whoever he was fighting for.

The first swing was caught by Walker. He twisted the right arm and brought his knee up. It crunched into the Mouth's ribs. A stray swing from the enemy cracked Walker in the mouth.

The two grunted with each hit.

Walker backed up. He tripped over a heavy pile under his feet: one of the unconscious punks. The Mouth struck him in the gut. The punch lifted him from his feet, and the big man grabbed Walker's arm and whipped him. Walker slammed into the wall beside the broken open supply closet. He took note of the massive hole in the door and shook the pain off.

The Mouth dove for him, and Walker sidestepped. The attacker cracked into the cement wall and yelped. Walker spun around and grasped the Mouth by the back of the neck.

"Get off me, maggot!"

"You talk too much."

He slammed the villain's face into the supply closet door. It felt good. So he did it again and again. Chips of wood popped across the room like confetti. Blood poured from cuts in the victim's face with each strike. Walker kicked the Mouth into the closet door, ducked low, grabbed the first thing he saw inside, and bounded backwards as the large man dropped. The villain thrashed about and tumbled into shelves.

Walker laughed. "And you're the leader of a gang? Very sloppy!"

The Mouth roared and sprang up. His square, bulging face burned like a valve withholding too much steam. He reached for Walker's neck. Three feet away. Two feet. Spittle splashed Walker's cheek. The villain's fingers tightened . . . then a metal clang sang through the basement.

The villain's charge suddenly ceased, and he collapsed.

"You didn't even see me take this from the closet, did you?" Walker held out the wrench and tossed it aside. The bang echoed as it landed on the floor. "You really are sloppy."

Groans escaped the fallen opponent. "Cheater."

"Says the punk using brass knuckles."

Walker crouched beside him. His skull and gut ached. He'd be feeling those bruises later. "What do you know about the Inner Light?"

"Upstairs." His bloodied teeth spread in a greasy smile. "They know you're here."

"I need a name. Where do they hold their victims?"

"I don't know what your obsession is with those whack jobs." The Mouth spat out a teaspoon of blood. "It's enough trying to deal with escaping cops and crusaders without people like you and those cultists making things crazier. We'd be better off without this magic junk."

"Our powers and this magic are two different things. We're born with powers—this magic comes from another source. Not that you'd understand. If you play around in the dark too long it becomes impossible to see the shadows. Who is upstairs? Hopefully, not just your lackeys."

"If *he's* here . . . then you're already a corpse. The darkness walks."

"That moving shadow?" So he wasn't seeing things. "That's one of them?"

"Hey," the Mouth slurred. His eyes rolled in back in his head. "My power has a large range. What do you *think* is waiting upstairs? Forget the Inner Light. You'll be full of lead before you get to the top step."

The big man's head rolled back. Walker let him sleep.

He tried the emergency exit, but it was a waste of time. It had been boarded and cemented over just as the windows. Walker's earlier guess was right. There were no other ways out. He didn't have three spare days to dig through boards and brick, especially since Mouth's minions would eventually make their way downstairs. He had only one way out.

Walker dusted his hands off. A firing squad waited at the top of the stairs. Beyond them was someone in the Inner Light. Finally, he would get answers.

The dead would have their vengeance, and he could finally rest. All he had to do was fight a small army and destroy a god.

~

"Are you okay, Walker?" Shana asked.

Walker clutched the transmitter. "You were listening, huh?"

"I've called the police. They should be there soon. I hope." She paused. *"You didn't use your knives?"*

"I wanted him alive. I'm not a masochist." He climbed the steps. The eerie silence surrounded his echoing boot steps. "Sit tight and maintain radio silence. I'll be done soon."

"Just wait down there until the police get there, Walker. Don't be stupid."

"Can't. If we want a lead on the Inner Light then I have to get upstairs. Need to move."

"Stop and think about it for one second!"

"Quiet!" Walker snarled. "This is my chance—maybe my only chance. I can't let them slip back into the shadows. You think your sister is the worst they've done? Families have been obliterated, good people have been broken to bits, and this city has no idea. If there's even a one percent chance of ending this tonight I'm going to take it. Now shut up, and let me work."

Shana let out a deep breath. *"Just don't die, Walker."*

"Can't do that until you learn my first name, can I?"

"Not the time for that."

"See you soon."

Walker turned invisible and leaned back as he swung open the basement door. Bullets blazed by him. The gunfire shredded the wooden entranceway to pieces and drilled shots into the opposite wall. The raging typhoon of metal and old wood of the decimated door screamed past his ear as it tore apart. Stone sprinkled from the shattering wall across from the new opening.

Finally, after a minute, the barrage of automatic and semi-automatic shots tapered off. Broken rubble tumbled down the stairway. He pocketed a broken stone the size of a golf ball.

"*The Abyss That Speaks*," a burly voice shouted. "What did you do to the Mouth?"

Walker wasn't stupid enough to respond. More shots crashed into the entranceway. There was only one way to escape without becoming a stain. He waited for his opening.

"I think we got him," the same voice said.

Another one scoffed. "You can't know that."

"Then you go check."

"No way."

Walker's chance had arrived. He leaned out and threw the small stone toward the bar. His power masked the beginning of its flight, but the rubble lost its cloak when it flew six feet from him. However, it hardly mattered. No one was looking where he'd thrown it.

A bottle of scotch behind the bar cracked with the hit and tumbled down. It smashed open against the boards below though no one could see the mess behind the bar from their vantage point. The goons turned their attention towards the ruckus, and some fired upon it.

"How did he move that fast?" one said. "There's nothing there!"

Another swore. "Does he have speed pow-ers? A Physical Type?"

Walker brandished one of his knives.

He sidestepped out of the stairs and made a quick count of the room: twenty total men. Some, like the bartender, had exited before this mess commenced. He moved towards the pillars on the left side of the room.

Walker threw his blade to the center of the crowd. The knife struck the hand of a gangly man with a shotgun. The thug screamed and fired into the ground, spraying splinters across the floor. Shouts erupted as Walker hid behind a wooden pillar.

"Teleporter," a fat man with a handgun said.

The one next to him swore. "Shut up, Molloy."

Walker let two knives loose. One stuck the shoulder of a man near the front door. The sec-ond hit the leg of a man with an automatic four feet way. Both screamed and dropped.

Then the lights went out. The seventeen remaining men looked about. An odor of ash overtook the alcohol and turpentine. Walker fol-lowed their confused line of sight upward.

A figure garbed in black robes descended to the center of the room, landing hard with boots against the boards. The punks all turned to face him, their mouths agape.

"It's the Abyss!" a man with a beard shouted at the cloaked man.

Another agreed. "Shoot!"

Bullets fired from all over the open bar-room cutting in at every angle at the black-robed figure. Walker dove under a table while the weapons went off. Shredded wood flew all over the room. The cloaked man bent back and forward dancing as the shots pummeled him mercilessly.

After a moment, the shooting stopped. But the cloaked man remained standing.

"What is this guy?" Molloy asked.

The robed man lifted his gloved hands from his sides and stretched them outward. His fingers dislocated and popped. They clicked like a lighter would, sending out sparks, and burst into flame.

The blaze jumped from the cloaked man's hands like two whips and lashed across the bar floor. Four men were struck and launched with the strikes. They immediately caught ablaze and screeched, rolling along the floor. The others fired wildly at him.

Sirens screeched blocks away, but they were hard to hear over the chaos in the bar. Walker's window to get answers was closing.

The invisible man scooped up a fallen handgun and slid across the ground. He aimed and fired two shots between a tall man's legs, striking two others in their right kneecaps. They fired blindly at walls as they fell under the lashing flames from the robed man. Walker rolled to his feet and ducked by another table.

Then he caught movement out of the corner of his eyes. He dove backwards, and a shotgun blasted. Drywall and rotted wood burst from the wall beside the pillar. The shooter had seen the handgun's flash when it fired. Walker cursed silently. This was why he preferred knives.

Walker rolled forward and tossed another blade. The shotgun man caught it in his right forearm and dropped with a scream. Walker left the handgun under the table and moved out.

"What a hero," the cloaked man said. "Maybe we should have a contest. Can I kill more than you can save, Abyss?"

The burning men had all ceased moving,

though the flames still clung to their clothes and devoured them whole. Chaos ruled the room.

If this were a contest then Walker was losing. But the Bulldogs weren't all total morons.

"Screw this!" a younger punk said. "It ain't worth it."

"Where you goin', Paul?" the chubby man beside him asked.

"This guy isn't human. This isn't right!"

Paul ran through the front door out into the streets. He was soon joined by four more. Tires screeched outside with sirens blaring not far behind. Megaphones and flashing lights filled the rain-soaked night through the windows of the darkened bar. The cops were here.

The man in the cloak dropped his whips. They burned away to nothing before hitting the floorboards. With a single bound, he swiftly leaped up and twisted into a thin stream of mist. The smoky stream vanished into the upper level of the bar and towards the winding stairs that lead to the roof.

"*I'll be waiting, Abyss.*"

The remaining men glanced away at the wrong moment. Walker tossed two more throwing knives, hitting one punk in the shoulder and left hand. As that goon fell, Walker did the same to the lanky man beside him.

White spotlights shone into the windows casting tall, malignant shadows like dark waves into the Neon Beetle. Walker scooped up a fallen shotgun and moved on the final three men.

"This is insane. Who is *this* guy?"

"Just shoot him!" the second man shouted.

"Shoot what? I thought he went upstairs!"

The third spat. "No wonder he took out the Mouth. But if we get him before the cops come in, we'll get some crazy cred."

That was when he blinked into existence before the three. They jumped; their faces flushed vomit green, but they still moved to fire. He brought the shotgun butt into the nose of the first man, and spun it hard into the gut of the punk beside him in a single motion. The second man doubled over as the first fell with his nose gushing blood. The third punk tried to aim his shot through his friends but couldn't get an angle, swearing at his tormenter. Walker threw the shotgun into the goon's face, smacking against the nose as he dashed in. Walker kneed the punk's midsection. The final man gasped and fell limp as his weapon clattered to the floor.

"Only reason I didn't use a knife," Walker said, "is because you didn't fire through your pals. You're welcome."

The young punk stared on incredulously as he slunk down.

Walker glanced around the room. Empty, aside for the fallen. He turned invisible once more, and reclaimed his spent knives from his moaning victims. None of them had any fight left.

But he still wasn't finished.

Walker climbed the stairs behind the bar, and the sprinkler system burst on. Voices from megaphones called from outside as water doused him. It wouldn't be long before the police charged inside and made arrests. He passed tacky wallpaper and old broken furniture on his way up towards the roof. He strode out into the night, and the exit door shut behind him.

Rain instantly doused his clothes. Down on the street below, a large group of civilians crowded around police barricades. Many he recognized from the apartment building. The major ones missing were Shana and Desmond.

A voice whispered on the rooftop behind him, "*The Abyss That Speaks.*"

Walker froze. The downpour clacked

endlessly in the night, but the voice chilled harder.

"I know you are up here," the cloaked man said. "I saw the door open and close. Let us not play games. If you want answers, and I think you do, you are going to show yourself."

The Inner Light was finally here. Walker's instincts told him to go for his knives, but his curiosity held him in check. He needed answers before all else.

Walker turned around, slipping back into existence. His violet eyes met the face of a slim figure in large dark robes standing behind him atop the exit of the roof access. The black hood fell deep over the speaker's nose, and the sleeves ran past fingertips. Teeth like jagged yellow pebbles flashed a sneer. The figure leaped down to meet him in a tornado of dark cloth.

"Who are you?" the being asked. "Are you a man or something greater? We have heard much through rumors among the lesser knaves. You are *The Abyss That Speaks*: the specter that haunts our every move. You are a myth as great as we are and quite a thorn in our side."

"Only a thorn? Didn't your master teach you about underestimating enemies?"

"You defeated many pawns tonight. That is impressive, I admit. Have you ever wondered how much more you could accomplish if you drank the right blood?"

Walker slipped free a knife and rammed it forward. It plunged into the hood of the agent. Walker twisted and slashed the blade free. Black ooze slipped down the handle of his knife.

The cultist remained standing even with a blade in his brain. The darkness where his eye sockets would be shimmered a crimson red diamond pattern. Of course, it wasn't enough to kill him. Black blood solidified where the knife stuck.

"Where is Alma?" Walker asked.

Rain knocked against silence on the roof.

Then the cultist spoke. The voice remained cold and hard, without mirth.

"How do you know her?" it asked. "As far as I am aware, there are none remaining who know what has become of the maiden. What is your name, Abyss? I am Garou."

"They call me Walker. Now that I have you, Garou, you will finally answer my question. Where is Alma?"

"The Inner Light owes no man explanation."

"Even hydras eventually run out of necks to slash. I will cut off the snake head of your master, but I'm offering you a chance, Garou. You only get the one."

"She is within your grasp. I will even tell you where to find her."

"Liar."

"Not at all. Barrie Heights, 103 Eustace Avenue. There you will find what you seek."

"What is she doing in that dead zone?"

"You only need trade your services to us, and we will release her to you. All will be explained. We will work well together."

"I don't take jobs from scum."

"Look close, Abyss." Garou lifted his cloak. "You will lay eyes on what you truly need."

Inside the empty cloth of the mannequin being, Walker saw Alma. It was only for the briefest of moments, but she was there. Wild curly blonde hair, small freckles across a thin jaw, and a wry smile, she shone as a lighthouse in harbor fog. She hadn't aged a day since her disappearance over a decade ago. Her familiar rosy cheeks and laughing eyes were exactly the same as he remembered. He could almost touch her and pull her back from the dark.

But not quite.

Crushing pressure fell on his gut and his shoulders. Reminders of old failures returned. He could not save her then. How could he think he would reach her now? It could not be so simple. Garou smiled at his misery. This vision was little more than the faint hope of a dying star: a trick. Walker had been around this business too long to think otherwise. The girl flickered like the candle of a memory he had long since forgotten. This thing was calling him in, but it wasn't Alma. She would never do that.

Or maybe she would.

As doubts assaulted him, Walker pulled back. He really was getting rusty. It was time to wake up. No, she would never pull him into the dark.

He drew another knife. Garou stared at him sideways, oblivious to the weapon.

"What do your eyes see in the dark?" Garou asked.

"The end of your pitiful existence."

Walker swiped the knife across the cultist's neck. Garou's head fell from the robes into the rain. The inky black ball exploded against the stone roof like a ripe watermelon. The robes fell away with the shape into the downpour just as humidity is blown out by a rainstorm. The monster had died.

It was over.

Walker turned back toward the street when he sensed a disturbance.

A whirring clicked twenty feet above his head. He glanced up to meet the drone. The floating beach ball-sized orb was not supposed to be out yet, but thanks to the police presence it was certainly called in early. Modeled after drones of the past, these experimental ones were essentially painted metal spheres that flew in a fixed pattern thirty feet above from the rooftops in the worse areas of Summerside. Microscopic cameras implanted on every side took infrared pictures and sent them back to the police. With the cops currently downstairs, response time would be fast. Unfortunately, this lone orb of circuits was already staring down at him.

"*Did you kill him?*" Shana asked. "*What happened, Walker?*"

"Not now," he said. "I've got a bigger problem."

The sphere hovered down to the roof of the Neon Beetle. The cops must have altered this drone's flight pattern. At times like this, he regretted his power not actually turning him invisible. He had nowhere to run and it would be on him in seconds.

Walker bit his lip and drew two blades. He would have to take it down.

"Intriguing," Garou said.

The black slime where the cultist lay dead pooled together, and funneled into the air like an ashen tornado in a single flowing movement toward the sole drone in the air. The gunk melted into dark incorporeal smoke as it soared through the downpour and whipped by Walker. Garou's ephemeral form misted into the metal ball of the drone and consumed it as a lion devours lambs. The black form totally enveloped the approaching sphere. The beeping and clicking of the drone instantly silenced as sparks and wires sprayed out of the gathering smoke.

"What is this madness?" Walker said.

"Walker? What are you talking about?"

The sparking drone turned toward Walker. Garou floated about in a ball of darkness, infrared lights shining down like headlights through its form. He had merged with the lone drone. His body became solid once more, floating in the air. But he had changed. Metal bits and bobs became embedded in his form and robes like they had always meant to be there. The infrared lights bored into the invisible man from Garou's elevated position. The machine parts of the drone he absorbed had grafted to his flesh and bones.

"How much magic do you have?" Walker asked, eyes narrowing.

"The better question," Garou said, blood dripping from the corners of his mouth, "is who you were talking to before. Would that be the woman?"

Walker raised the knives before him. "You'll never find out."

"Won't I?"

"Your runes don't make you a god, Garou. Batteries run out."

"I can handle much more than a common human can. Allow me to demonstrate."

Garou's physical form cracked and warped into mist once more. The smoke substance spun in the air and swooped down for Walker. Knives slashed at the strange figure, and thick slime from the slashes sprayed into the downpour. But Garou didn't stop moving.

The mist twisted into Walker's earbud. It

funneled inside as if spinning down a drain. Walker whipped the transmitter to the ground and stomped it. But it was too late. Only a small puddle of dark sludge from his attacks remained in the rain; Garou had gone. Walker was alone on the roof.

A bang from the street below caused him to jump. The crowd shouted and hollered.

He glanced down over the ledge. The police stormed the bar, and the crowd cheered them on. Then it hit him. Shana was alone in the building, and Garou had somehow found her. No one else knew what had just happened. He wasn't sure he understood it himself.

Walker sheathed his knives and ran for the scaffolding. A megaphone blasted from down on the street calling for the surrender of the Bulldogs, oblivious as to the real situation. Walker descended to the streets, his boots banging against metal steps. Raindrops fell heavier on him.

He touched down on the street. The crowd remained transfixed on the bar while the police charged into the Neon Beetle, riot shields ready. He let them do what they needed to. Through the rising chaos, Walker ran for the apartment building.

~

Walker charged into the front door, slipping through the crowd by the entryway and into the foyer. The halls beyond the foyer were empty, but not unscathed. Blobs of black sludge dripped from broken plaster walls, disintegrating into nothing on the scuffled red carpet. He barreled onward towards the basement. Outside, he found Brandon slumped against the doorway. The boy bled all over, with cuts from head to boots.

"Brandon!" Walker shouted.

He didn't answer.

Walker bent beside the boy, and seized his collar. "Wake up!"

The boy blinked, his words slurring as he struggled to consciousness. "Are you gonna finish me off?"

"Don't be a halfwit. Tell me what happened."

He coughed and groaned. "The girl and the old man untied me and said we had to leave. We got to the top of the stairs and this thing came out of her earpiece. It tore into me. The old man took her with him while I tried to distract it. Didn't last long."

"Which way?"

"Emergency exit. Down the hall to the right." Brandon closed his eyes and winced. "That thing is a monster, man. Worse than you."

"He's not invincible." Runes weren't inexhaustible, but they could still do a lot of damage if allowed too much freedom. "He just thinks he is."

The speed Walker ran surprised even him. Because he hurried down the hall so fast, he didn't notice he was back outside until the night breeze blew the heavy rainfall back into his face. The building was already far behind now.

Narrow alleys covered in graffiti loomed like gargoyles. Spilled trash greeted his boots with soft squishes. Light whispers of wind whipped against the old brick and chain-link fences. Hair stood on the back of his neck as he watched the shadows break under lamplights.

He crossed the labyrinth of twisting alleys, passing such nonsense graffiti as *Blood for the New Age, Honor Lives!* and *Someone is Aiming at You*; eventually he recovered the trail of dark sludge staining the building brick. The muck was dissolving in the downpour. Garou's trail led to the end of an alley with a split open fence at the end.

Walker turned invisible and crossed out into the open.

The parking lot rolled out before him, completely barren with all the lights burnt out and most of the vehicles long gone. In this part of town, that would be for the best.

But one light still shone in the center of the parking light. Under the lone streetlamp stood Garou, still wearing dark robes but now fully formed again. Before his feet lay an older man strewn out on the pavement, unconscious. Blood streamed from cuts dashed haphazardly across Desmond's chest and arms. Garou stood before the girl, Shana, with her arms outstretched in defense in front of the fallen man. The cultist seized her by the wrists.

"Stay away!" she shouted. "He's already hurt."

"I wasn't finished yet," Garou said.

"Haven't you monsters destroyed enough?"

"Spare me, girl. Your sister doesn't have quite the power we are looking for. Tell me, please, what yours is. You might have exactly what we require."

Walker stepped silently through the rain

toward his prey. They were twenty feet apart when Garou noticed him.

The machine man's skin radiated a healthy white sheen matching his perfect white teeth with a smile that could almost pass for human. The only thing stopping him from appearing normal were the metal circuits and slabs where his right arm, left hip, and throat should have been. Sparks popped where veins blended into wires. Black mist steamed around his artificial pieces. Garou's eyes shone infrared, twitching where the blood-stained color appeared eternally marked on the irises. He threw Shana down to the pavement and turned towards Walker.

"Abyss," Garou said. "I thought our business concluded. Do you not wish to save the one you were looking for? I gave you the right location."

"You don't know me too well."

Garou outstretched both arms towards Walker. "Let us rationally discuss our goals. You want the one you seek, and I want this one. We have no conflicting business!"

"You can see me now. The drone you absorbed gave you that ability, huh?" Walker dropped his invisibility. There was no point wasting the concentration on a power that wasn't working. "When you hit the drone back on the roof I suppose you took it whole."

"I swallowed it," Garou said, tapping his steel neck. "I see everything in red. And I look forward to seeing much more of it in this lot."

"Walker," Desmond croaked. He pointed to Walker's left. "By the puddle. Use it!"

Several feet away under the tire of a van lay the shotgun Desmond had carried earlier. Walker sprinted for it, and Garou was right behind him.

The night air slipped across Walker's back as he dove for the gun. Garou brought his patchwork arm down like a flaming hammer. Walker rolled, letting the appendage strike pavement. He swiped the shotgun as he rolled forward. The fire from Garou's strike flashed out in the falling rain. Walker spun backwards away from Shana and Desmond, and Garou followed him into the center of the lot.

The formerly invisible man fought off a shiver from the rainwater and pushed a shotgun shell into the flap of the weapon. It clicked. He loaded the remaining four shells as he dodged strikes from the enemy. At the same time, Shana dragged Desmond behind the van. Walker made sure the cultist kept his attention on him.

Garou frowned. "Violence is what a Crusader resorts to. You are better than this, Abyss."

"I thought you knew my reputation." Walker pumped the shotgun.

"The void is full of people like you, Garou."

"Be sure to save a spot for me."

Walker fired. The roar of the echo bounced like a cannon in the vacant lot, but the shot hit its mark. Garou screamed as his flesh split open, and black sludge sprayed the rain-soaked pavement. He weaved but wouldn't fall. The wounds were already closing. The rain fell harder.

Walker reached behind his back for a metal knife. The long blade cooled his sweating palms. In one motion, he grabbed the tip, whipped his right arm out, and let the weapon soar. It whistled through the night air, slicing rain in its vertical spin. The knife struck between the metal slabs of Garou's throat.

The mechanical man fell to one knee, gagging.

Walker sprinted forward, readying the shotgun at his side. The intense downpour was making aiming difficult.

Black liquid mixed with blood pooled on the rain-soaked pavement. Garou thrashed about like a drowning victim. Walker was already upon him before the enemy could react.

He moved to fire at Garou's eye . . . then stopped. An eerie feeling ran like cold fingers down his spine. Inside Garou's flesh small round stones shifted around like worms. Walker's screaming instincts made him jumped back.

Garou ceased choking and let the gaze of his dark eyes fall on his opponent. He grinned. "You are no amateur. I was ready to gut you, but you saw my rune and recognized it for what it is. As long as I have it, your attacks are in vain."

The cultist tore the knife from his throat and threw it to the ground with a metal clank. The neck gash stopped its bleeding, as did the shotgun wounds. "And I was so looking forward to the look of terror as I slashed your throat open."

One glance at Garou's right hand showed it all. His fingers outstretched, and sharp tips the size of letter openers awaited his opponent. He'd let the knife hit him; he'd let the shotgun strike him. Garou wanted Walker to get cocky and close.

"You can't win, Abyss." The enemy flashed teeth coated red, white, and black. He breathed hard as his eye markings bled thin red streaks down his cheeks. "You can't kill death."

The knife formerly embedded in Garou lay a foot from Walker. He picked it up and inspected the metal. The heavy stream from the sky licked at his blade as he wiped it clean against his coat. He kept his shotgun at his side. No sense in wasting the shots.

"But I can see your runes," Walker said. "Your eyes. You must be a low man on the totem if they're this weak. Your self-control is lacking."

Yes, that was it. Walker nodded slowly as the calculations came together. If he could do enough damage, and if he could last long enough, he could take this monster down. He could win. Now he just needed to hold together to do it.

"I have all the control I need." Garou frowned. "Do you know what this world was like before man destroyed it? Paradise. Magic pulsed through rolling mountains, the open foaming seas, wild and majestic beautiful animals, and the swaying, towering trees. Earth was a world fit for the gods. We could have been those gods, Abyss.

But the magic left this world behind long ago, and we are left with the false light of humanity to guide us until the sun destroys us all. Eventually, the dark wins, and we lose."

"There are words escaping your mouth, but they're as empty your head."

"He's not wrong," Shana said. She had sidled up behind Walker, flinching. Thin streams of crimson red bled from her nose. "I saw it. He really believes this. But there's something else. I saw a girl near Bernard Street, Walker. Her name is Alma. She's waiting in the Galleria Hotel." She clutched her head and leaned against him. "She's who you were looking for, right?"

Garou pointed a claw toward her. "I was correct! You *are* what I want. You will help bring that world back. Think about it, Abyss. Can you not imagine a world different from this sham? Let us fix it, and make it what it should be!"

The cold helped Walker focus. He closed his eyes and thought for a moment. Alma shivered in the cold far away from him, but she was closer than ever before. Then he looked at Shana, leaning against him. She fell over, and he caught her in one arm. Her power must have overtaxed her mind.

"You can't fix it, Garou," he said.

"What was that, worm?"

"You think that you can patch up a leaky canoe by putting your finger in it? How about a dam? Everything still flows. Existence itself is a tornado; it rips you apart if you fall to the edges, and crushes you with debris when you don't expect it. There's no way out: it will eventually swallow you whole. That storm has always been here. Digging your head in the sand and hoping for it to go away changes nothing."

"You monumental fool," Garou said. He snarled. "We're trying to save this world!"

"We already have people for that, and you aren't one of them."

"You know it is hopeless, and yet you press on." Garou shrugged. "So be it."

Walker whispered to Shana over his shoulder. "Go get Desmond and get out of here."

Her brow crinkled and softened, letting defiance quickly melt to concern. She stared at him sideways. "Who?"

She did overwork herself. He sighed and pushed her up again.

"The injured man by the van. Go help him aside the building, and I'll deal with this."

"Oh, that's his name?" She blandly nodded. "You'll be okay?"

"Me?" He laughed. "I'll be expecting a hot meal when I get back there."

She patted his arm. The smile that spilled over her made his heart skip a beat. She reminded him of someone. Not the best time for that. He glanced away before she noticed.

"Thank you, Walker," she said. "I'll be waiting."

He let the queasiness in his gut subside before he answered. "Shotguns are loud. Better cover your ears."

Footsteps splashed through rain puddles behind Walker toward the van.

"Where is she going?" Garou said. "Does she not want to see her sister?"

"Shut your mouth, Garou."

"I was told that the girl—Marietta was it?—had a family. Of course, we tried prying into her head, but that's far too messy of an affair. We aren't very gentle with our abilities. You might melt the cerebral cortex or tear out a sumptuous frontal lobe. Quite disgusting!"

"Shut up, Garou."

"The point is that families with powers

sometimes have other members with similar powers. It isn't that common, but it does happen. I wonder what we can rip out of that pretty girl of yours. We can help dull the pain of her lost sister, or we can turn her inside out if she is useless. The tongue is always a treat to rip out. Her screams will be soothing."

The shotgun roared. The spread struck Garou and embedded itself in the truck to his left, breaking a headlight. But the monster was already in motion.

Chunks of black blood fell from the cultist's cloak, yet his full-toothed smile remained. Garou slashed his claw, and the shotgun flew from Walker's hands. The enemy brought down his second arm slicing flesh. Walker's left shoulder bled.

"Are you already dead, Abyss?"

This insane cultist moved as if he didn't understand runes at all. There had to be a limit to what they could do before the body gave in. Not even stolen drone parts could change that. Garou was beginning to slow and he didn't even realize it.

"I'm not dead," Walker said. "But you will be."

Walker sprang forward, his knives lashing out. Blades clashed against claws and rainwater danced atop the colliding strikes. Garou's eyes continued leaking bloody tears.

"Is that it, Garou? You have some regeneration, fire, transmogrification, and alchemy abilities. Not very impressive. Are they grafted to you? Is that how it works? All it does is make you a cockroach instead of a spider to step on. Bugs still get squished, in the end."

Garou flashed his stained teeth like a wolf at prey. "We aren't born with powers like your kind, Abyss. We had to take what we were owed to make things right. And I have taken more than any other."

White heat shot through Walker's left shoulder where the claw had cut. Blood pumped out of the wound. He kicked forward and jammed a knife through the cultist's outstretched right palm. Garou laughed and fell back, breathing hard.

"What are you giggling for?" Walker asked. "Still seeing red?"

Garou outstretched his injured claw, and it glowed. The wind around the two changed. Particles and water molecules chilled and clattered against his swirling black cloak. The pentagram markings around his eyes pumped even more life force out. Ice emerged from his palm! The very air encircling him froze and sharpened underneath the pouring rain. A serpent of ice twisted from his slashed hand and lunged for Walker's neck. Raindrops froze around them, clattering to the pavement as it cut through the night.

Walker slashed at the oncoming ice snake. Chips bounded, but the frozen beast didn't stop. Ice tore at his neck, slashing skin. The snake dropped and hit the pavement.

Ice bounded as the serpent chased after him as if he were a mouse dinner. Walker sidled through the parked cars to his side away from Shana and Desmond. The snake glided through the air after him, smashing against the vehicles and bursting windows and car paint. Broken bits of chrome and windshield fell across the pavement in showers of scrap. Garou slowly stepped through the downpour after him, mumbling away. Walker circled around the enemy, stretching the snake all over in awkward patterns. It twisted and bent after him without mercy. The ice obscured Garou's view, but the serpent did not care.

Garou appeared to notice Walker's game and raised his left claw in defense just as the knife was thrown. Walker's blade pierced the palm. He sprinted up and over the knotted ice body and brought down his second knife into the enemy's left shoulder. Garou flinched but kept his goofy smirk as flames formed on his hands.

He had Walker where he wanted him. The claws gripped against Walker's shoulders and tightened. Walker groaned as his skin tore. Bones popped, and flames burst from the claws as the snake flew closer. Garou laughed between heavy breaths.

Then the smile faded as a creeping realization set in. His hands were melting.

Garou screamed. Black sludge slipped from his skin and into the pavement. The fire in his body extinguished in the rain. Circuits and wires dripped with rotted flesh into the pool where Garou's feet had been moments earlier. His body was disintegrating, just as the rain began to lighten.

He was dying.

"You seem confused," Walker said, stepping back. The ice snake from the spell cracked and clattered to the concrete around them. "I apparently know your limits better than you. Did you not notice the more you used different abilities, the more your eyes bled? Your body can't use so many at the same time. Heavy duty regeneration, alchemy, flames, transmogrification, and elemental water and ice, all at once? Even those of us born with abilities know that. No wonder they sent you out to deal with these stupid gangs. You're a failure."

"No! I am not the failure." Blood poured from Garou's ears and mouth. "Spent energy is not enough to do this!"

"No, but this downpour is. You didn't realize when I cut your head off and you replaced it with the drone parts, but your body has been slowing for some time. How are you this clueless about your runes? Please excuse my laughter. I'm enjoying watching you cry a bit too much."

Garou fell to his knees and clawed uselessly at the pavement as he appeared to sink into it. He was no more than sand being beaten down by the tide. Smoke plumed outward.

Walker picked up the shotgun. "Any last words?"

"What are you, Abyss?" Garou asked with a quivering grin.

Walker readied and pumped the shotgun.

That was a lousy question.

"The next time we meet," Garou slurred, his features blurring in the rain and the black slick, "it will be in the void."

"Goodbye, halfwit."

Walker fired, and the shot blasted Garou's skull. The head burst like a tar balloon streaked with blood. This time he did not reform.

Walker pumped the shotgun again, and fired the remaining shot into the black slick where the corpse had been. No sense being wasteful. The remains smoked into the sky as the puddle dissipated.

He turned on his heel and saw both Shana and Desmond limping towards him. The old man was biting his lip, but the girl took slow steps. She tripped into Walker's arms.

"Hey, Shana," he said. "What's wrong?"

"I don't . . . remember." She buried her face into his chest as her words fell weak and limp. "What happened to Desmond? Who were you fighting?"

He looked at Desmond who only shook his head. The old man took his shotgun. "This is why I don't like her using that power. One day, this is going to be permanent."

Walker looked down at her. "You don't need to worry about it."

"I don't?" She looked up half asleep.

He easily lifted the drowsy girl into his arms. Without waiting for her protests, he began his return to the apartment. Desmond trailed after him eyeballing where Garou had vanished.

"My name is Percival," Walker said.

She looked up at him with her lips parted in genuine surprise. "That's a good name."

"Yes."

Within seconds she had fallen asleep in his arms.

Up ahead, Brandon stumbled out of the exit. He waved to the pair, still clutching his bloody sides. At least, he was still in one piece.

"What's next?" Desmond asked Walker. "She help you find who you were looking for?"

He blandly nodded still looking down at the tired, soft face nuzzled against his chest. "I'm going to help her back upstairs, and then I'll go."

"But you're bleeding."

"I am."

The rain would fall deep into the night, beating against the brick of the old building, but it didn't matter. He clutched her tight as he brought them inside with Brandon following. They made small talk, walking through the empty halls. Everyone else was still outside watching the cops busting the Bulldogs. No one had seen the real battle behind them.

Nothing had changed. No one had ever seen Walker, not really. Once he got Shana to safety, he could move on. She would recover and eventually allow herself to have a normal life again. At the same time, he would find her sister and Alma. The Inner Light's time was at an end.

Soon enough, he would be back in the rain. The towering buildings and cloud-capped grey skies would stare down on his miniscule form, but no one would see him coming. No one ever saw the Abyss until it was too late.

He clutched his wounds as he planned his next move.

The night wasn't over yet.

LAST EXIT TO SHADOW CITY

I.

The pit in his stomach grew larger the longer Rhodes spent staring into the lopsided shade of the old train tunnel. The far too bright orange evening sun blasted down against the rail yard behind him, shading it even further. The thought that there was more to this place chewed at the back of his tired mind. He couldn't escape that ineffable urge to turn away.

It's too bad he was paid up front, otherwise he wouldn't even bother.

He crossed the hodgepodge of tracks towards the tunnel with his hands in the pockets of his light coat. Walking alone was always a risk in Summerside. But even though he was unarmed, he was not helpless. A rail yard like this provided him with plenty of ammo. Having powers had its advantages.

"Why are you here?" the yardmaster had asked. The middle-aged man's cigarette-smoke-stained-office was plastered with disorganized papers, but the yardmaster himself was more out of sorts. He scratched his unkempt grey beard. "I've seen your rates. This is a below your pay grade."

"I've got a hunch about this place," Rhodes said. "Listen, you called me here. What do you care about why I chose to take this job?"

"I called you here because you're known for fixing problems. Some of the conductors and security guards reported hearing voices at night, and cameras have caught folks sneaking in but never coming out for a long time now. It might be nothing, but the rumors get worse every year. There's no evidence anything has happened at all, but we still keep getting slandered. We'll pay you for a full day's fee if you stay overnight in the yard to investigate. Of course we can't afford your normal rate. Do you have a problem with that?"

He didn't, of course. A job that paid meant more money in his pocket and money for the family, especially Charlotte. She was nineteen now and his secretary, without any life of her own. It was a thankless job, working for her dad, but she never complained. Heck, she was the one who set up this appointment for him. She deserved better.

And she had been having those dreams more and more. Charlotte hadn't had them since she was five, but within the last year they had become more forceful; a world that looked like Summerside, but wasn't. The red skies and pristine white buildings she spoke of seeing sounded like an alien world. Dilapidated Summerside couldn't be any more different than that. She dreamed a place where shadows moved on their own, and they wanted to devour her whole.

"There are shadows there," she said. "But they act like people. They believe they're people."

He patted down her ruffled blonde hair. "They aren't?"

"No. Inside them is a dark force . . . I don't even want to think about it."

Her dreams became wild nightmares of magic and mayhem in the dark world. But Summerside was a city of vigilantes, not magic. Perhaps, if she could get over this problem, she could get a job at one of those government firms. Until then, she would have to make due as his secretary. She didn't seem to mind that too much.

For now, it was enough to just get more high profile cases, and then maybe he could finally retire from the game and focus on his family. But underneath, he knew that wasn't going to happen. This sort of job was in his blood, and he could never truly leave it, even if it left him.

Several freight cars rolled in through the tracks. Already, they were winding down for the day, the sound of screeching breaks becoming rarer and rarer. Rhodes preferred they disappear. If he had to deal with a criminal, he'd rather fewer bystanders around.

Summerside would never change. This city was a crime ridden hole with more criminals than one could shake a police baton at. On the plus side, it meant more jobs for outsiders away from the government-endorsed firms, like him.

Rhodes leaned against the concrete wall inside the shadow of the tunnel and lit a cigarette. From here, he could see the larger buildings in downtown looming like the giants of old legends. The ugliness of the ancient and damaged structures remained a constant reminder of the bad old days. No wonder Charlotte had bad dreams about this place. He let out a puff and began his stretches.

Thirty-eight was not so old, and he was in really good shape; but age was still age, and it could creep up at the worst times. He wasn't that spry kid playing hero anymore. A sharp pain shot through his shoulder as he rotated it. Rhodes hadn't been in the game in years. Now, he mostly played cleanup for the small fish that slipped through the nets. Most might find such a job pathetic, but it was a load off his mind.

After making sure his hamstrings were sufficiently exercised, he called home to remind them he was not coming back for the night, and then began the wait until nightfall. A heavy pressure tightened on his shoulder like a fist-sized slug shooting it. His bones told him this was going to be one of *those* jobs.

The evening sun dropped behind the skyscrapers beyond the tunnel entrance. Soon enough, it left him alone in the dark of pure night. The minutes rolled into hours as he paced.

Finally, he fell back against the tunnel wall.

"I need another smoke," he said.

"*You are one of them.*"

Rhodes froze. His steel eyes scanned the rail yard. "Who is it?"

"*I have been waiting for you.*"

"And where have you been doing that?"

Before he could manage a plan, cold breath blew on the back of his neck. His bones involuntarily chattered, and his shoulder clenched. He was leaning directly against the stone wall, so where was this air coming from? He slowly swallowed his nerves.

"You're a Stone Elemental type, are you?" He kept his teeth steady as he spoke. Having his back to the enemy was a bad way to start this. "No wonder they never heard you coming."

"*My powers are far beyond that, as your kind well knows.*"

"What?" Rhodes had seen too much over his career to know what this villain was referring to. "Be that as it may, you're disturbing the people here. Find another place to haunt."

"*It will be done.*"

The cold air shifted, and Rhodes whipped around. Instead of a man, he found a pair of long spindly dark arms spiraling from the shadows. They snapped like a lasso against his face and right arm, cutting off his cries. The shadow limbs slung backwards with him—into the stone wall!

But he didn't hit a solid surface. Instead, he melted into a midnight black space where cold and humidity pummeled his bones. Rhodes choked on the lack of air in this new night, and the world rushed by in sparkling twilight.

This shadow dragged deeper into the dark; where sights and sounds were myth, and life and death were as indistinguishable as a reflection in muddy water. His lungs crushed in on him.

And then, as if by magic, he could breathe once more. Hard white light brought him back to consciousness.

However, he was no longer in Summerside. In fact, it did not look like he was on the same Earth at all anymore, but some twisted version of it.

He plummeted out of the darkness and into the humid night of a new dark world.

That earlier instinct was correct. He should have run away.

II.

Rhodes hit the pavement in a roll like a thrown oil drum, landing on his side. The world tipped and twisted. A hardened chill bit at his insides like a wild bear, clashing with the sun-baked pavement burning under his clutching palms. Breaths fell hard and slow, and his brow poured sweat with every heave. Shivering knees made it hard to stand up.

He knew the thing that had pulled him through the wall was there behind him. He needed to move to meet it, but the rest of him would not obey his commands. It was as if he had been deleted from existence before his particles were forcefully reassembled whole once more.

Finally, he managed to catch his breath. "What power was that?"

"*I already told you,*" the voice echoed around the darkened railyard. "*I am beyond your kind now.*"

Rhodes forced his pounding head up towards the source but the shadow had vanished. Instead, he found the railyard a whole different place.

The red Armageddon hue of the sky soaked in an eternal blood-colored sunset. Stars punctuated the harsh view. The dots of light pulsed like pin pricks of blood seeping out of tiny wounds.

But the sky wasn't the only new sight. The train yard had also changed.

The battered down tunnel allowed the sky

to bear down on him as if a mad bomber had blown it open. The dislodged rails and shattered train cars strewn about showed this place had been abandoned long ago. Rust and trash were all that met him there.

The city beyond the railyard was different. The buildings were no longer crumbling and left to decay but had been made whole and polished immaculately clean with a bold white paint job that gleaned in the harsh light. His headache flared again as his focus failed.

This was the place Charlotte had seen in her nightmares. This was a fake Summerside.

"What did you do?" Rhodes asked into the wind.

"*You can die a slow, rotting death in the real world.*"

"This is what you did with the others who came through the tracks."

"*Be certain to keep your mind longer than the last ones. You are all so very weak.*"

"Tell me who you are."

"*You'll learn it when you're dead, regardless.*"

"Stop!" Rhodes said. "What do you have to do with my daughter? Hey!"

Out of the edge of his peripheral vision, a

long shadow moved along the damaged tracks. It shot like a snake down the rails and under the cars before disappearing entirely to the dark.

Only the cold, yet humid, breeze blowing from what felt like above remained. He was alone in this place, and without answers.

Rhodes scanned the empty yard before running back to the tunnel wall—it was solid. He couldn't exit the way he came from. That shadow had his only means of escape.

Without a second's pause, he ran the track towards the city. Someone had to be there. He hit the streets and headed north towards downtown.

At the same time, the streetlights shot on, bright white searchlights shone down the empty road like beams from the sky. The sun had set above him, but the dark crimson sky remained. The lights streaking across the ground had no source that he could discern, but he still kept out of their slow and sweeping range.

Would those shadows Charlotte mentioned be arriving soon?

But the streets were vacant. Only his steps bouncing off the streets filled the empty white city. He thought he saw black air form out of the ether before him, but that impression died when he heard glass breaking.

A man in black sidled out of an alley ahead of him. He held a katana draped over his shoulders and had his face painted like a mad geisha. The stranger approached, one foot awkwardly crossing the other like a tightrope walker moves.

The painted man smiled. "I knew someone would come through again."

"Come through?" Rhodes asked. "Where am I?"

"Paradise, they say. But they're crazy. It's a graveyard to people like you and me."

A wolf-like howl pierced the city air. The fragrance of wild flowers blew on the breeze before melting to burnt flesh. Stars twinkled and pulsed above like stars should not as if they were reacting to this sudden change. The man's smile glinted wickedly as he drew his sword toward Rhodes.

"I wonder what I will get for my ninth kill in this place. Getting trapped has its benefits."

"Were you sent to do me in?"

"Sent? I was brought here same as you. The only difference between us is that I will continue to stay. I consider this place a gift. You will be food for maggots."

Rhodes took a step back. It was still possible for his day to get worse. But this man did strike his interest. He had also been brought here. There had to have information.

"I don't want trouble," Rhodes said. "If we work together we can find that shadow."

"Thank you, but no. That shadow is my savior."

The swordsman approached. Ragged breaths escaped his painted visage as his battered black boots scampered across the road. The sword slashed for the neck.

Rhodes ducked under the first swing . . . and the sword itself followed him! The metal blade coiled like a snake and bit down at his shoulder. Rhodes winced at the bloody wound.

Leaping backwards, Rhodes watched the sword crunch into the pavement. Stone shattered and flew out. The blade receded and hung in the air. The metal snake of a sword remained attached to the aggressor's hilt. His dead eyes followed Rhodes, sword dancing above.

"I don't need to kill you," the attacker said. "But it is what I do."

"Do you attack people in their dreams, too? Or is that just something your glorious savior does?"

The killer whistled to himself. "You know who he's looking for?"

"He's looking for my daughter? Why?"

"Why don't you make me tell you?"

Rhodes calculated his odds. He had no weapons; he was exhausted, and he was still disoriented from his arrival here. Not to mention his disadvantage in an open area with no room to hide, and his opponent was a Metal Elemental with a snaking sword.

"Okay," Rhodes said, raising his hands. "What do you want?"

"A challenge. Come with me."

The man in the makeup beckoned Rhodes toward him. He did not relax his guard: the blade bobbed in the air above Rhodes' throat as he made his prisoner walk at his side.

They slunk through the winding, barren streets. Shadows flickered around the clean corners of the towering buildings, but vanished in a blink. They were being watched.

Rhodes risked speech. "You're Richard Archenault, aren't you?"

"They call me *Arc*," he replied. "Swordsman of legend."

"Nobody called you that, to my knowledge. You were a merc who killed anyone they asked you to. I don't even know how many confirmed kills you have. You're also a Metal Elemental that can control and warp objects like swords."

Arc chuckled. "You're informed. Are you with one of those government firms?"

"No, I work for myself. I was hired to inspect the train tunnel due to all the disappearances and rumors."

"And now you're here. Welcome to paradise, amigo. This is where the shadows converge to create their own world."

"So then you know why he wants my daughter and you also know where we are."

"I don't care where we are, as long as I can hunt. He and I are not so different."

The pair turned a familiar corner into an alley. Rhodes remembered a similar spot in Summerside. The narrow area led into a small apartment building behind the immaculate trash cans. He'd been there on a domestic disturbance job weeks ago. It looked as if this city still had similarities to the real one. There would be a few places to go inside the structure, but only a handful that wouldn't get him trapped by this assassin.

They descended stairs to the bottom floor and toward the back entrance. The floorboards creaked with age. He'd been in there before to retrieve a stolen ring. With his enemy right behind him, Rhodes had one chance to get this right.

Rhodes stomped his right foot down, and the resulting vibrations went through the floorboard. His power searched for what he was seeking. His thoughts gripped the nails, and he threw them upwards with his mind. The man behind him screeched, and Rhodes dove sideways.

The air above sliced open. Arc's sword twisted, slicing across his back. Rhodes spun and rolled across the freshly-scrubbed red carpet, letting the blade miss its mark. Using the pull of his power, he raised his hand. Nails fired like bullets upward through the floor where his enemy was still standing. They struck Arc in his left arm and neck through his foot. Blood spurted from the holes in his skin. The sword turned back toward Rhodes as the running man rolled back up.

"Villain!" Arc shouted.

Rhodes ran as fast as his legs would allow him to run. The sword pursued, stretching and bending like an attacking cobra. He shouldered the hallway door open and dove into the empty apartment. Nicely constructed walls and cleaned chairs sat around a beautifully white space. The window was at the rear beside a large couch. The shouts behind him grew close—as did the sword. He lifted his arms before his face, sprinted forward, and dashed the length of the apartment. In his run, he jumped through the window, and glass shattered over Rhodes. Cuts burned across his body.

Wind whistled by him in his one story drop. He landed in the trash cans from earlier. Metal clanged down beside him. The sword had spilt the garbage containers, spraying trash all over.

Rhodes reached back and touched the sword, letting his power flex. It rippled into the sword as he tried to feel around for it. The weapon whimpered at his touch. He recoiled from it, and the blade receded back up the building into the window where howls cried out. Rhodes lifted an eyebrow at the sight.

That sword held a secret. Now he just needed to find a way around that blade.

The long alley went on for what could be miles, but he ran it like he was a young man again, his temples burning with his lungs. There he found a metal chain-link fence that blocked the way to the rear end of a Burger Barn restaurant on the opposite side.

Smashed glass rang out back at the apartment far behind him. Arc was on his way.

Rhodes touched the fence and held it with his mind. His power pulled it apart, unraveling weaved metal. He used some of it to heal over the cuts from his window jump, and he put the rest down. All that remained of the fence was a disassembled mess on the pavement.

He opened the exit to the restaurant then fell back to the alley to attract Arc's attention. Rhodes tucked himself behind a dumpster across from the demolished fence and waited.

The assassin finally stepped out into the alley with a limp. His off kilter movements gradually vanished with very step. Since he was a Metal Elemental, he must have used the metal nails to heal his injuries. But dead was dead, and a removed head or a blade through the heart wouldn't heal if a Metal Elemental lost their life before realizing what had hit them. To win against one meant attacking hard and fast. Arc certainly knew this better than anyone.

"Dissection sounds like such a good idea," Arc said.

The jagged assassin stumbled down the alley, his foot at first limping, then sliding upright, and then walking straight. Soon enough, even his grimace had vanished. From behind the dumpster, Rhodes watched Arc's white teeth flash in a grin as he approached the fallen fence.

Elemental powers allowed an element to be one with the body and could be bent and warped into the skin, flesh, or bone, to heal any wound. A fence wouldn't pose much of a threat to one. However, they weren't invincible. It was one thing to be shot and use the bullet to heal the exit wound, but it was another to be outright killed by the force of the initial shot. Swords worked the same. Rhodes couldn't rely on a lucky hit. He had to get the assassin by surprise.

Arc stepped on the downed fence and smiled at it. Rhodes clenched his teeth. He could just impale the piece of trash, but not until he got answers. Capturing him came first. But the assassin was not going for the door. Arc kicked at the fence.

"Do you really think I would fall for such a simple trap? This is—"

The crash the dumpster made when Rhodes kicked it was loud enough to wake whatever dead lived in this world. He held back a groan, more from exhaustion and less from pain, as the wheeled garbage bin was made of metal—and he had softened its properties when he hit it. The reverberation sang through his bones as the dumpster shot across the alley towards Arc.

The mad man sidestepped towards the restaurant at the same moment, almost involuntarily. His assassin's instinct worked against him.

Rhodes jumped forward, shielded from view by the dumpster, and popped out beside Arc. The assassin didn't see him right away. Rhodes landed on the pavement and gripped the fence with two objects—his right hand, and his mind.

The fence coiled upwards like a hungry anaconda, sliding along his legs and holding Arc's flailing limbs still. His sword clattered to the cement, as did the assassin a second later. The fence squeezed Arc tight. His jaw striking down cut off the curse on his lips.

"That was careless of me," Arc said. He wriggled against his tightening restraints. The fence, held by Rhodes' thoughts, was unbreakable now. Even if Arc was a Metal Elemental, he could not override another's control. "But a loss is a loss."

"Be a sport and tell me what your messiah wants with my daughter."

"I can't tell you what I don't know."

"You know."

"I suspect you have a higher opinion of my intelligence than I do. Blood is what I live for, not knowledge. Wherever I go, there I stay, then I move again."

"Then perhaps you know who brought you here." Rhodes tightened the hold with his thoughts. The links creaked and Arc choked on his breath. "You aren't that dumb, right?"

"I'm not in the habit of giving my enemies anything to work with. Oh, do you hear that? They've found us."

"I don't hear anything." Rhodes spoke the truth. "And I'm not letting you out until you answer my question."

"And if I don't? I could just break out of this and cut you to bits that way."

"You can't. I touched the fence first."

"You must be experienced at this. How many of my kind have you killed, big guy?"

"We're both Metal Elementals, Arc. You know as well as I do how dangerous these powers are, especially in a city. I know my own limits, as I'm sure you do."

Rhodes held the fence in his power's grip. As long as he had it locked in his mind, Arc could do nothing about it, and there was no chance Rhodes would loosen that hold. The same worked for Arc's sword, but that was on the pavement and out of his reach.

Rhodes picked up the fallen blade with his free hand and inspected it. An odd sensation behind this weapon brushed against his thoughts. It was almost as if it were speaking to him.

Before he could speculate further, a whisper intruded on the edges of his mind.

"*Run!*" it said.

"Who are you?"

"*The sword,*" a young girl's voice replied. "*There is no time to explain it now, but you must run. The shadows are coming!*"

"I still don't see or hear anything."

"*You just got here. It takes time to adjust. Trust me, they're coming!*"

He perked his ears but barely heard anything. However, he did begin to see strange sights.

The air wavered like heat on a desert highway, the humidity reinforcing the impression. Every now and then, black pin pricks of shadows shot across his eyes like a camera flash. A presence existed in the darkness.

"What did she tell you?" Arc said. "The shadows are almost here, right?"

At the edge of the alley, he finally saw it: dancing figures like marionettes barely visible to the naked eye. They closed in with giant strides and long, intangible legs. Monsters? No, it was the shadows Charlotte spoke about.

And they were coming for him.

He put the sword to his side and abandoned the fence, rushing through the alley. He didn't stop to see if Arc escaped whatever was coming. For now, his brain, along with the sword, was telling him simply to escape.

Rhodes dashed into the open door of the restaurant. The inside kitchen was as immaculately cleaned as the rest of the city. The dishwasher and perfectly stacked plates could have been mistaken for brand new. He continued out into the dining area over immaculately swept and washed floors where even the folded table cloths and chairs had been carefully lined up and ready for whatever party was about to begin. Perhaps, it had been set for the shadows.

He continued out into an empty street. His sight and sense of smell wavered for but an instant. The polished pristine buildings morphed dark grey, and an unmistakable scent of blood broke the clean air. And outlines of people, at least what he thought were people, mindlessly traveled the sidewalks. Just as quickly as his vision came, it departed.

"*Hey!*" the young girl said. "*Down the alley ahead. We have to make it to the church before Arc does!*"

"Why, what's in there?"

"*My brother. He'll kill him if he gets back first.*"

"You know anything about this weird world?"

"*Later. Please hurry!*"

Rhodes bounded into the narrow alley, hoping that his earlier vision was just a hallucination. The taste of blood stuck to the back of his dry mouth. This city was alive.

And yet, he thought of Ben and Charlotte as he ran. No matter what happened, he could not leave them alone. They were strong, but she couldn't afford to lose her family again. Summerside had taken enough from her. Corinne could look after their son and daughter, but the last thing he wanted to do was leave her with everything. That was his other job.

This city hid secrets behind every masked wall. Could he even return home again, or would it crush him? There remained the possibility he would never see home again.

As he kicked in the door of an emergency exit, he feared what might be waiting on the other side. It could be anything at all, and that scared him more than he would ever admit to anyone. This was what tortured his daughter every night.

He would make sure that would end tonight.

III.

"Where are we?" Rhodes asked the sword. "And your name would be good to know."

The alley brick and stone warped the more he ran through them to a black craggy material somewhere between stone and salt but with the familiar boiling heat of the city coating the atmosphere. The sky remained its familiar red through the jagged edges of the nearby roofs.

Voices echoed through the shadows, re-verberating against his thoughts. Harsh and abrasive barks like tribal chants pounded off in some intangible dimension adjacent to his eardrums. But it all sounded like gibberish.

"*I'm Amanda,*" the girl's voice spoke. "*I am the sword.*"

"A kid?" He thought a moment. "Can you tell me your power, Amanda?"

His voice was as flat and level as he could manage, which is far more than he expected. These shadows brought children here and they would pay for it.

"I'm Mr. Rhodes, Amanda. Why don't you come out of that katana?"

"*It's easier this way since I can't walk. I'd just get in your way.*"

His boot struck a loose pebble, causing his heart to nearly jump out his throat. The stone dashed against a fence, momentarily breaking the silence. He listened intently but heard nothing. After a beat, he took a breath. He wasn't being followed.

"I see," he said, ignoring the sweat trickling down his neck. "You can transform and contort your body to metal. That's a handy power, if not very common for Elemental Types. Arc's ability was more traditional, like mine. Were only Metal Elementals like us brought to this place, Amanda? That shadow looked to be hunting our kind."

"*He has a grudge, I guess, so he goes out looking for us. Beats me. That big shadow is their leader, I think.*"

"Do you know what they want? I think they're targeting someone close to me."

"*Arc's been holding us captive since we've been here. I don't know.*"

"It looks like Arc was working for them, even though he's not."

"*You can't explain anything to Arc. He's crazy, and he only wants to hunt. That's why he took my brother—to make me help him. He doesn't care about escaping.*"

"Did he use you to hurt anyone, Amanda?" Rhodes bit the inside of his cheek before continuing. "Other than me."

"*He just uses me to try out different sword types. But, no. There were only two people here after me and my brother showed up, and they were taken by the shadows before Arc got them. Touch those things and they can swallow you whole. We've been alone awhile. That's why he's so extra excited to see you."*

"The feeling wasn't mutual. How much further until we get to the church?"

Rhodes finally emerged from the warped black alleyway back into the crimson light of night. The barren parking lot stared him down with not a single car to keep him company. But that funeral stink remained in the heavy air. A force hovered just out of his perception, just like the girl had said earlier. Those shadows. If Rhodes wanted to survive and protect this child, he had to see these things. He focused on the empty lot, and a headache rose in his brain.

The wind bent and changed. Air cleared, and crimson clouds parted. He looked to the skyline. What was once a pristine city became an abomination of shoddily constructed buildings leaning against ancient dirty crags and black cliffs. This city was an illusion.

Rhodes choked back the exclamation he'd almost shouted. This wasn't just a power like his, or Arc's, or even the girl's. This was a whole new ability. He'd dealt with those whom had mind abilities before—Mental Types—but they were not only the rarest form of powers, they did not operate like this. Mental Types tended to need physical contact on their target to use their powers, and the ones that didn't had limited scope. They could obscure sight, hearing, taste, or smell: but not all at once, and their powers broke when they slept. They could not cast an illusion that could trick groups of people over the range of an entire city for an extended period of days or weeks. Powers had limits. This was not a power—it was beyond that.

Rhodes wiped the sweat from his crinkled brow: now to find the boy, and then get some answers.

He followed the Amanda's direction through another alley and back out into the street. Soon he had learned how to focus his senses to see both the illusion—what they wanted him to see, and the reality—what actually was. It took training his reflexes and assumptions to keep focus. In this place, reality needed discernment, and those without it were doomed to walk blind.

People passed him on either side, only they weren't people at all. Men and women hunched as they crossed the length of the sidewalk soundlessly, a shade of what a real human would look like. He could not determine if they were real or not, but they did *exist*. They had no skin or solid mass but carried a basic shape of human anatomy such as long legs and arms that blurred in and out of this plane. Unlike the one that had brought him here, or the voices just beyond his ears, these were not hostile. He could not even determine if they knew he was there. These shades merely walked by as if an elemental force guided them toward whatever predestined fate waited.

He tried to touch one, but when his fingers got close, a hard frost ripped through him. Touching felt like a bad idea.

The smell of sulfur watered his eyes as he passed the crowd, but the girl said nothing. Whether it was because she couldn't see or smell them, or because she didn't want to call attention to it was unclear.

He flowed into the darkened crowd, avoiding their touch, and passed two streets before coming upon the church.

Unlike the rest of this fake white city, the church's form remained the same regardless of illusion or reality. The gothic stone structure towered above the rest of the block, broken and battered by neglect and the old construction of crumbling rock, rotten wood, and blackened stain glass windows inside steel bars. It was as if the world around it was cleansed, but this place was left to fall apart. Perhaps, this city was still under construction.

Large wooden doors creaked like cawing crows when he pushed them open. Insides of moist and cracked pillars and pews waited, with only the heavy humidity following him inside. That dead silence returned again. Dread clawed the back of his neck like a bird of prey.

At the end of the pews, he reached what was supposed to be the altar—or what should have been the altar. There was nothing there that should have been. No crosses, statues, candles, or even the altar itself. All that remained was one lone boy, tied on the floor with tight ropes. He was unconscious.

The boy wore a simple red t-shirt and matching shorts with sneakers. He was just a normal kid around nine or ten. Before Rhodes could do anything, the sword in his hand began to warp and bend.

The steel surface of the blade twisted into the shape of a young girl. Her skin became pale again, like most Elemental Types, and clothes not dissimilar from the boy's returned to her as she became whole. Her legs had clearly not seen much use, as they were far thinner than the rest of her—and she was already small. Amanda slunk to the floor and took hold of the boy's shoulders.

"Danny?" she said. "It's me, Danny. Amanda. We're gonna get you out. Wake up!"

Rhodes was stricken by the similarities of the pair. Hair like steel wool, slightly round faces, close to matching clothes and thin eyebrows—they had to have been twins. When the boy blinked awake to show his smoky grey eyes it only confirmed his suspicion. They matched.

"You're okay?" Danny said, with a rasp.

"Thanks to Mr. Rhodes." She pointed to him. "He beat Arc, and he's going to get us out."

"How did you two end up here?" Rhodes asked. "I was checking out the tracks at the station when that shadow grabbed me."

The boy coughed. "I wanted to see if the rumors were true, so I checked out the tracks after dark. Amanda followed even when I told her not to. The shadow came from behind when we were looking at some graffiti."

"Who is that shadow, and what is Arc's relation to it?"

"No clue, man." The boy's jaw clenched.

"That psycho dude attacked us when we landed here. He got us pretty fast. Told Amanda to become his sword, or he'd kill me."

"Don't mind it, Danny." She patted his shoulder, and the boy flinched. His bruises made Rhodes sick to his stomach. "Mr. Rhodes is a Metal Elemental like me. I think his powers are more about the mind."

They indeed were. Rhodes explained how he controlled metal with thoughts and touch. He could not manipulate and lengthen or warp it like Arc, or transform into it like the girl, but Elemental Types of the same kind usually had little in common except affinity for the same element. And Metal Elementals tended to stay in the city where their powers were most useful, and out of the spotlight, where they wouldn't be watched. Carrying weapons, like knives, brass knuckles, or guns were strictly prohibited for his kind without a government license. There was no telling what they could do with an unlimited arsenal. His earlier battle with Arc was proof of that fear.

"So how about it, Danny?" Rhodes asked. "What can you do?"

Rhodes helped the boy up and guided the two of them in the pews by the front. He needed to keep them calm, so he kept his tone as cheerful as he could.

"I'm not an Elemental," Danny said. His skin wasn't as pale as his sisters, which led credence to his words. "I'm an Abnormal."

"Oh, are you?"

He blushed. "Yeah."

Abnormal Types weren't as rare as Mental Types, but they were less common than Physical and Elementals, simply due to the fact that they were unclassifiable. Abnormals especially were hard to pin down. Their powers could be anything since they were not tied to the body and mind like the other three types. But siblings both having powers was rare enough; never mind those that each held different types.

Rhodes smiled softly. "What can you do?"

"I call it *vertigo*. One touch and I can flip your world around for a minute. Right is left, up is down. But I need to touch the bad guy first, and I can only do it once every fifteen minutes. Someone like Arc was only fazed a little, and he worked past it to get me."

"I thought the shadow was only looking for Metal Elementals. Why did he grab you?"

The twins glanced at each other and silently had a conversation with their clouded grey eyes. This was a sibling moment he couldn't understand, so he waited for them to finally finish.

"Mr. Rhodes," Amanda said. "Please don't spread this around."

"I don't gossip."

"Okay, well, you can't tell anyone this, but Danny and I have been practicing using our powers together. I armor him, and he uses his touch to hurt. We haven't tried it on any criminals or anything, but we did try it out late one night against some mouthy jerks in the park."

"That was stupid, but I guess that's a kid thing to do." Rhodes ground his teeth, wishing he had a cigarette. These kids couldn't have been older than ten. "So you followed the rumors to these tracks and got pulled into this mess. I get that. But that sword psycho is another problem altogether. If we could all work together, we could track down that shadow and get out of here. I have to try to explain this to Arc, even if it is hopeless."

"Yeah, right." The boy scoffed. "We've been here for a week, and that piece of work has left me here to starve. I mean, I don't get hungry or anything, but he did leave me here."

"None of those shadows came in here?"

"They ignore the place. That's why *he* left me here like that."

Rhodes paced the rows with his hands in his coat pockets, and his eyes on the large arches of the church ceiling. He should be able to figure out at least some of this before Arc arrived. Even a slight clue would give Rhodes an advantage, but it would still be a gamble. There was still no proof that there was any way out of this world or that Arc even wanted to find it. Rhodes was halfway up the row when he stopped dead. The key was not about the shadow or even Arc at all—it was in figuring out why this world existed in the first place. Why did Charlotte even see this place to begin with?

The other shadows were not like the one who brought him to this place. These static and lifeless creatures might not be anything but illusions. But that couldn't be since they very clearly had autonomy and shape. However, that wasn't enough to prove they had anything like minds or souls. This could be yet another trick, just like the false visage of a pristine white city he spotted when he first arrived here. None of this came together.

What was this world for?

To his right, there was a creak. His head moved before his eyes, allowing him to miss what jumped up and lunged for his head. A long metal snake slashed his face, leaving him to twist. Skin split on his right cheek. Before he could gather his wits, the attacking object sunk back into the pews and slunk like a cobra back into the shadows of the church pews. A careful thought made him realize that it wasn't a snake—it was a sword.

He shot his glance back to the front where the children were sitting. The two still talked among themselves, oblivious to the attack.

A slight scraping scratched along the surrounding pillars and spread along the church floor. That one sword-like snake was not his only weapon. He called out to the kids before he ran for them.

They were surrounded.

IV.

Rhodes rushed to the front of the church. He shouted to the children, but both were slow to move. The sound of shuffling steel on marble brought the hair on his neck standing up. The snake was moving somewhere nearby.

Danny shoved his sister out of the pew when the steel whipped across his face. It lashed against his shoulder, spilling blood across the bench. He fell down to the floor beside his sister.

The snake blade bobbed and weaved forward.

Rhodes cursed as he dashed towards them. He wasn't going to make it.

Amanda shouted to her brother. "Move, Danny!"

The girl's slight frame warped and bent, turning into a thin stream of glinting metal. She had become steel. Her new form split and twisted around her brother's hands, becoming armored gauntlets. At the same moment, the sword bit down on him.

Danny raised his hands to his face, and the attacking blade bounced off. The boy rolled backwards as the sword receded back into the pews once more.

Rhodes approached Danny and stood in front where the metal snake had been.

"How many swords does he have?" the older male asked. "Stand back to back. Don't move out of this position. He's waiting for us to make a mistake."

"He came here with one longsword. I don't know if he found another one somewhere."

"If he's been spending his time hunting and needed to use your sister as a weapon, then I'm going to deduce that he didn't. That sword of his moves fast. You'd think the thing would lose density as it expanded."

"It thins," the boy replied. He rubbed his injured shoulder. The slash thankfully wasn't deep. "But he can use other metal things to add to it. Amanda says he did that with her, too."

Rhodes felt his shoulders tighten. "Sick and dangerous. I can't let this maniac free."

"How are you gonna stop him, man? He moves too quickly."

"We can use my power, but it's risky. We're going to have to survive for at least five minutes without any protection or leaving this spot. If you can handle it, then let's give it a shot."

The boy fell silent. Rhodes didn't blame him. Danny had only been freed for mere minutes and was being asked to put his trust in a stranger. Rhodes didn't even know if his plan would work. It was simple and could easily be seen through . . .

if the enemy was expecting it. Rhodes had to bet that Arc's bloodthirst overwhelmed his common sense.

"She says she'll do it," Danny said.

"Can she split into two like that for other objects?"

"Amanda can become anything up to the size of a big sword. But more than two things are harder for her to move. It's easier when they're smaller. Why?"

"I need two daggers. They don't need to be big ones. Can she do it?"

"She can."

"She can hear me now?"

Danny nodded. "Yep."

"How far does her telekinetic range in that form work?"

"I don't know. We've never testing that out much. Usually, we have to touch."

"Amanda," Rhodes whispered. "I'm going to need you to do me a favor. I know you want to protect Danny, but to do that you're going to have to do something dangerous. It's not any risk to you personally, but you need to trust him to me for a few minutes. Can you do that?"

His power had been straightforward, a

simple telekinetic bond with metal objects. He'd used it to trap Arc before, and the assassin probably had an idea of why. This meant Rhodes would have to approach his predicament differently. He hoped that both his and her telekinetic connection would close the distance he needed to take Arc by surprise.

"She will do it," Danny said. The boy handed him the gauntlets. The metallic objects warped into small daggers in his hands. "What are you going to do? Why daggers?"

"I'd rather not say it out loud. Just watch. I might not look it but I'm good with blades."

Rhodes crouched low beyond possible sightlines of the surrounding pews, and brought the daggers to his sides. His arms stretched out as his knee touched down.

"*What am I doing, Mr. Rhodes?*"

"You'll see," he whispered. "I'm sure you'll figure it out fast."

The knives dashed out of his hands with a push of his thoughts. They hovered an inch from the floor as they shot both to the rear and the front of the church.

The blades reached both the wooden doors at the front and the spot where the altar should be at the rear. The two began their upward ascent when the boy suddenly yelled. Rhodes kept his concentration on the knives, and he looked up to the source of the noise. A snake sword leaped for Rhodes' neck.

Danny kicked the metal serpent, sending the sword slightly off course. It scraped the side of Rhodes' neck, and blood trickled out the wound. Rhodes rolled sideways, and the weapon twisted back, biting into his left side. His ribs flared. He took the blade and threw it aside, cutting open his palms. The sword slammed against the floor, and Danny stomped it down.

"Are you okay, man?"

"Get away from it!"

The sword bent at where Danny had stepped on it, slithering up his bare leg. The boy yelped, struggling in vain to grab at it despite the weapon's wild animalistic movements. It swirled upward, despite Danny's struggles.

A brand new metal vine branched out of the sword and wrapped around the boy's wrist. He stifled a cry.

Arc supposedly fed his swords for additional reach. This must have been the result.

Rhodes threw out his left hand and made a

bid for the blade. It sliced into him, even as he tightened his hold on it. Danny stumbled out of its contractions, even as Rhodes pulled it loose.

"*Mr. Rhodes!*" the girl exclaimed.

"I'm dealing with it! Keep looking around up there." Blood and skin grinded under his tightening palms. "He can use multiple blades at once—even inside the one he's already using."

Danny gasped at Rhodes' wounds. "Are you alright, man?"

Sharp pains slashed through Rhodes. "I'm fine!"

"*Mr. Rhodes. Up here!*"

The flying knives brushed against the high arched ceiling, and both pointed their tips to a pillar in the far left end of the church. A dark fig-ure moved behind it.

"*Be careful, the sword made a web of metal all over the floor.*"

"Got it. Danny! Follow me."

Rhodes whipped the snake aside and bounded onto the pew before him. The sword swung around mindlessly as he dove. Danny jumped up on the bench after him.

The wood whined with every step Rhodes made along the length of the bench. Danny stumbled behind, saying something about the bottom breaking. Small bits of blade bored their way from below, poking up through the pew. Rhodes leaped to the next row with the boy not far behind.

As he hopped, the older man glanced across the floor and saw what Amanda was speaking about. Thin webs of metal matriculated over the length of the church. Arc must have found a plentiful source of steel. It had to have been from the bars outside the windows. Now he had more than enough metal to cause a problem.

The pillar was a row away when Rhodes stretched out his arms. The two floating knives shot back to his open hands like magnets to their opposing poles. The boy shouted as the bench broke under them. Metal crashed through the pews. Rhodes leaped for the pillar ahead.

"*The metal is like string all over the floor,*" Amanda said. "*It all leads back to him.*"

"Follow me!" Rhodes shouted to Danny.

Rhodes leaped the last bench as wooden pieces popped up underneath his boots. A thin metal stream crashed against his kneecap. Rhodes winced and kicked it away. They landed the carpeted floor beside the row of stain glass windows.

Danny slammed into his back.

"Are you okay?" the boy asked. "That looked like it hurt."

"I'm still standing," Rhodes said, flashing a reassuring smile. "Look out!"

Arc jumped in on Rhodes. The sword he held was a thin blade, not much for show. The attached metal broke off as he lifted it in a raised stance.

The assassin brought the blade down on Rhodes' shoulder. Rhodes arched the knives upwards, and steel reverberated. Arc reeled, and Rhodes kicked at him. The strike cracked against the enemy's sternum. Arc ejected saliva from his mouth.

Rhodes threw the daggers back to Danny and then scooped broken metal from the floor. He shattered it into twelve pieces with his mind. The six inch pieces floated above his head.

A light flashed in Arc's hands and a small knife slashed the air for Rhodes. The defending man lifted his right arm, and the blade buried into his wrist. Rhodes stifled his scream, but Arc had already turned and ran.

"A-are you alright?" Danny asked.

"I'm fine, Danny. Do you have the daggers?"

"Right here."

"Good. Keep her with you. We need to catch him before we worry about me."

Rhodes felt the small knife Arc had thrown sinking into his wrist, a warm sensation filling the inside of his punctured skin and veins. It would be a few more minutes before he could absorb the metal to patch his wound, but first he needed to catch up to Arc.

They followed the assassin up a small set of stairs into a rear office area for the parish. Despite the large room size with desks jammed up against each other it was cramped. Arc cut between the desks, but Rhodes wouldn't have it, charging through the rundown wooden husks instead. Without a clear sightline, he kept his orbiting projectiles by the door. The desks crunched and cracked under his weight. By the time Arc looked back, Rhodes had already bounded through the last wall towards him.

He tackled Arc to the floor, and the pair rolled around. Fists and elbows flashed, crashing against and bruising skin as they thrashed about. Arc growled like a rabid dog as he pummeled Rhodes without mercy. Unfortunately, healing took energy, and Rhodes was running low on it.

"If you can't beat me then what chance do you have against the shadows?" Arc wheezed as he punched. The pair rolled to their feet, still slugging away at the other. Arc held Rhodes by the lapels, and the two fell against the opposite wall, dust pluming. The boarded window beside the killer shone pale light across his creased brow. "You can't kill shadows anyway."

"Yes, you can," Rhodes said. "We can escape. You just need to help us do it."

"A lion doesn't help a gazelle. I'm going to put your head on the memorial at Calloway Row. The shadows will appreciate it before they find that girl they want."

"I'll appreciate it when I crush your bones."

Rhodes gestured his fingers, and the shard projectiles shot across the room. Arc ducked, and they slammed into the boarded window, cracking through the other side. Muted, unearthly moonlight broke the darkness. The second floor overlooked a parking lot floors below. Arc flinched as the light beat across him, momentarily loosening his grip on Rhodes.

That was when they noticed Danny had

slipped in beside them. The young boy punched at Arc, stunning him more than hurting. Rhodes spun the assassin around and he stumbled out of Rhodes' hold before the window.

"What was that supposed to be?" Arc asked. "A warning shot?"

"Hit him straight on," Danny said to Rhodes.

The older brawler moved in when Arc did a strange thing. Instead of attacking the man before him, he hopped backwards. Arc had thrown himself through the window! Broken pieces of board dislodged from the frame as he fell.

Arc's screams faded with his drop. There was a crunch as he landed against hard pavement. Somehow he was still breathing down there.

Rhodes looked at the boy. "Your power caused that?"

"Yeah," the boy said. "He won't be moving right for a good minute. Up is down to him."

"I'm sure getting up is going to be hard for him, as will be drinking without a straw."

From the edges of the window emerged a moving shadow, floating in like a cloud of mist across water. It scraped against the floor. The flat sheet of dark death formed against the far wall by the office entrance behind them.

"I thought shadows couldn't get in?" Danny whispered.

"Not until we're let in," the thing said. "We're always let in, eventually."

Rhodes' stomach boiled. He inched towards the exit, and the boy followed. They both recognized the shadow that had brought them here.

"Why are you showing up now?" Rhodes looked to make sure Danny still had his daggers. Thankfully, he did. "I've been here for ages."

"I had to confirm, and confirm I did. You are who I was waiting for."

"How do you figure? I'm not an assassin like Arc."

"You're more dangerous. You are the one who tore me apart, and, in return, I will return the favor. Then I will eat that crying child you took from me. What do you think now, *hero*?"

Terror slowly pried its way into Rhodes' thoughts. He had heard that voice but once almost twenty years ago. Back when he was a young kid starting out in a firm, he quickly rose through the ranks. A monster of a man with some sort of unknown power broke into an apartment complex and killed several, taking a baby as it escaped. Rhodes cornered the monster and cut it to pieces. He'd saved the baby and had raised her himself. And the villain died in the encounter.

He saw the monster die, and yet here it was as some sort of shadow.

Rhodes hands trembled as he tried to hold his posture, but it was impossible. This creature died, and the dead don't come back.

"Revenge, is it?" Rhodes finally mustered.

"First, I gut you, wear your skin, and return to my city. Then I find the baby and do what I was going to in the first place. It will be so much fun doing it as you."

Memories of finding Charlotte on that rooftop flooded into Rhodes. This was the freak that took her parents and was ready to take more lives. But she was his daughter now, and she had a good life. This monster would never come near her again.

Screaming laughed up from the street outside the window. Before he could react, even more moving shadows began to slide in through the new opening. Danny shouted and pulled Rhodes towards the exit. He reluctantly followed as the laughs chased after them out into the crimson night of the fake city. Rhodes knew those screams. Arc was being devoured.

Soon enough, the same would happen to them.

V.

The pair passed down winding stairs and reached the street again. Danny tossed what looked like a gauntlet to Rhodes. It morphed into a solid bracelet around his wrist. The boy also had one on.

"*This way I can talk to you both,*" Amanda said. "*Did you know that monster?*"

"Quiet," Rhodes whispered.

Danny still trailed behind him. "Don't worry, man. They're not coming."

Rhodes chanced a glance into the black void of the street behind them. Only the usual rouge moonlight on the sidewalk and slinking ephemeral bodies could be seen.

"That thing wanted to kill me back in Summerside. Why would it stop now?"

"*You knew it?*" the girl said.

It wasn't a story Rhodes told to anyone simply because it was impossible, and it led to being forced out of the hero profession, but there wasn't any point hiding it. The past had returned to kill him, and these children had a right to know.

He scanned the black mass of crowd and dropped his pace to a saunter. If those things weren't threatening him, he wasn't going to waste energy running. Memories prickled in the back of his mind with every moment spent in the quiet of the silent mob.

"A long time ago, when I was young, I was an agent for the government. I got out of the game before I turned twenty. One of the reasons is because of what I saw when answering an emergency call late one night."

"Was it a shadow?" Danny dodged a crowd member that nearly bumped him. "Go on."

Rhodes ran it through his mind one more time before he finally divulged his secret. It had been so long, and yet the memories remained so vivid.

The report had mentioned a suspect with an abnormal power attacking an apartment building. The villain had barreled through the halls, injuring everyone in his way as if unaware of their existence. He snarled like a coyote and growled like a bear as he moved. It was only when he tore the hinges off the door to one apartment on the seventh floor that any semblance of humanity returned to him. That was when the villain deliberately murdered the young couple living inside. The murderer then took off with their baby, for whatever reason.

That was when Rhodes got the call since he was close to the scene. He cut the criminal off on a rooftop and faced it one on one with his floating knives. The bloated monster with purple skin like a corpse and long nails like claws caused his skin to crawl. That was when the misshapen and naked figure with eyes blacker than coal attacked him.

"He was insane," Rhodes said. "He went on about *his* city and how people like me were holding him back. That wasn't unusual for villains, but the way he moved and the way he spoke were at odds with how he looked. It was almost like he was possessed."

"And you fought him like Arc, right?" Danny said. He laughed. "You beat him!"

"I did fight him."

And he did beat him. Rhodes dismembered the attacking beast, sending its remains off the roof to the street below. When it struck down the monster dissolved into nothing, leaving no semblance of a corpse. He didn't tell the children the first part, but he emphasized the second.

"*What about the baby?*" Amanda hurriedly asked. "*She was alright, huh?*"

"I took her in as my daughter. She had no other family. The problem was that there was no trace of that criminal. The guys upstairs thought I lied and let the criminal go because I was scared and weak. I showed them the bite mark on my shoulder, but it wasn't enough. Eventually, I was blacklisted, and ended up quitting."

"Lame!" Danny shouted. "What kind of heroes are those? How could they doubt one of their own?"

"The more important part is that the monster didn't die. It's here. It spent twenty years trying to find me by abducting any Metal Elemental it could and bringing them here. It wants Charlotte again. It wants to finish the job. Where even are we?"

"*Arc went all over this city hunting for life.*" Amanda paused, most likely trying to avoid the memories. "*He told me there were other people here, but they hid inside broken buildings. It's like that* shadow said: they can't go where they're not invited so the people are safe in the areas not taken over by illusions, like the church."

"Then where would we find them? We can't run around here all night."

"Try the old church in Calloway Row. If people stayed away from there in Summerside, then maybe it's the same here. This place is weird, I don't know."

She wasn't wrong. This upside down city had been playing with his senses since arrival. The miraculously maintained buildings took over for the old relics strewn about Summerside. The abandoned and desolate railyard and the decrepit church were all the reverse of what existed in the real world. This artificial place stunk of something worse than even that city of crime did.

They passed between the huddled masses of dark fog barely resembling people. Danny's cut shoulder bothered him so Rhodes silently slipped into a drug store. Who knew what they had?

Sure enough, the inside was cleaner than a hospital room and smelled just as bad. The two held their noses. Huddles of ashen people-shaped creatures awkwardly browsed the aisle as if they were there to shop. Rhodes and Danny tried to pay them no mind as they searched the surprisingly stocked shelves, when the two reached the shelf where the bandages should have been, they quickly made a discovery.

The boy read the sign above: "*Sparw dna Segadnab?*"

"Wraps and bandages, backwards. Just like a mirror. Weird that there's no store signs outside, but they're in here. Take one out of the box and see if it's real."

"It's a bit weird to do something like that without paying."

"Something tells me nobody pays for anything here. Just see what it looks like."

They wrestled open a box and removed a bandage. It had a slightly sticky texture, but it was solid enough. But Rhodes refused to trust it. Instead, he removed his jacket and slashed fabric off the back.

Rhodes slapped the makeshift bandage on Danny's back. As he was placing it, the older man's shoulder bumped against a black blob of a man. He bit his lip as reverberations clinched his nerves.

A small explosion of darkness overtook him and then clarity prevailed. He blinked, and the world was as it should be. Normal people in suits and skirts walked the aisles picking pharmaceutical products and buying them at the manned cash. The aisles and rows looked just as cracked and dirty as they always did in Summerside, but the people smiled and laughed despite it all. This was the city he knew so well.

Then he blinked again.

The world returned to its false state, and Rhodes recoiled. His back knocked the shelf over, and he threw out an arm instinctively against the approaching Danny. The shadow Rhodes had struck passed before them, oblivious to their presence. They leaned into the shelf as the thing approached the cash at the front, appeared to pause as if paying, and then left. Rhodes let the boy go and breathed. The nerve muscles in his arm still rippled from the earlier contact.

He fell backwards and bumped into another shadow. This time nothing but visions of a broken flaming city filled his mind. Blood trickled from his nose as the stench of death bit into it. Rhodes jumped back flat against the shelf.

"Are you alright, man?"

"Don't know, but don't touch those things. Whatever they are, they think they're people. I saw what they pretend to be." He explained a bit of his vision before beckoning them towards the door. "We shouldn't be in cramped spaces."

They strode the streets for what felt like hours, humidity and fatigue beating down upon them. While his wounds were healing, none of his stamina returned. At this rate, they would never reach the church.

Hallucinations broke his concentration. He was starting to see the world *they* wanted him to see, and his muscles numbed. This was the reason Arc returned to the safety of the church. Those spots must have been safe from this sensation. Sanity was a casualty of living here for any extent of time. It was no wonder that shadow didn't chase him outside—it didn't need to.

"Down here," Danny said. "Normally, I'd take the subway, but we can't here."

There was no telling what would await them underground where shadows ruled. Rhodes followed the boy's directions up the street. His legs worked against him, and some unseen force pushed harder than gravity. They soon crossed a shallow alley and reached a barely lit street.

More shadow people crossed their path. There was no escaping them. But what was worse was that Rhodes was starting to see less of the shadows, and more of the people they were trying to be. His control was failing and his skull was ringing like a train whistle.

The pair ascended steps towards a duplex. Danny knocked on it without pause.

"We can rest here, man," the kid said.

After a beat, the door flew open and revealed the figure of a normal boy. He looked Rhodes up and down as if he didn't see Danny at all, which was just as well, because the boy in the doorway would have been left speechless. He greeted Rhodes with a chipper tone.

"*What's wrong, Mr. Rhodes?*" Amanda asked.

Rhodes struggled for the words. "It's Danny."

"What?" both siblings asked at the same time.

The boy in the door titled his head. "How do you know my name?"

Rhodes thought quick before either sibling could interrupt him. "Acquaintance of your mom and dad. I know your sister, Amanda, too. Her legs are bad, right?"

"No, they're just fine these days. Why

don't you come in, Mr. . . .?"

"Rhodes," he replied. "I'm just Rhodes."

"Welcome to the Kessler residence, Mr. Rhodes. Mom and Dad are right inside."

The boy left, and Rhodes waited a moment on the stoop, his heart twisting against his ribcage. This creature mimicked Danny perfectly aside from the positivity.

"What did you see?" The real Danny side-eyed him. "I only saw a shadow."

"*Me, too.*"

"It was you, Danny. That shadow was you. You two stay here. I'm going to go in and see if I can learn anything, as long as they're talking to me."

"Don't be crazy," Danny said. "That wasn't me! You can't trust those things."

"This might be our only clue." He handed the boy his bracelet, and Amanda's voice left him. "You two will be safer if you have somewhere to run to."

Rhodes swallowed his pride crossed the threshold. Instantly, a lukewarm chill like thick mud trickled through his nerve-endings. The throbbing of his brain and bones refused to cease, leaving him with little option other than to keep moving.

He would get his answers and get the children out of here. He would exit this shadow city intact. He was almost certain of it. *Almost.*

If that voice whispering in his ear wasn't laughing so loud, he might actually have believed his words.

VI.

Rhodes still had one foot in the real world, wherever *that* was, and this dark world, wherever *that* was, when he entered the home of the shadow child. It was almost as if he were on the cusp of a place, a state of mind, just out of his grasp. The veil was right there; he just had to pull it back.

But he couldn't afford to stick around here. Not with a family waiting back home, and two children behind him who needed his help. These things were also after Charlotte. The bells wouldn't ring for him just yet. If only the rest of this death world saw things his way.

He passed through the narrow hallway by the sloping stairs into the back room where the stench of rotting wet wood attacked him. Three figures sat inside the living room, two of which were nearly human but not quite, with oblong skeletal shapes for bodies and slightly crooked faces missing simple pieces like eyes or hair. The third figure was similar to the boy before him, nearly fully formed and almost real-looking, only this one was a girl with tied back hair and a welcoming grin on her small face. The fake-Amanda jumped from the couch when she saw Rhodes and guided him to the chair before them. He wearily fell into it.

"Mr. Rhodes!" she said in a tone between flat and warbled. "It has been a long time."

Rhodes fought off a double take. "You know me?"

"We do, hardly."

"What about your legs? You can't walk."

"No way, of course I can! I can do everything here."

Her tone warped, but his warbled. His tongue slurred, like he was losing control of his thoughts.

"What are you doing in here, man?" Danny asked.

Rhodes looked up to see the real Danny standing by the archway to the hall. He held his sister at his side and placed her down against the wall. None of the shadow beings noticed them.

"You're not really Danny or Amanda," Rhodes said to the ones on the couch. They didn't flinch at his assertion. "So what are you, and why can I see you?"

Fake-Danny waved towards him. "Don't worry, Mr. Rhodes. You're just getting used to being here. Give it some time, and you'll be reborn, like us."

"Reborn?" That was a word that rubbed him wrong. "You're just shadows. The actual Amanda and Danny are still the real ones."

"We are them," the girl shadow said. Her pleasant smile creased at the corners. "Soon, we will be the only them. You, too, Mr. Rhodes. I can sense you being reborn right now."

Rhodes smiled back at her, his eyes slowly sliding shut. He had figured it out but too late. He wouldn't be getting up from the chair again. His tired muscles wouldn't allow it.

"Are you talking to the shadow?" the real Amanda asked. "How are you doing that?"

"I'm dying," he said, simply. "This world eats you. I was wondering why neither of you had the same problem as me, but that's because you both spent more time in the church safe zone.

You've also been in steel form, Amanda. I've been running around without any protection."

"I have no protection," Danny said. "But I'm not fading as fast as you."

"You aren't as hurt as me. I healed myself, but my energy isn't returning. It's fading."

"When it's time," Fake-Danny interrupted, "you will be whole. One will come for you."

Rhodes' body stiffened. He couldn't let it end now. If he did they could still get at Charlotte. Then there were these kids. Rhodes made one last gamble with his new found sight between planes. He concentrated and watched the window across from him.

In the distance were black skies behind crimson clouds where only hot wind blew across deserted desert fields, and no living being roamed. But there were forms, very faint objects, shining deep in the depths of it. He imagined the face of that monster—the one he had sent here so long ago—and found it. It shambled mindlessly along the rooftops.

The monster was a shadow now, a faded memory of some forgotten farce of a man, but its bulky and ridiculous form remained an intangible mess.

Rhodes needed it to be here and called to it with his thoughts.

His enemy heard his silent pleas, panting like a dog that had been called for dinner. It slipped and slid along rooftops, hunger on its mind. It wanted to devour him whole.

He blinked awake, and the shadows grew even fuller than before. No longer could he even focus on the real Danny and Amanda. All that remained were these remnants of them.

Fake-Amanda's cheek twitched as if it were pinched. "I am proud that you have accepted what will become reality."

"It's not reality." The words poured slowly from Rhodes' tongue like honey. "You're not real. You're a shade of it."

"No, we *were*. Soon, we will be all that is. That will make us real. There is nothing else."

"Enough!" Danny shouted.

The boy swung a blunt object. Fake-Amanda screeched as the metal bat swung through her and puffed her into a cloud of smoke. The fatigue in Rhodes momentarily faded as he focused on Danny's appearance. Where did he come from? Was he in the room? Rhodes had forgotten.

The boy had bruises all over his face and panted hard. He stared down his doppelganger.

The fake Danny roared and leaped for him but met the same fate as his false sister. The bat crashed through him. Not even dust remained.

"They got you because of your powers, man. Amanda and I were talking about it. That's how they got Arc, too. You use too much of your powers, and you get tired, right? It's like stretching too much and getting so worn out you can't walk. Notice since leaving the church that no rest we do makes any difference?"

Of course, it had to be the case. The shadow city drains and takes. Stamina was valuable, but it could always be restored. It was no wonder that shadow wanted Arc after him. It drained him much faster, and, without the church or another safe zone, there was no way to escape this trap. The only question was what Danny did to get this clarity to see these shadows clearly.

"I beat myself up, of course!" The boy grinned stupidly. "Amanda wasn't up for it, but it wasn't like she could stop me. We need you to help us out. Can't do that if you leave us now!"

"Thank you," Rhodes said. He couldn't

hide being grateful, even if the kid was dopey. "I feel less tired somehow."

The two parent shadows never moved. It appeared they were not yet formed. Rhodes sighed. The three of them were safe now.

"But that big shadow is on the way here, and I can't move too well," Rhodes said. "So, I'm going to need one last favor from the two of you."

"Amanda says she's game. I am, too."

Rhodes tried to make a plan, but with his mobility all but shot, it would be a gamble. When he focused on that shadow that had brought him here, he thought he saw something inside where its heart should be. This was Rhodes' only clue to defeat the shade. "Give me gauntlets, Amanda. And stay close, Danny. You might be able to do something."

"*He won't do anything*," a voice said from above.

Without arguing, Danny threw the metal bat to Rhodes. It morphed in mid-air to the very gauntlets he had asked for. Rhodes caught and wore them the very moment a large black beast dropped through the ceiling. Wood and plaster rained down on them, as the giant shadow landed on Danny like a giant water balloon. The boy yelled as he was absorbed into the black mass.

"*Help him!*" his sister shouted.

Rhodes leaped off the chair, but he was too slow. The beast burst out the front door and into the street. Rhodes moved at a sluggish speed, an embarrassment for an emergency like this.

He grit his teeth as his muscles groaned. "I'm going to send this thing to oblivion."

The drained man stumbled out of the duplex and into the stoop, leaning on the railing. He just knew that if he fell again he wouldn't be getting up. Unless he killed the monster here, they would become shadows just like the rest. His family would never forgive him for that.

Pushing deep down for his last bit of energy, Rhodes let out a groan and stumbled down the stairs on stiff legs. This time, he would finish the twenty year feud permanently.

VII.

Rhodes reached the middle of the road with every bone and muscle in his body throbbing. The night before him flashed in a constant barrage of lightning strikes which illuminated the world in muddy darkness. Whether it was because he was seeing the world as the way it truly was or because he was dying he couldn't discern. At last, before him in the empty street lurched the shadow that had brought him here to begin with.

The monster clutched Danny's shoulders with shadowy claws that blended effortlessly into the night. If Rhodes squinted, he could almost grasp the figure of the former man it once was.

"You did all this to get me?" Rhodes said. "You hurt all those people, invaded my daughter's dreams, and attacked children. Why? Because I stopped you? If it wasn't me, it would have been someone else eventually. Your kind is always the same."

Deep growls issued from the mask of a face the shadow held. "*Your* kind is everything wrong with the world I left behind."

"I was doing my job of stopping murderers like you."

"And what a job it is!" the shadow said. The boy winced as the claws sunk deeper into his shoulders. "Chaos is truth. It is what this insane universe is at its core: a confusing and untamed wilderness where only the clever and the strong survive. And people like you dedicate yourselves to lies instead—lies that the weak must be rewarded for their weakness. You clip the wings of the strong fliers, the ones who know the truth, for the ones who should have no power. Your backwards nature denies reality, and it is what has caused the broken Summerside we have left behind. This place is the new reality. These shadows are who we all really are."

"You're hurting the boy."

The shadow roared. "You prove my point! Who cares what becomes of one who can't handle himself? There are no rules. You and your kind constructed them for your sick world. Crusaders? They fight reality itself. I did not create this shadow city, but I welcome it over that lie you call reality. There is no reality in the lies your kind peddles."

Rhodes inched closer as the shadow went on. His fists tightened in the gauntlets. Close enough and he could spring for the boy. Rhodes needed to keep the thing talking.

"Fine, okay, you're right. If you want to take it out on me, you can. I agree that you have the right. I killed you, after all. I don't regret it, and I'm not going to apologize. But I didn't make the rules up—that's where you're wrong. Summerside is just like any other city trying to get along since the world almost died so long ago. Innocents exist. We can fight and kill each other all we want, but there are those that want no part of it. I'm not going to get them involved."

"And why not?" the shadow said. "What does it matter? They're going to die regardless. See this city? This is far beyond me. Soon enough, this will be Summerside. There is nothing to fight against except our reality. You will all die. This boy." The shadow dug his claws in more, and Danny whined. "This boy will die."

"You don't get to decide that."

"Spare me! I'm beyond you here. The shadows are stronger than all—powers or no. We are above whatever random creed or cause you humans cobble together and call morality. There is nothing here but chaos: true reality."

He was almost in striking range. Rhodes only needed one more push, and he could attack without being touched by the enemy. The gauntlets were his only hope of winning.

"How many Metal Elementals did you kill looking for me? Did they all die in this world by your hand? You can't even fight anymore, can you?"

"I don't need to. Were you wandering

around looking for more like you? I regret to inform you that they're all dead. They were weak and struggled for air as they sunk under the waves. There is no hope for you here, wretch."

"Do you even remember your name?"

For the first time since Rhodes had arrived, the shadow paused as if parsing thoughts. It was as if this notion had never occurred to him before.

"Could it be that whatever you trafficked in to give you those powers also took something else? Why did you attack that apartment, anyway? The police looked into the victims and could find no links or possible suspects, except one. A man who had no other ties to anyone or anything. No powers, no motive, just a loner who kept to himself. The victim's ex-boyfriend. She hadn't even been with him in years by that point."

The shadow growled. "You test my patience."

"You might have forgotten, but I remember."

"Stop!"

"Horace Abalone."

The shadow screeched and threw Danny aside. Rhodes leaped the distance and brought up his gauntlets. The former human slammed a claw down, and metal reverberated in the night. Rhodes forced his right hand forward and plunged it into the chest of the shadow. It wailed and brought its left claw up. But the limb waved impotently. Danny had gripped its arm tight.

Horace shouted, clearly unable to understand how they were able to touch him. But Rhodes understood. The shadow had lost its cool and allowed itself to physically manifest itself too much in order to kill its opponent. Danny let go, but his power already kicking in on this monster.

Rhodes' right arm twisted in the shadow's chest. A shrill shriek broke from the intangible lips, and light twinkled inside the pit. Rhodes pushed deeper, his goal just in sight. Cold and crushing pressure squeezed down on him. Sleep threatened to choke him to death.

"You're the only shadow different than the others." He easily dodged a swing from the shadow. "They did give you something, Horace. I'm going to take it."

"Let me go, worm. You already killed me. You can't do it again!"

"I'm going to set you free."

Rhodes squeezed down on the silver light inside the shadow's chest. With his last remaining strength, he pulled the foreign object out. His muscle spasmed as black ink splashed out around him. The ephemeral form of Horace howled.

"No," the shadow said. "You can't just—"

But it never finished. The shadow trickled away into the night like dust in a desert wind. Its screams blew away to nothing in the breeze. All that remained of Horace Abalone was a memory.

"It's gone!" Danny said. The boy rubbed his shoulders. "What was that thing?"

Rhodes concentrated his attention on the round curved silver stone in his hand. Faint heat trapped inside oddly soothed him. This was the only aspect of Horace Abalone that was different from the other shadows. It must have been the one thing that kept him tethered to the real world. It had to be linked to it in some way. Rhodes focused his thoughts on returning back to Summerside and hoped his gamble would pay off. The warmth in the bauble slowly swelled.

"Hold on to me, Danny. It's working."

The boy grabbed Rhodes by the wrist without asking questions. The world warped and twisted around them, dancing shadows disappeared into nothing but memories on the fringes of Rhodes' mind. Of his surroundings, only Danny remained, still beside him.

"*What are you doing with my rune?*" a husky voice said from nowhere in particular.

Rhodes snarled. "Taking it where you will never see it again."

Within seconds, he vanished from the false reality, leaving the shadow city in whatever hell it existed in.

VIII.

Rhodes threw open the door to the yardmaster's office. The middle-aged man was snoring into his desk. That was just as well, since the hour was near midnight. Rhodes kicked the side, shaking the cheap plastic.

The yardmaster jumped up, panicking until he noticed it was Rhodes.

"Oh, it's you." The exhausted man scanned Rhodes' torn clothes and battered body. "Where did you go? I paid you to stay here all night, not to go out and get into bar fights."

"The problem's solved. I chased a bunch of kids off; one got prissy, and I clocked him good. They won't be coming back."

He yawned. "And I should just trust you?"

"You know my track record. That's why you hired me. Give me a call if they return."

There would be no sense telling the fool what had happened since sunset or that Rhodes had been transported to a whole other shadow city. It was gone now regardless.

No one could ever know about that place. Thankfully, the kids had agreed to keep quiet.

The portal that rune opened sent them back into this world, on the same street where they fought Abalone. Traffic swerved around them, and the kids were confused. Rhodes was simply grateful that he could breathe better, and his energy began to return.

He sent Danny and Amanda back home, and, when he was sure they were inside and safe, took a taxi back to the railyard. The dark skies made it look as if the same amount of time had passed in both worlds since he had first left this one. Thankfully, no one would have missed him for that long. It was a small price to pay to destroy any path back to that world.

"Fine," the yardmaster said. He yawned. "You can go. But if anything comes up—"

"I'll handle it," Rhodes said. "I always do."

He exited into the night without a further

word, and the yardmaster went back to his desk.

In his pocket, Rhodes felt the rune between bruised fingers. He would have to ask around and knock some heads to learn the story behind it. Whatever made Horace Abalone into that monster could not be trusted, and there was no telling if that world really was safe and locked off for good. But at least, that monster was dead. No one would suffer from Horace Abalone again.

As he passed the tunnel where he disappeared from, Rhodes remembered back when he first fought that monster nearly twenty years ago. That moment should have ruined his life, like it did his career, but the opposite occurred. Instead, his family began from that moment. At the same time, those shadows consumed Abalone, who could not deal with the reality of this city. His type were all the same. They needed to fashion their own world to escape it—they needed their own illusions.

But eventually, all artificiality falls away, and the truth remains. They are left with a prison of their own making that they locked themselves inside.

This was the real world. No shadow could ever replace it.

Rhodes didn't pay it any further mind. Villains would always be the same, hoping to get something for nothing. No matter how old he got, certain things remained the same.

Rhodes exited the tunnel and railyard back into the real Summerside. He couldn't help but feel grateful to be back.

He called up Charlotte. "I'm coming home. How are you sleeping?"

"You're not going to believe it, Dad. I slept like a log. It's just like it used to be. That creepy dark world is gone."

Rhodes smiled to himself as he walked the sidewalk towards the subway. Streetlights brightened his path forward. "That's just what I like to hear."

LUCKY SPIDER'S LAST STAND

The woman had just finished wrapping Spider's bandages when he heard a rumble. He quickly recognized it was an explosion. She fell against him, her small shoulders against his chest. The two tumbled to the floor in a deliberate embrace as the grenade's smoke plumed outside the cracked warehouse window. He checked her over and found no wounds.

Her soft, supple skin and intoxicating fragrance distracted for just a moment. Spider was her enemy, and yet she had agreed to reapply his bandage so easily. He was the villain, and the heroes were coming to rescue her. Her concern baffled him.

Yells and gunfire from the men downstairs brought Spider to his feet and then the door. The hideout had been found out. He patted the girl on the shoulder and told her to remain quiet.

Her soft brown eyes stared into his, silently questioning his very being. This distraction wouldn't do. The boss wouldn't stand for failure like this. Spider had standards. The boss might be dead now, but Spider wouldn't abandon his ideals: not even for the girl.

The door locked behind him, and he slid the key into his pocket. The scent of burnt wood and charred brick assaulted him instantly. He straightened the collar of his blue suit and crossed the decaying hall to the stairs. If he was going to die, he would face death like a man.

The building had been set ablaze a decade ago after a criminal with fire powers sought revenge on some fat hacker holed up in his bedroom. That was back when the war between heroes and villains was at its peak. This place was left to rot in Barrie Heights with everything else the scum destroyed in their war for Summerside. But that was ages ago, and those villains were long gone, killed or imprisoned by the heroes. It had nothing to do with Spider.

Burnt floorboards creaked ahead, and Spider went for his gun. He tasted the blood before he smelled it, as if a walking corpse had found its way out of the grave. That was when he saw the intruder emerge from the shadows.

A man wearing a custom, homemade, closed knight helmet and visor out of the fourteenth century and holding two sabers strode across the open floor with giant strides. He wore thick dark brown pants and heavy boots, which were the only indications that he might be sane. The rogue wore no shirt and his abs, pectorals, and wide shoulders were covered in blood down to his blades. The awkwardly-tempered silver close helm agitated Spider with reflecting moonlight from the shattered windows.

Spider raised his firearm and called out. The psycho continued toward him, unabated.

The gang had barely escaped last night's raid with the girl; Spider was still exhausted from running and keeping watch for the cops. It was as if the wannabe hero knew all that.

Of course, he did. That was when the realization hit Spider. This was a Crusader.

Spider clenched his teeth. This wasn't an official black mask wearing hero. He was not sent by the government or by the cops. These heroes were illegal, and dangerous.

"Stop right there, Crusader," Spider said. He raised the firearm, and tasted the bile at the back of his throat.

"That will not stop me."

Spider fired. The bullet struck the intruder in center mass. Blood spurted from the wound, and the Crusader reeled.

But it wasn't enough. The Crusader stood straight again, and the bullet leaped back out of the wound. The spent shot clanked uselessly against the burnt floorboards.

Spider fired again with the same result. The insane man advanced again. The scent of fresh blood hung in the air.

His anger rising, Spider threw the gun aside. This Crusader was a Physical Type; his ability was obviously self-healing. Matching him one on one would not happen. Running for it was Spider's last recourse.

"Are you thinking of running, Spider?"

Sweat poured down Spider's neck. "Are you Ragnarok? The illegal hero who kills mooks like me?"

"I am," Ragnarok answered from under his close helmet. The visor was so thin that no face could be seen. "You are Lucky Spider, the one who has the Police Chief's daughter captive."

"Yeah."

One of the sabers clanked at Spider's feet. He blinked at it and then at Ragnarok.

"What's this for?"

"I have seen your work, Spider. You are a strong warrior wedded to a false cause. Your dishonorable friends paid the price, but you are not like them. There is honor in you. Pick up the blade, and let us see your true strength."

"You have powers. I don't."

"I can heal, true. But does that matter if my head is missing from my shoulders?"

Spider watched the fallen saber with hungry eyes. An itch gnawed at the inside of his brain, and a thrill ran deep in his spine. Could he actually win? He would have to. This was his last chance.

Spider scooped up the saber, keeping his eyes on Ragnarok. The Crusader never moved.

After the rise of powers, heroes were given a free ride. If you had a good power and were in with the government, the world could be yours. Normal folks got nothing. That had changed over the decades. The rise of illegal heroes, Crusaders, struck a new sort of fear into the dark corners of the underworld. No one knew what they wanted, and they didn't care what the rules were. Death meant nothing to them. You could bargain with a crooked hero but never a Crusader.

And now Spider was facing one. An inexplicable smile broke across his lips.

"Why a saber?" Spider asked.

"Because you are good with one."

Spider hefted the saber in a practiced grip, raising the blade in a wary guard as he and the Crusader took their distance.

"The loser forfeits their life," Ragnarok said.

"I know how you work."

Spider moved in without waiting, swiping at the Crusader's open arm. Ragnarok dodged, and the two blades clanged. The fighters danced their swords in a swirling symphony of strikes.

Blades crashed, and the boards creaked underneath, kicking up black ash and rotted wood. Skin sliced open between the two warriors, and blood leaped out of the wounds. No matter how many swings they exchanged, Ragnarok only closed in. Spider soon found himself with his back to the burnt wall.

"Look out, Spider!"

That new voice was Bull, screaming his heart out. The chubby man stumbled around the corner, clutching his bloodied arm and a gun in trembling fingers.

He fired wildly. Two bullets struck Ragnarok in the back. The hero dropped with the shots. Bull continued shooting and pumped the corpse full of bullets.

Spider slid on his back to the floor against the wall. Somehow, he wasn't dead.

"Where's the whore?" Bull yelled. He gestured for Spider to get up. Blood streaked down his dirty face as he looked over Ragnarok's corpse.

"Damn Crusaders."

"He's not dead, Bull. Get out, quick. I'll get the girl."

"Just cut off his head. I filled him with lead. It's gonna take him a while to wake up, right? Well, finish it."

The hero *had* said that; Spider could end it right here. But should he? Blood was still leaking from Ragnarok's wounds, and he remained still. Spider took one step toward the Crusader, his own wounds crying out. The infamous Lucky Spider lives again!

Wooziness gripped him. Crimson blood

had stained Spider's navy blue suit from head to toe. The bandage the girl had wrapped him with was sliced apart. His breaths fell hard. He had to finish this fast.

He stood over Ragnarok, sword ready. He'd actually lived. The boss would be so proud.

But the boss was dead.

Cold chills pierced his heart and dripped down to his stomach. The massacre last night had killed most of the guys. He had looked after the girl—Michelle. The others wanted to serve her to the cops in pieces, but the boss said it was up to Spider. The boss had always trusted Spider's judgment to keep him alive. Things always worked out. But Spider had failed the boss in the raid last night. He was gone now.

And why did the girl look at him like that?

He lifted the sword and then brought it down. His anger beat out his frustration.

The weapon pierced into the rotting board beside Ragnarok's head.

"Get moving, Bull," Spider yelled out. "He's going to wake up any second."

"I'm always awake," Ragnarok whispered through the visor.

The Crusader braced his hands against the

floor and nimbly leapt to his feet in one easy motion. The bullets jumped from his wounds.

Bull swore and ran back out the way he came.

"You call that a friend, Spider?"

His body heavy, all Spider could do was consider the Crusader's words. The gang would always be like this. "Guess not."

Spider tried to smile, but the world slanted. He dropped to his knees and then to the floor. Moonlight from the shattered windows blinded him.

"We must do battle again, Lucky Spider," Ragnarok said.

The world blanked out, and ended.

When Spider awoke, he was lying in an alleyway. The rising sun punched him hard, clashing against the cold alley brick. Graffiti and trash littered the moist pavement assaulting the rest of his senses. He lifted himself out of the garbage and inspected his surroundings. He wore a long coat over his torn suit, and the bandage around his right arm had been reapplied. The girl's scent lingered over both. He plucked the sleeve and realized it came a bit short. It looked the same as her coat. Why did she patch him up once again?

He stumbled out of the alley and sunk into the crowds. The work day had begun. People gushed around Spider like a raging river.

Despite the urge to return to the guys, he knew they were all gone. The girl had been returned to her home, and the day was saved thanks to that Crusader.

And now Spider had nothing.

But he felt something in his pockets. He dug deep inside. He found the life savings he had squirreled away from the guys, all in a set of envelopes. The girl couldn't have known about it, so who put them there?

The man with the sword.

He remembered Ragnarok's last words. They would meet again. Spider turned on his foot and walked from the busy streets. There was enough in his savings for a small apartment or a new arsenal. Spider *could* have his revenge against that man.

At that moment, he could do anything.

But Ragnarok won, and Spider lost. A deal was a deal. Lucky Spider was dead. He thought of the girl as he disappeared into the crowd. What did she see when she looked at him? He would find it for himself.

WHEN THE SUNSET TURNS RED

I.
JAILBREAK

"It's okay, there are no real names here," Arlen said, spreading his fat hands open. The two men crammed in on either side of him in the small cell groaned in agreement. "It's just you and me tonight, anyway, John. We can begin your initiation now if you would like."

Chambers pursed his lips as if deciding how to respond to this new knowledge. He didn't come here to talk to the overweight man in the suit, nor did he want to sit in this jail cell listening to him blather. He had other plans. He wanted to be free of this world of death and corruption, and yet here he was trapped in it again.

"My name isn't John," Chambers said. "The only reason I'm here is because this lot of idiots got into a brawl with an undercover cop in front of the park."

The small cell filled with a dozen other men all murmured to each other at his words. If they weren't all covered in cuts, bruises, and welts, across their torn clothes and ruffled hair they might have been ready for another skirmish. But they were in this place for a reason and not about to stop playing it cool.

Arlen cackled for a second before abruptly ceasing. "Our police force refused to do their job. This means it is only natural the people would have to do it for them, John."

"Stop calling me that. Some gang of greasy thugs stormed the drug store by the park, and you all formed a lynch mob to drag them all out. Then I got pulled into it just for being there."

Chambers ran his fingers through his slicked back black hair and narrowed his green eyes at the crazy fat man. Arlen's smile remained unperturbed.

"What were you doing at the pharmacy, John? It's not your neighborhood. I have never seen you before. No one here has ever seen you around before. You had no place there."

"I go where I want."

"So you say. Please go away, now. You are tiring."

The rest of the prisoners had dispersed and wandered the cell. The wounded men walked the cement floors. They stared out the bars down the hall to where the guards were located, and street-lights poured in through high windows. They were certainly planning something.

Chambers had given up on this city long ago when he realized he could never make a difference with it. People like Arlen were every-where, scurrying like roaches under rotting sofas. But despite it Chambers couldn't hope that one day he could change something, even slightly. That might never happened, but there was always a chance the city might be at least a little cleaner. Just a small spark was all he needed.

Chambers sat on the bench by the wall and folded his arms. The last thing he wanted was to spend the night in jail, never mind in a Summer-side jail of all places. He'd been around long enough to know how bad the criminal element can get around here. This wasn't as bad as it could get.

"You've got the time, Shane?" Arlen asked the man to his left.

Shane peered down the hall. "Ten after midnight."

"Just as hoped."

Chambers pulled up his shirt collar. "Someone is willing to bail you out? What a sucker."

"That isn't your business, John."

"Fair enough, chubs."

Hair suddenly stood on the back of Chambers' neck. A motor rumbled outside, and it was getting closer. Chambers jumped up, but it was too late.

The entire building rocked, and prisoners fell over shouting. The motor ceased entirely, and a new sound emerged. Pops shot outside the station as did officers yelling. Cops ran down the hall beyond the cells towards the front of the building. Every prisoner shook themselves awake in confusion. All of them, that is, except for Arlen.

The ventilation system whined and creaked above their heads letting in the smell of oranges rotting in the sun. Wooziness struck Chambers, and his eyelids threatened sleep.

"They're here," Arlen said. "Now for business."

Before Chambers could ask a question, the chubby doomsayer slipped a small round object from under his tongue and swallowed it. None of the other dozen thugs did anything of the sort. The smell from the ventilation strengthened with every passing moment. The other cellmates soon drifted off into slumber as they slumped over. Arlen grasped the bars and squeezed. They bent under his strength.

Chambers pulled back on the madman's shirt collar but couldn't budge him.

"I've no time for you, John."

A bout of dizziness sent Chambers blinking. "Since when did you get powers?"

"Apparently, you know more about me than I first thought. I would have liked for us to be friends, but it's much too late for that. See?"

The men in the cell dropped like flies, as did the cops running in the halls towards the front of the building. Chambers' vision softened and faded, but still he clung to Arlen.

"I regret to inform you that this not my power, John. I am powerless, like you."

"You just—," he said, slurring. "You just bent the bars."

"It was a gift. I've no power like the diseased calling themselves protectors of justice or the like. But I'm generous. Here is my gift to you."

Arlen placed his palm on Chambers' forehead, and a rush of black illness filled his thoughts. Death, misery, and cinders of what remained of humanity, all merged together to form a cohesive picture of negative beauty in his brain. Chambers vomited before his head landed against the jail cell floor like a cement block.

"Enjoy the vision of our new tomorrow, John."

Chambers twitched and mumbled in his darkening world before sleep swallowed him. The last thing he saw was Arlen throwing open the cell and roaring in triumph.

II.
VISIONS OF RAGNAROK

"Drink the water if you start to go under."

Chambers forced his eyes open as the slumber barreled down on him. The other men in the cell had already fallen into sleep. If he hadn't bitten his tongue he would have joined them.

This wasn't simple gas in the ventilation. When taking the job, he was told to watch out for strange magic, but Chambers didn't believe it. Why should he? Powers might exist, but Magic didn't.

Chambers crawled back up and wobbled out the open cell door. Aside from a set of boots thumping far ahead, the building was silent. With a grunt, he leaned against the wall and slid forward down the hall towards the evidence room. Sleep threatened to pull him into its thrall, so Chambers slapped his cheeks. He had never screwed up a job before, and he wouldn't start now.

Chambers remembered the man knocking on his apartment window as he slept. The large behemoth of a man beckoned him to approach the fire escape he sat on. A vigilante. Chambers' heart had nearly jumped out of his chest when the man wearing a knight helmet called his name.

When he calmed down, the vigilante offered him the wad of cash for a job.

"You're giving me full pay upfront?" Chambers asked.

"I know your work." He put a small nylon bag down on the fire escape. "You always do what you say you will."

"So do you. You're that vigilante that's

been all over the news for rescuing the mayor's daughter. You don't need my help. You can do it yourself. You've *done* it yourself. Didn't they even call you Ragnarok?"

"My time is just about over," he said. His helmet jangled with a nod. "You want revenge for Sunset Red, correct? There is no better man to ask about their fate than Arlen James."

Ragnarok descended the escape into the dark alley not once looking back. But still Chambers didn't understand his presence here.

"This is a lot for only one man," Chambers said. "Who is this Arlen guy?"

"You will see when you reach him. I've left the rest in the bag. Good luck."

That was the last time Ragnarok had been seen in Summerside, as far as he knew. No more rumors about the vigilante surfaced, and that was weeks ago. But now, here Chambers was carrying out that madman's final request as if he owed that guy something.

Chambers shoved his way into the evidence locker swearing the whole way. Of all the stupid jobs to take, he had to agree to this one.

Since every cop in the building had fallen asleep, he easily entered the evidence room and found his own supply of taken goods in storage. All he had was the water bottle his employer had given him and his pocket knife. The locker slammed shut as he sauntered out, stepping over prone policemen in the way. He downed some of the water, and his head swam with each sip.

The headache pumping in his skull wafted away like a deflated balloon. He removed a handgun from one of the cops and kept moving towards the back of the station.

Down the hall, he rounded on the interrogation room where rough voices whispered back and forth. Chambers kept close to the wall to make sure he heard every word.

"Hit him again," Arlen said.

Someone grunted. "He's almost awake."

Chambers focused on each voice as they tried to wake a prisoner in their midst. Not one of the others did he recognize but he counted at least four men were inside.

"Wake up, Commissioner," Arlen said. The sound of smacked skin reverberated out into the hall. "I need answers."

A gruff voice mumbled. It had to be the sleeping Commissioner.

Arlen whistled. "Sergeant, you told me the

Commish here knew something about our missing shipment of blood casements. But the Lieutenant over there told me that the truck was never found. Which of you is lying?"

"Neither of us," the higher pitched man said. He was apparently the Sergeant. "It was never found, as far as the public knows. But I heard word that the Commissioner assembled a task force to investigate what else they found in that truck. Graffiti and about three dead men with bullets to the brains. Three of our missing men. Who else could he be searching for?"

"So it wasn't the police that executed those men? Curiouser and curiouser!"

"I'm not telling you anything," a smoker's voice said. He coughed violently. "What is the meaning of this attack? Who are you, and why are my men helping you do this?"

"Those are a lot of questions, John. I hate to stifle such a curious mind, but you need to remember that I asked you first. Where is our truck? We checked the impound lot; we browsed evidence, and we have men on the inside. Someone is holding it."

"It's not in Summerside," the Commissioner said. "It's already been destroyed. We got word from someone higher up."

"Oh," the Sergeant said. "The Brother isn't going to like that."

Arlen sighed. "Our precious sacrifice has been co-opted. You can kill him, Lieutenant."

The clicking of a trigger hammer caused Chambers to swing around the threshold with his own stolen weapon ready. Four men including Arlen waited around a man tied to a chair in the center of the room.

Two of the cops drew their guns, but Chambers fired first. A shot slammed into the chest of the taller man and the follow-up put two in the second's breastbone. The third got off a bullet that went wide before Chambers popped his skull. Arlen put up both hands as Chambers sidled into the interrogation room and around the table. Three down meant the crazed man was alone.

"Who are you?" the Commissioner asked. "Are you from another department?"

On the floor, the dead men's skin melted away, as did their bones. Their clothes sizzled to nothing leaving only empty space where their bodies had been. Chambers swore.

"He is no one, John. In fact, he is in this as

deep as I am." Arlen winked at Chambers. "Is that not right?"

The sound of screeching sirens settled on Chambers' nerves. The cops could not be allowed to take him. Not now.

"Let's go, Arlen. We're going for a walk."

He shoved Arlen out of the room, leaving the Commissioner in the chair.

"Where are you going?" the Commissioner said. "What happened to their bodies? Someone explain this!"

"Stay put," Chambers said. "Cops are on the way. This guy owes me answers."

"If you say so, John. Please just don't shoot. I don't condone senseless violence."

"Give your snake-tongue a rest, Arlen."

Chambers dragged the lanky scum down the hallway towards the emergency exit. The Commissioner called after in vain. Sirens sounded closer with every passing moment.

He forced Arlen outside an emergency exit, and the pair tumbled through the maze of Summerside alleys. Humidity instantly choked their breaths.

Cop cars whizzed by the alleys. Chambers kept his weapon aimed squarely between Arlen's shoulders as the overwhelming pitch passed over them. As much as Chambers wanted to put two in the back of his skull, the last thing he needed was an obvious corpse leading back to him—assuming this scum even became a corpse. At the same time, there were other questions that needed answering, and Arlen had them.

They slipped out the alleys blocks away from the station. There, the tall hill covered in tombstones awaited. The pair passed through the gate and through a line of trees towards the graveyard.

St. Ambrosia was an ancient cemetery, older than Summerside itself from before the rebuild. Many of the graves had been desecrated long ago, and few names remained due to the chaos that was life back then. Nonetheless, he did know some of the more recent burials in this place and one in particular he needed to visit.

"Very morbid, John. Are you found of luring victims to their plots?"

"Don't make any cute moves. I'm going to show you something, so keep up."

He pushed the killer conman through the freshly-cut grass and trimmed trees into the dark of the night. No one ever visited after sunset, not even kids on a lark. As he moved forward, his stomach crumpled into a tight ball. His head told him he was being watched, and his heart told him to leave; but the poison in his soul needed this man alive, at least for now. No matter what happened, answers came before anything else, and he would get them.

Halfway up the winding pavement roads the duo met a maze of cleaned, yet cracked, graves. They stopped before one in particular. Chambers stood behind Arlen who read the name as if he were a dyslexic five-year-old.

"Jamie and Rose Hunter. Died three years ago. Do I know them, John?"

"Jamie was a member of a now-defunct group called Sunset Red. His sister was gunned down in front of his apartment. Two days after her funeral, he was thrown from his roof. Graffiti sprayed on the pavement said *Blood for the New Age* on it. For the last three years, random people have been disappearing all over the city, and rumors of a blood cult have been going."

"Oh gosh, that sounds horrific. But I won't deny it looks bad! We were going to kill the Commissioner, so I can see why you would make that connection. It's just misguided paranoia."

Chambers jabbed the barrel into Arlen's spine. "What's the blood for, buddy?"

Arlen kept blandly staring at the grave.

"Thinking up a lie won't save you," Chambers said. "You're going to get on your knees, and I'm going to end you humanely. Be grateful. This is a fitting end to a monster like you."

The fat man dropped to his knees and sighed. "I was hoping you were better. Revenge is pathetic. All that time and energy wasted on the dead-and-gone instead of what is to come. You should be exhausted of focusing on such frivolities."

"This isn't revenge, punk." Strangely for him, it wasn't. The longer he remained around Arlen, the more his brain and gut churned, and his hair stood on end like a mad anxiety breaking through. "This isn't about honor, justice, or anything personal. It's what needs to be done."

"And you call me crazy. What gives you the right to execute me?"

"It needs to be done. I can live with the consequences." Chambers drew back the hammer on his stolen weapon. "So everybody else wins."

"Slow down!" a voice shouted. "No need

to be wasteful."

The graveyard stirred dozens of feet away and around them. The silhouette of a man crossed out from behind one of the birch trees and through the graves emerged a baker's dozen of men wearing suits after him. All were surprisingly-well-coifed despite the location and time, and each held an automatic rifle. A chorus of clicks held Chambers still with his gun on Arlen.

"You don't want to die," the new man said. His voice boomed like a politician practicing before a mirror. He adjusted his black tie and cleared his throat. "No one wants to die, friend. We will settle this like civilized men. I am Olaf, and Arlen's ally. Consider letting him go, and I might have answers for whatever questions you may have."

Chambers watched the men aiming their weapons from the shadows. They might be far, but they still circled him. The only gap was the path before him down the hill behind the grave and through the brush. That would make him an easy target. "Answers or not, your friend here will die."

"Goodness, sir, there is no need to be so violent. Did Arlen do you wrong?"

"Not anything worth shooting him for."

"Then why are you so willing to execute him?"

"Because he should die." A savage thought twinged in Chambers' brain. That ridiculous notion of evil he thought of when he looked at this guy kept flaring up. His job was to stop the murder of the Commissioner. He should be finished with this mess. "Your friend is scum."

"You don't even know me, John."

"One look at your disgusting smile is all I need."

"You are acting like a child," Olaf said. "Not a gentleman. We might as well put you down now. There is no room for such lowlifes in our city."

"Tell me who your top guy is." Chambers kept his barrel trained on Arlen's skull as he scanned the well-dressed goons. "New player in town? Affiliated with the mob? The gangs? Or just a bunch of rich fools with too much time on your hands? Tell me, and I'll let this crazy go."

"Pining for membership?" Olaf asked. "Was this just a silly attempt at courting us with your thuggish traditions and antiquated sense of belonging? No. The Inner Light makes offers; it doesn't take them."

"You didn't quite answer me. What kind of group steals blood trucks, assaults a police station, and sends out hired killers to find just one member? You're just a plague on this city."

"Not quite, sir." Olaf flashed a toothy grin. "We exist to lead what remains of humanity to the Promised Land beyond the shadows. We have had enough of this world of unclean powers and wish to start anew in a land untouched by mud and dirt. But peace requires sacrifice. The world demands sacrifice."

"Did you eliminate Sunset Red?"

"That is a name I have not heard in a dog's age. Perhaps, we did finish them. Why should you care if a hive of wasps has been torched? Were you a member?"

"I was," Chambers said. "Taking them out requires skill. I assume you got the Grounders and Haze, too. You must have some skilled men, or powers, in your arsenal."

"Powers are for the impure. What is your name?"

"That doesn't matter. You're planning on killing me anyway."

"Very true, and good point. My curiosity

has reached its limit. I bid you a good day."

The men raised their rifles, and a chorus of clicks cried out. Chambers had debated on firing first when a single thin red beam streaked through the black night and overhanging lamp-posts. A sniper. He was the first one to notice it tracing Olaf's skull.

The resounding crack cut through the darkness, crushing into skin and sending a mist of red blood out of the enemy's head. Olaf didn't utter much of a cry before his corpse rocked back.

"Sniper!" several men screamed.

Chambers hopped the grave behind him and dashed down the hill without waiting for further activity. The sniper gave him an exit, and he wouldn't waste it. Chambers weaved through gravestones and neatly-trimmed bushes on the way back down. Gunfire erupted behind him, and some shots broke stone and burst bark around him.

He slipped through the steel gate and turned back to see his pursuers. A sharp piercing pressure rocked his left shoulder. He'd been shot. His bleeding wound burned.

Still Chambers ran on. He weaved through abandoned warehouse lots as his arm sang with pain. Warm blood trickled down his bicep. Foot-steps far behind pounded against pavement.

The tables had been turned: now he was the prey!

III.
DOWN BY THE RIVER

Chambers slid back to consciousness. The cold steel girders pressed against his flesh which clashed against the warm wind. He pushed his back against a metal beam and looked out over the canal waters as he regained his composure. The breeze set his shoulder ablaze.

He slipped his pocketknife free and slashed a piece of white shirt out from under his coat. He stuffed the fabric between his teeth and removed his jacket.

A count of three allowed him to calm his nerves. Then with a thrust, he dug his knife into the wound. The shirt piece in his teeth absorbed his agony.

He had been shot before. This was part of the game. Much as he would have preferred to get the bullet out in a more sanitary manner, there just wasn't time, or an opportunity. Right now laying low took priority over health.

The aching caused his jaw to clench. This never got easier.

Down in the water, shallow from a particularly dry summer, he spied figures wading through the hip deep canal. They skulked slowly in his direction. Slowly, it dawned on him that he might have seen them before. However, they soon vanished like a mirage, leaving Chambers alone under the bridge again.

Chambers let out a muffled yell as the bullet popped out of his arm, banged against the steel girder, and splashed into the now-empty canal below.

He removed the piece of shirt from his mouth and tied it around his armpit. He slid his coat back on and grimaced at the resulting pain. The makeshift bandage would have to do.

"I think I heard something this way," a voice said.

Chambers stiffened and went for the filched gun. The weapons had two shots left. He had quite nearly forgotten firing blindly behind in his escape. Another firefight would go badly for him.

Footsteps tapped over the bridge. He

counted three men.

Wooziness passed over Chambers. He rubbed his eyes and pinched the bridge of his nose.

He'd heard stories about a merciless hunter of the night—someone called *the Abyss* who used knives and disappeared into the dark afterwards. Perhaps they had finally crossed paths. Chambers swallowed his breath. This night couldn't go any worse.

Loud pops followed by gurgling brought Chambers back to life. Bullets?

A horrid scream erupted from the bridge, and a black shape plummeted past Chambers over the side. It was a man in a suit with combed black hair—one of the graveyard thugs. The well-dressed pursuer splashed down in the water, his body bobbing for air before the canal swallowed him whole. He never came up for air. It was as if the body had disintegrated.

Silence ruled the night again, and Chambers waited for a sign. This could have been the sniper from earlier, but that didn't mean the gunner was on his side. Summerside was never that simple. The Inner Light had to have rivals, and, hopefully, they weren't the psychopathic type.

"But you're not like that, Billy. You think you are, but you don't know."

That fool had gotten into his head again. Even after death, he was a pain in the neck. All Chambers wanted to do was what he was good at, but the city had enough murderers to make up for the surplus of gutter scum, assassins, and wanna-be villains. Then there were the people with powers and the vigilantes on top of it. Why did he come back to this city? He didn't need Sunset Red, and he didn't care when they were destroyed. They had wanted his head, after all. And yet for some unknown reason he still thought about it all the time.

But he had no need for nostalgia. Chambers clutched his gun and perked his ears.

He caught a glimpse of the canal below, and a wave of cold fear washed over him. Was the water moving again?

"I'm coming down there," a new voice said. "Hold your fire. I am unarmed."

The harsh tone betrayed the words this man spoke, but Chambers kept his trigger finger ready. Metal rattled as the speaker descended the stairs.

But the figure wasn't quite what Chambers

expected. Instead of some hardened thug, a plain, forgettable brown-haired man in a suit approached him through the maze of metal beams. At least, he *almost* looked plain. The longer Chambers stared into the eyes the more his hair stood on end.

The eyes turned hard emerald before passing into a bright green glare like the moon shining through fog. Chambers aimed at his heart.

"Easy, William," the man said. "I'm just laying my cards on the table." The skin on his face warbled like a mirage. Within a second, the façade of this man's appearance lifted and revealed wild charcoal black hair atop a ghostly face as pale as bone. He wore a thick leather jacket to match the stranger's demeanor. The black mask around his eyes reflected moonlight. "You did well tonight."

The gun never wavered from the vigilante's chest. "How do you figure?"

"I've been keeping a tab on you since you came back to town. You did well hiding, but I have ways of finding what I need. Tonight was different from your routine. You weren't meant to be at the police station. You were keeping your nose clean. Why did you get involved?"

"A crazed vigilante paid me to stop a psycho from killing a cop. That's as far as my involvement goes. I bet you know the guy who hired me."

"Regardless of that—he paid you to stop a murder. Mission accomplished. Go home."

"The men I killed vanished into the air. I want to know what happened."

"They're not dead—they went back to their master. Leave. It doesn't concern you."

"Spare me the moralizing. You just killed three men."

"Three?" the masked man said. "You miscounted. I sent Floyd down into the bay where he had sent many before, and I gunned down Jacky for the men he tortured to death weeks ago and for the one he was about to kill. Ray was just a fresh-faced rookie in over his head. I let him go. None of them are dead. The Inner Light members can't be killed that easily."

"You're well informed. I suppose this gives you more of a say than me."

"I know more than you," he said, without a hint of condescension, "because I was given the ability to. I have three powers. One I was born with, one I was given, and the third as a result of the first two. But I don't mean to belittle you. I watched you in that graveyard. You perceived an error in Arlen without knowing why. I can aid you in using that talent for greater things."

Chambers chuckled. "I don't even have your name."

"You can see it in scribbles all over this town. I am seeking those who will put a stop to the festering wound that is Summerside before it is infected further. We are short on time. I wish to hire you for a job. Tomorrow evening at six. Go to St. Donovan of the Plains Church on Faust Avenue. A man named Terry will be there. Tail him but keep your distance. Report to me if he goes anywhere other than his home. That is all."

"Without any pay?"

He pointed to where the thug fell into the canal. "You were already paid."

"It's like talking to a bull."

Another job so soon sounded ridiculous. He was already half dead, and he let his emotions lead him to this situation. Why was he even in Summerside?

Chambers slid back against the beam, and a light like sunrise glinted off the waters below. He remembered Jamie and Rose. Were those two trying to tell him something from beyond the grave?

No, he was losing it.

The man in black stood still as if waiting for Chambers to make a comment. But before he could say anything to his rescuer, consciousness left him.

The last thing Chambers heard were words from the strange man,

"Someone will be with you soon."

IV.
FOR YOUR OWN GOOD

The pain kicked in, and Chambers woke with a start. A sturdy mattress lay under his fingernails, and his eyes opened to the darkened room of some motel. The closed blinds let in a sliver of sun which cast faint rays along the shaggy grey carpets at the foot of the bed. There an older woman stood, grasping a torn piece of what looked like fabric as she sat beside his removed coat and shirt. Her eyes widened at his sudden alertness.

After a second, it hit him that she held the piece of shirt he had wrapped around his shoulder. The woman swallowed her voice and pointed at his shoulder. A fresh wrapped bandage had been applied to his wound.

She wasn't bad looking as far as stressed out doctors go. Chipmunk cheeks and chestnut hair helped to disguise the dark circles under her tired eyes. She wore no jacket over her yellow blouse and slightly dumpy form, which was just as well since the humidity in this room could have choked out a bear. She slid on a pair of sunglasses and lifted a leather bag off the bed.

He rubbed his numbing shoulder. "Did you bring me here?"

"I was called." She packed what looked like forceps into the bag and tucked it under her arm. "*He* already left. Before that, he said you know what you have to do."

"You're with him?"

"We don't do names. He already knows enough for the both of us. But I will give you some advice." She glanced at the ceiling before she spoke again. "Two pieces, actually."

"You cleaned me up. I guess I can listen to what you have to say."

"First, no heavy activity with that shoulder. Even on your upcoming job—whatever that entails." She took a deep breath and turned towards the front door before she continued. "Do yourself a favor and stay here until you absolutely have to leave. No matter what you might see. It's for your own good."

"Was I hit with poison?" He rubbed his eyes. "I am feeling a bit groggier than usual."

"*He* touched you. I've seen what one touch from him can do. If he's hired you, he's certainly going to test you first. You'll see things—people. It will start at any time you're awake. I'm not sure; I've never seen it myself. No matter what happens, don't panic and stay put."

The masked man did say something about having a power. Three, to be accurate. That had to be a lie since no one who had a power had more than one. Chambers leaned back in bed and let out a sigh.

"Okay," he said. "I'm staying put. Thanks for the patch up, doc."

"I'm a nurse, and you're welcome. Remember: stay put!"

The door shut, and he turned over in the bed. The clock above the television told him it was five in the morning.

Powers or not, he had until the evening to decide whether to take this job. Even though the masked man had helped him out three times so far, Chambers wasn't sold on this wannabe hero. He never even wanted to come back to Summerside, and wouldn't have if . . . if . . . whatever reason was he there for?

A migraine burrowed in his brain. He ran palms across his forehead.

This used to be so easy. Do the jobs, get the green, and move on. But work thinned; the money got dull, and moving on was impossible. His head mercilessly ached as he tried to push the thoughts away. That sunrise poking through the blinds wasn't helping.

He sat on the bed's edge. His dry lips cried out for water, and he needed to think of anything else.

The figure of a man in a green suit leaning against the bathroom door provided that very distraction. It took all of Chambers' experience in the game to not show his surprise.

The man in the suit had tied-back rusty-gold hair and a thin face with only one faded cut that ran between his smoke-colored eyes across his small nose. Chambers froze when he realized he wasn't seeing things. He knew this man, and he couldn't be standing there. But he was.

"This is his power," Chambers said. "He

makes you see things from your past."

"It's not quite what he does, Billy. Do you think he would be setting off so many rumors around this town if that was all he did?"

This thing spoke. Chambers shook his head. "So it's hypnotism."

Jamie Hunter chuckled just like he did when he was alive. "Always the skeptic, Billy. It's good to see you again. I'm honored that I get to be your first visitor."

"First what?"

"When he touches you, it takes hours for the power to fade, depending on how hard a shot he doses you with and how strong a constitution you have. You needed it. This was the only way he could get through to you about what's happening in this city."

Chambers let his feet feel the carpeting under his toes and forced himself up. He tripped as he approached the mirage of Jamie. The fake man smiled even as Chambers punched it, hitting nothing but air. The wall shook, but the false visitor remained undeterred.

"Don't make it harder on yourself, Billy. Accept this."

"*Accept this*, he says." Chambers barreled

into the bathroom and twisted the sink tap. He vigorously splashed his face. "I've accepted a lot of things in my life, Jamie. The world ended centuries ago when powers appeared—or magic as they called it at the time—and everything fell apart. Finally, after centuries of endless back and forth fighting, we pulled it together. But nothing changed. Summerside is as bad as anything I've heard about in the old world. How many times do I have to accept that putting a bullet in a monster is inevitable? That it's never going to end any other way?"

Jamie's voice remained unshaken. "It will end, but not the way you want it to. Calm down. You always had better sense than I did. Why else did you run from Sunset Red? That's why you're the only one of us that didn't get iced. The world is changing, but it's not going where you think it is. There is a war brewing in the shadows. You can be an agent to prevent worse things from coming. You can do something. You don't have to be a failure like I was."

"You were just doing your job."

Jamie laughed softly. "You didn't know this, but I failed my last mission. After you ran, Sunset Red went off the rails and started taking on more disturbing work. I was supposed to end a bunch of teenage kids on the town one night and gather their blood for a service. Not only did I refuse, but they then used me as bait to lure out enemies—the Inner Light. Too bad they didn't expect to be eaten by those monsters next. Now you're all that's left, because you were smarter."

Chambers stared up at his reflection of bloodshot eyes. "Which one of them did it?"

"That's not why I'm here. This isn't about me. I'm telling you to take this job."

"And if I do, will you disappear?"

A sad grin spread across Jamie Hunter's ephemeral face. "You're going to see worse than me before the day ends. Just don't give them too much thought if they don't speak."

Before Chambers could say a word, Jamie Hunter vanished like mist in a high wind. The room became barren once again. Only the ticking of the clock kept him company.

Chambers threw on the shirt left by the bed and his coat. He stormed out of the motel room and into the hallway. Harsh sunlight smashed his eyes and headache.

"Forget this," he said. This masked man thought too much of himself if he believed he had the right to do this to anyone. He was just as bad as Arlen's pals. "I'm out."

Chambers exited out into the early light of Summerside, his head still pounding. He passed through the crowd on their way to their morning destinations. Men in suits and women in dresses, just like always. He never thought more of them than that. They were part of another world than his. Why was he supposed to care about what happened to them?

This was just the way things had to be. Nothing changed. Nothing ever does.

But his mind began to play tricks on him. Chambers saw others amongst the madding masses—sprinkled amongst their numbers were those he knew more intimately. Men in suits, well-coiffed and dapper, and punks in shabby clothing and smudged, all stained with blood trickling from their foreheads or seeping through their suit jackets and shirts watched him closely from inside the slow stampede. Their dead stares showed neither hate nor pity—just emptiness. They were all dead.

He knew this because he had been the one to kill them.

Some attempted to push through the living, seemingly unaware they were spirits, and passed through every man and woman on their way towards him. Chambers quickened his pace, nearly knocking over an old couple on their way to the nearby furniture store. He apologized as he passed, his voice trembling far too much.

The only place he could think to go was the church the masked man had told him about. It was either that or let one of these corpses touch him and that notion terrified him more than death.

But the dead men did not remain consistent. They vanished, reappeared in other places, and some showed their faces more than others did. Lips moved on all of them, but whether they had any voice was impossible to discern in the morning noise. He had simply hoped they would go away.

They never did.

Chambers sweated as the cold of the living crowd pressed on him tighter. What would happen if the dead reached him?

He tried not to imagine his potential fate and dashed down the street. There were still twelve hours until the scheduled time, but he couldn't wait.

Death had found him and would not let go. He fought off the urge to laugh. Wasn't this what he wanted? No, not from corpses. Not like this.

Chambers ignored both the noise of the city and the silence of the dead as he hoofed it through the sweltering Summerside streets. He couldn't die yet—not with a mission to complete—and thanks to Jamie, if that was really him, he knew what he needed to do. Those who ended his friend's life and those like him would pay. Arlen's crew had much to answer for. This was Chambers' last chance, and he would take it.

Not even the dead would stop him.

V.
I WANT TO LIVE

The humidity enclosed on Chambers even as the morning sun evaporated behind the giant wooden doors of the church. A straight carpeted path through pews waited before him. Light organ music played from near the altar. The tall raised roof became shadowed by the sun shining through the stain glass. None of those dead men were anywhere to be seen inside.

It took two hours of running through the streets and crowded blocks, but now he could ease up. Incense tickled his nostrils and brought a grin to his face. Never had he been so happy to smell that junk.

He crossed the pews towards the front, passing spiral pillars and lit candles along the way. He sat and leaned back with his head facing the ceiling. Finally, some relief.

"Can I help you?"

An old priest loomed over him. Chambers stifled a yawn. "I hope so. Do you know a man named Terry? We need to have a few words."

"Hopefully, not violent ones."

"Too tired for that. I didn't get much sleep last night. Men in masks can be royal pains."

"Have you heard of The Seeker? He's been in the news quite a bit recently."

The name struck Chambers like lightning, frying thoughts in his mind. He had heard that name before—the name of the unknown vigilante destroying the minds of criminals. Some babbled incoherently before ending their own lives, and others went mad in the nut house. However, those that survived seemingly unscathed from their encounters graduated to worse and worse depravities. Just dealing with what little he had seen showed Chambers how impossible that had to be. You couldn't just ignore these ghosts.

As interesting as that might have been to speculate on, another question remained. Chambers had someone to find.

"He said Terry regularly comes here around six in the evening," Chambers said. "You probably don't believe me, but I'm not here to hurt him. I'm here for information."

"I can't tell you about him, but if you stick around you might meet one who does. By the way, Mass is beginning in less than an hour. Consider attending. It will do you good."

"I'm not sure about that, but thanks."

"Thank you for coming." The priest took a step towards the rear of the church.

"Wait," Chambers said. He clasped the priest's forearm. An idea struck him like a hammer to the head. "What do you know about magic?"

"Those who wish to use the supernatural for their own personal ends are committing a great evil. Have you been involved in it?"

"*Involved* is the wrong word. There are people who practice that stupid junk, but does it have anything to do with powers?"

"Those are a natural phenomenon as far as we know. People are born with them. Those who would use magic want power beyond even that. Why do you ask?"

"I'm not even sure myself. Does Terry come to Mass?"

"Not daily, but someone who knows him might come by today. It is possible. Please stay. It would be good for you."

The priest moved to the entranceway where an old woman had just walked in.

Chambers checked his phone and saw that was just after seven. He rubbed his forehead, hoping to get the aches out.

He needed to get his priorities in order. There was a takeover going on in the Summerside underbelly. The Seeker was one of the few aware of this war, and he wanted Chambers with him.

But he had no reason to join that loon. Chambers' ties with the underworld had been forcefully severed long ago, and those involved with him were no longer among the living. He could return to his quiet life and forget about any of this. It had nothing to do with him.

"I wish it didn't," he said under his breath.

Before last night, he might have still thought he was unrelated to this. Sitting in the church, he couldn't help but mull over the dead following his every move and what that would mean for him. What would a city run by this Inner Light be like?

When Chambers looked up again, he quickly noticed other people taking their seats. At least two dozen elderly and mothers with their children filled the pews. The organ quickly sounded, and the people stood for their service. He had apparently lost track of time.

At the back, he spotted one younger man, possibly around his age, kneeling and apparently at prayer. He was divorced from the rest and kept his sandy hair lowered and tucked between his arms. As the rest sang, he remained isolated in his own universe. He didn't once move even as the music came to an end, and the priest began speaking.

Chambers quietly shuffled over and took a seat beside the kneeling man.

The man didn't look up at him. "You're not used to churches, are you?"

"They make me nervous." Chambers made sure to keep his voice just low enough. "Do you happen to know a man named Terry? It's urgent."

"Terry doesn't like to be disturbed by strangers. He's a paranoid person."

"I don't care about his phobias. There is a group of dangerous people, and he might have the key to finding them."

"The world isn't going to end by tonight. He will be here later. Can't you wait?"

Chambers clicked his tongue. "I wouldn't be bothering strangers if I thought I could."

"This is about the shooting from last night."

"Shootouts are no strangers to Summerside. I'm looking for someone who wants to do a lot worse than shoot people. Terry knows who I mean."

"I'm Terry, and I can't help you. All I can tell you is that there is a force in this city that wants to crush us into paste, and we can't fight it. I've seen stuff you wouldn't believe."

"Where do I find Arlen, Terry? He's the one, right? I just knew in my gut, deep down past my experience and cynicism that this man was evil. What do you know about him?"

"I know about as much as anyone who escaped an attempt to be nailed to railroad tracks.

The one thing I've heard is that a man wearing a tattoo of a lotus has been hanging around at the Purple Rose Club on Crescent, and he's been asking for me. But I don't know if he's involved with this. Maybe he's with you."

"No one is involved with me. They're fishing. Nobody has approached this guy because they think it's a trap, and they're right. These guys want The Seeker and think you know him."

Terry finally looked up at Chambers, and an expression dawning on his ugly mug like he had just discovered grime on his shoe. He shook his head. "I don't know The Seeker. I don't know anyone anymore except dead men. I just want to live."

"You will," Chambers said, standing up. The priest had begun to read something about a man named Omri. This was his cue to exit. "Thanks for your help, Terry. I can handle the rest."

"Don't tell them I sent you."

"You didn't. I won't tell them anything. It's going to be a good talk."

Chambers slipped out the exit before anyone noticed him leaving. He made a straight line through the alley on the side of the church. The subway wasn't long off. He had to get back to his safe house and stock up, then he could get on with this.

The key was Arlen. Ragnarok had sent Chambers after him for a reason, and that group in the graveyard proved the vigilante's hunch about them correct. Maybe his type knew what they were doing after all.

"You are still stupid, Billy. Slow as ever."

Chambers stopped dead in the middle of the church parking lot. Only a handful of old beat up cars and a few trucks sat in the empty space. For a moment, he had begun to believe that the voices had returned.

"It hasn't worn off," Rose said. She appeared beside him like the morning sun. That familiar smile dawned on her pale lips under the wild strawberry blonde hair he knew so well. "Lucky you, huh?"

He tried to respond, to give her back what she always gave, but his tongue refused to flap. His instinct to pretend everything was normal flared up in some negative space in the back of his brain. Sweat glistened on his forehead.

"It wasn't your fault, Billy. It wasn't even Jamie's, and don't think I'm unaware you blamed him for a while! I should have skipped town, and I didn't. I knew what was coming, and I convinced myself it would all go away. I'm even dumber than you are."

"I—"

She sighed wistfully. "Don't force it. Why are you so certain Arlen deserves to be killed? Your moral compass broke long ago, or so you told me many times. I thought you were planning to live the rest of your days as a vagrant."

"That was the plan." He choked down the lump in his throat, pushing down the pit in his stomach. "Things change. Are you and your brother going to show up for the rest of my life?"

"That man only gave you a small dose. The fact that you've only suffered just this much is impressive. You've heard stories about what he can do with his touch."

"Then why doesn't he charge in and deal them all like this?"

"Powers have limits, Billy. The more he touches the more he risks losing himself to it. Right now, he is out of commission because of what he can do. That's why he sent you on this job instead of pursuing it himself. You are needed."

Chambers pushed forward through the alley and into the street. Rose followed beside him, passing through pedestrians. Not one person noticed this impossibility.

"The pay better be worth having my brains scrambled."

"You'll have a lot worse than that scrambled. For once, use your ears and listen."

"I'm sorry, Rose." It was as if his lips spoke words he didn't understand. The hole in his stomach filled for a moment, and his breathing paused. He forced a smile. "For everything."

"I might have been wrong about you. You're good at what you do, I've always known that. But you need to be better than that. What's coming next will push you far more than this. Follow that man. You need each other. Until next time, Billy. Take care of yourself for once."

The moment he reached the subway platform, Rose crumbled into dust and faded into the non-existent wind. The mass of people flooded around him for the next train, unaware.

Soon, the subway arrived, and the men and women in suits and dresses piled into the cars. He joined them and held onto the safety rail as they packed around him, and the train pulled

331

out.

It was unlike both the Hunter siblings to be on the same page. Usually, he had to be the ones to stop them from butting heads. At least now, he had a bead on the ones who attacked the police station. He would get to the safe house, get his tools, and move out, before that Seeker even knew what happened. That guy wanted to hire the best, and he would see what that meant.

In several of the subway seats, he saw shady men with bloody wounds staring back at him, muttering under their breaths. Of course, the crowd didn't notice.

Chambers gripped the bar as they soundlessly watched him. He would just have to trust the nurse when she said they were harmless.

She was right about one thing. He should have stayed in bed.

VI.
CARELESS

The dead men didn't need to touch Chambers to get into his head. They couldn't lay a hand on him—they were dead after all. But just looking at them made his spine shiver and sweat. Chambers got off one stop early, his muscles barely holding back from trembling into paste.

He had replayed their final moments in his mind when he gunned them down, felt every flash of pain in their flailing corpses as the bullets split skin and bone and life gave way to the embrace of death. Their feelings, hate and fear alike, sloshed through him like ice in his veins. By the time he reached the stairs out of the station, his knees had started knocking together. He had seen everything they wanted him to.

But he also saw more than they intended. He viewed their entire lives, from the first day of school to their first offense and every escalation afterwards. They died as they lived, and he had little pity for them just like when he killed them. However, a strange seed had sprouted down in his gut. It wasn't guilt or regret, but some new emotion beyond them that he had never experienced before. He wanted to be sick but refused to allow his anxious brain and jittering bones to do it. This feeling fought against him, and he pushed right back at it.

When his nerves settled, he finally stepped back into the daylight again. A fog somewhere inside had cleared and left him strangely lighter.

The sun welcomed him like an old friend, and he moved through the streets towards his destination. He checked to see that no one had followed. Hopefully, those feelings would not overtake him again.

The neighborhood was usually empty during the day, and it wasn't any different then. By eight in the morning, everyone who mattered had gone to work, was already looking for some, or was sleeping for their night shift. He met a few mothers and elderly couples on his way to his building but none suspected anything. Chambers mostly worked at night, and they knew it without knowing what he did. He passed them on the way into his apartment.

Rose's words still echoed in his ears as he put on his shoulder harness and both Eagles inside them. He loaded them and placed spare clips into his plain grey briefcase, as he always did before a big job, and changed into a new dark blue suit and jacket. At the same time, he put on his boots with the hidden knives inside. Hopefully, he could avoid bloodstains on this mission. Rose would want it that way.

Before leaving, he noticed a note on the floor tucked under his doorframe. He glanced over it and saw that it was signed by the very man who had set that power loose on him. The Seeker knew where he lived. Chambers read the note out loud.

"You're not going to listen to me, Billy, but you need to wait for the allotted time. Otherwise, you will be alone. Should you take this into your hands, realize that there is no turning back. Do the smart thing. Do what Rose would have you do."

Chambers felt his lip curl in a smile, but anger was all that boiled underneath. He tore the note in half and ate the pieces. This masked man would be the end of him.

But Chambers wasn't far from insanity himself. Not after everything he had seen since Ragnarok approached him with the mission. The Seeker was right: he couldn't turn back from this now. But the memories of those dead men caused him to shiver. This job would require something different from his usual brute force. He needed to be someone else.

But he couldn't afford being sloppy or detached. Not when monsters were out there.

The trip through the city took no time at all. Most people had already reached their destination by now, and the dead haunting him had faded. By the time, he made it to the Purple Rose on Crescent it was ten in the morning. The place didn't open until noon which either meant waiting, or being creative. He'd never been good at either before, so he decided to try the latter.

When no one was looking, he slipped down a side alley. Chambers tucked his briefcase in between a set of dumpsters but kept his loaded guns on his person. The more inconspicuous the better, but he wouldn't go in unarmed. Behind the club, three built men wearing suits smoked and had a conversation in the lot. They cursed at him.

"We're closed," the pale one in the center said.

"That's not my business," Chambers said. "I'm here to see Arlen."

All three stared. The freckled one went for his phone, and the others whispered to each other. A nearby second floor window flashed, and he didn't have to guess that someone was up there and probably aiming at him. Perhaps going in guns blazing would have been a bad call.

The freckled man nodded to him. "How do you know Arlen?"

"We met last night. I'm John."

Freckles whispered Chambers' words into the phone, then hung up.

"Okay, John, you're in. He wants to see you."

Instantly, a swarm of well-dressed men poured out of the nearby alley and converged on Chambers. He put his hands up, but to no avail. Heavy weights crashed against the back of his head and stomach until he lost balance. The world went dark.

"Get his legs," one said. "Bring him in before someone sees."

That was all Chambers heard aside from Jamie's earlier words ringing in his ears.

"It will end, but not the way you want it to."

VII.
SUNSET

Pain pricked the back of his neck when Chambers woke up. The ropes behind his back held his wrists tight, and the chair under him squeaked. A strip of cloth whipped from his eyes, and light blinded him.

A crooked smile dawned across Arlen's bruised face. "I didn't expect to see you again so soon, John."

Harsh lights beamed down on Chambers, blinding him. A blur split through the light and hit him. The punches struck him repeatedly. Arlen stood before the light, casting shadows across Chambers' bruised body.

"Are you still looking to join us? Those pieces you were carrying sure looked like you meant business. That small knife was nasty looking too. Whose blood was that on it?"

"Mine," Chambers said. He coughed some from his throat. "I haven't had a chance to kill any of you yet. I'm getting rusty."

"Olaf nearly lost his head over your friend in the graveyard. Who was he?"

"I don't know him, but I have met the guy. He's a lot meaner than me."

The cold press of a gun barrel dragged against his heart. Arlen's empty smile widened.

"How did you find us, John? Be a good boy, and we might just let you into our club. Name the name, and you will get the VIP treatment."

Chambers leaned forward in the chair, pretending his head hurt worse than it did. He made note of the layout of the room. It was a small room in the basement. Two men lurched over on either side of him, and thin shadows passed under the doorjamb ahead. There had to be at least two other men in the hall in addition to the three surrounding him.

He gripped his hands and found more than rope had bound him. Loose handcuffs around his wrists jiggled.

"You wanted to know how I found you, Arlen. Let me tell you a story. Don't worry, it's short. I'm not much in the way of a minstrel. Do you know what Sunset Red stood for?"

"A group of villains who killed other villains for green. They used brutal force to instill a sense of dread in the underworld. It was sad that they thought it would work forever."

"That's the official line," Chambers said. His left wrist twisted, and the cuff on his bone bent awkwardly. He hid his grimace with a laugh. "From what I heard, the man at the top was a pessimist. He thought the world was in its sunset, and we were nearing the end. Even after centuries of chaos and trying to pull it all together, he still believed we were in the last moments. The redder the sky at sunset, the better things will be in the morning. That would be us cashing in on chaos. We fed on misery. All of our kind does."

"You believe us the same."

"I believe you'll end up a pavement stain just like Jamie, yes. Great story, am I right?"

"Ridiculous is what it was, John. You cannot hope to leech off what is coming, as your dead allies show. They tried and now they are but a faded memory. You either harness the potential or become worm food. I am not seeing any reason you should not also be worm food."

Chambers grunted, and sat straight up in the chair. The cuffs had almost slipped off. "I thought the same about you. But I didn't quite understand why. Now, I'm starting to."

"Being a member of a murderous syndicate has warped your mind. It's no wonder you think you must kill me without a second thought. You're broken, so I forgive you, John."

"Thanks," he said, surprisingly without sarcasm. "Forgiveness is a strange beast. I do apologize for wanting to kill you without a reason. It's been a hard day, and I've come to a conclusion. The more I deal with you the more I understand. I don't want to kill you anymore."

Arlen leaned closer, cracks in his smile showing on his trembling jaw. "It is good that we are becoming friends, but you were never going to kill me. Now give me what I desire. The man who shot at us."

"No, you don't understand. I said I don't *want* to kill you anymore." Chambers eyeballed the men on either side of his chair. They were too close to draw their weapons without hitting their allies. He found that agreeable for what he needed to do. "Times change, and I think I might be changing with them, it's true. I don't want to kill you, Arlen. But I still have to do it."

"You arrogant child." Arlen elbowed Chambers in the chin. Saliva splashed out between his clenched teeth. "Must I always explain myself to you clueless masses? I seek to bring the just towards the Inner Light. There, we will all reach our true potential. All of us. You saw me in the police station. You saw the dregs behind me fall to slumber while I opened the jail doors. That came from a higher place. That was only a small piece of what I was given from the depths of my poisonous existence. I was elevated beyond even those who ruled the world for so long with their powers. They are dying. Every year, less are born with powers, and we are better for it. However, my kind is only growing. We are on the cusp of something greater, and I will help us reach it.

What gives you the right to stop progress?"

"It's not a right, but that's beside the point. I know where this path leads, and you refuse to see the broken down bridge ahead of you. So I have to stop you the only way I know."

"You can't do that if you're dead. Death has that effect." Arlen reached for the gun in his holster. "That is one truth no matter who you are."

Chambers jumped. He spun sideways in his seat, knocking the guard on his right against a wall of shelves. Chambers charged backwards, shoving the furniture into the enemy's body. The chair broke against his weight and dropped the guard.

Arlen raised his gun but Chambers cross punched and sent the fat man spinning down.

The last man moved in, flicking open a knife. He grasped at Chambers' shirt collar and flinched when his victim gripped his wrist. Chambers stomped his foot, and the knife inside his boot popped out. He spun his opponent around and kicked the blade into the attacker's abdomen. The guard shouted and hit the floor, clutching his gut.

Arlen sprang back up and drew his gun

again. Chambers lifted the guard by the shelves and put him forward as a human shield. As they moved, he swiped the firearm from the thug's belt. Both Arlen and Chambers aimed their weapons at each other.

"Throw it down, Arlen."

"This is cowardly, but not unexpected, John. You wouldn't need to resort to this sort of behavior if you were on the right side of this room."

The hallway door flew open, and two armed men peeked inside. They also raised their guns towards Chambers. The man on the floor moaned and crawled from the room. Arlen backed towards the door.

"And now what, John? You aren't leaving this room even if you kill your prisoner. This is delaying the inevitable. You came to this place just to die."

"I'm not the one that's going to die here."

"Is something happening down there?" a voice from above asked. "What's with the ruckus? We don't want the cops sniffing around again."

"Everything is fine," Arlen said. "I am dealing with the problem. Go back to your work."

Chambers would not get through this

without a few holes drilled through him. The Seeker was right—he should have waited. Now, he had three obstacles blocking his only escape.

"This is silly, John. Should anyone above hear a single gunshot, they will find you. Just be cooperative. You can make it easier by telling me who the shooter from last night was."

Before Chambers could speak, and as if by chance, a phone rang in Arlen's pocket. He reached for it and glanced at the number calling him. After a sigh, he answered it.

"What is it, Michael? Can't you tell that I'm busy?" He crinkled an eyebrow at whatever Michael had said on the other end. "Wait a mi-nute. Who are you?"

A long pause followed. Arlen's smile re-turned before he whipped the phone to the floor and stomped it. He bolted out towards the stairs.

"Kill him!" Arlen shouted.

The two guards squeezed shots off. Their bullets punctured the human shield, and their ally jerked with each hit. Chambers had lost his bargaining chip.

Before the corpse dropped, Chambers charged forward. He blitzed through the door-frame while the shots kept striking their dead ally.

A bullet punctured his left thigh, and he shouted.

Chambers shoved the corpse onto the left guard and shot the one on the right. The guard fell, firing back and hit Chambers just below the ribs. Chambers twisted and gunned down the struggling man on the left. All three soon stilled.

However, their bodies morphed into piles of green slime before dissipating into the air leaving their clothes and weapons behind. It was as if they were never real to begin with.

A shot of regret washed through him like hard liquor, and the feeling passed just as a single shot tends to. He had no time to wonder: Arlen had escaped. He took a second gun from the pile of clothes and chased after his enemy.

The man he stabbed sat against the bottom stairs, clutching his stomach. He trembled, staring at where the three men had vanished. He didn't even acknowledge Chambers' presence. After checking him for weapons, Chambers abandoned the empty basement.

The wooden stairs led straight up into an empty dance floor with more space than any he had seen since Sunset Red's infamous offices. At least, it would have been empty had a gang of men not leaned over the bar to aim their guns at him.

They fired, and bullets slashed through the air towards him. He dove under a table behind a large booth to his left, hoping the hard angle would make getting a shot off difficult. He wasn't too different from a pinball flipper and they were a slot behind one too many bumpers.

The spread of tables across the carpeted area beyond the dance floor allowed far too much space and not enough hiding places. He was trapped and outgunned.

Bullets screeched against walls and splintered table wood. While Chambers thought up a plan, one happened for him. A cacophony of new bullets fired. Several screams erupted.

Almost immediately, the room quieted. Slowly, Chambers leaned out to check.

On top of the bar stood a familiar figure in a heavy black leather jacket with matching hair and skin as white as a ghost. The Seeker held dual Eagles just like the ones they had taken from Chambers earlier. The bodies behind the bar all melted leaving his savior alone.

The piercing green eyes from behind his dark mask illuminated the already bright room. Black blood streamed like tears, and hard breaths pumped with every step Chambers made towards

The Seeker.

"I found your guns," The Seeker said. "Thank you for leaving extra ammo outside."

Chambers slid out from under the table, and his savior threw him his two weapons.

"How did you know I left the ammo outside?"

"It is how you work against larger groups. There are few more obvious hiding places than dumpsters. By the way, Arlen escaped into the parking lot. Go. I'd join you if I could."

"There's still a man downstairs. He's the only one who didn't fade away."

"I had a hunch there would be."

"Are they dead? Dead men don't disappear like that."

The Seeker leaned against the bar and grunted, his eyes bled red tears. He hadn't been shot which meant his problem must have had another source.

"Not now," The Seeker said. "You still have a mission to complete. Get going."

"I'll hold you to that!"

Chambers rushed past his savior through the hall to the left behind the bar. Boots pounded against hardwood somewhere up ahead.

It could only be Arlen!

Daylight beamed through the door as he ran through. Almost immediately, gunfire burst and shots careened against the pavement and wall. Chambers jumped sideways and easily dodged the wide spread. Ahead of him, Arlen stumbled towards a car at the end of the lot.

Chambers steadied his aim and fired. The shot flew true, and the bullet buried itself in Arlen's back and dropped him.

Slowly, Chambers approached the gangster's crumpled body. The fallen cultist flipped onto his spine and swore.

"Show me the peashooter, Arlen."

Arlen nodded to his right hand where his trembling fingers let go of the gun. However, in Arlen's left hand he held a small round stone that was as red as congealed blood left outside too long. No light shone from the oversized pebble under the high sun, and yet a sickly glare reflected from it. Arlen's trembling hands slowly lifted in defeat towards the top of his head, before he suddenly shoved the stone into his mouth and swallowed.

Bloody teeth smiled at Chambers. "You should have stopped me from eating that."

"I normally would have shot you, but I was hoping you'd choke. It's not every day you see someone go mad right in front of you."

"Mad?" Arlen laughed between breaths. "Have you still not understood who we are?"

"You're dead men."

"Still on with that? This is what is coming to all of us. This is Justice."

Foam pooled on Arlen's mouth, and he trembled as if a seizure had struck him. Skin purpled, and veins pressed against flesh. His eyes rolled back in his skull, and he fell limp.

"Justice, huh?" Chambers said. "For once, I agree with you, Arlen."

The dead man stiffened, and his eyes snapped open. "Glad to hear it, John."

Arlen suddenly launched itself towards Chambers, screaming. His bones rippled like a corpse thrown from a bridge, and Chambers fired into him.

But he kept coming.

Shots sunk into Arlen's body like sand and popped uselessly out his back. They clattered to the pavement, without a slight bit of disfigurement. Arlen slammed against Chambers and grabbed his neck. Chambers choked, white sparks filling his vision. His guns fell from his hands.

"Do you see it, John? This is what you asked for. Can you see it?"

Crimson spots formed into pictures inside of Chambers' mind where bright shadows walked night streets. The size of humans with a thick dark mist rolling off their forms, these beings had little in the way of defining features aside from white orbs where their eyes should be. The shadows converged on him as the world darkened.

But a glint distracted him. In Arlen's neck, he found a white spot. It was very transparent and difficult to see, but it existed. He could only guess it was that stone.

Chambers swung his palm upwards into Arlen's chin. His head jerked back, and Chambers headbutted him. His skull rattled against Arlen's which loosened his enemy's grip.

He dove for his guns on the pavement. After landing on his shoulder, Chambers fired.

The shots to the chest and head popped through Arlen's flesh, falling out through the other side once more. He saved his last shot and aimed at the white spot in Arlen's neck.

The enemy didn't appear to care. "You haven't learned anything, John."

"I've never been much for it."

He fired the last bullet into Arlen's neck. Flesh parted as the shot struck the white light. The wound instantly closed. No more shots were left. Chambers dropped his spent guns.

"That was a waste," the shooter said.

Arlen laughed. "Suffice to say, I—"

The gangster froze, and his face paled before reddening. He choked and wheezed and dropped to both knees. Saliva ejected from his mouth, and small bits of pale stone, now silver, sprayed out with it. The pieces smoked into cinder as they touched the pavement.

"What? No!" Arlen growled and punched the pavement. "You've taken my escape."

"All those bullets, and you aren't even dead."

"I'd rather be!"

Arlen let out a bloodcurdling scream and rocked backwards to the ground. He convulsed uncontrollably. His eyes rolled back in his head, and his voice died out in an instant. Blood trickled from his lip, but he still only fell unconscious into slumber.

Chambers climbed back up at the same moment he heard the familiar cacophony cracking through the sounds of the city. Sirens! He bolted for the alley just as the cop cars screeched down the block. The Seeker had taken his hidden bag, leaving him with nothing but the empty weapons he already carried. Now he just needed to get away before the cops caught him.

He spotted the lights flashing in the parking lot behind him. Chambers slipped out into the streets and down the alleys. Whatever he was supposed to be involved in was over. For now.

VIII.
LAST SHOT

Chambers slid into his seat at the Silverback, same as always. An old blues song played on the jukebox, and some fools started dancing. He tipped his glass as a pair of regulars passed him on the way out. They told a joke he'd heard a hundred times, but he still laughed just the same. His ribs felt every bit of it.

The young night didn't stop the place from hopping. Despite living in such a crime capital, the people knew how to have a great time. He used to know what that was like once.

The bartender poured him another, and he

appreciated it. The past twenty-four hours had been an experience he wouldn't soon forget.

A soft set of fingers clapped his shoulder. The pretty waitress gazed into his eyes with her lips settled in a straight line. "What happened with that scary guy from the other night?"

"Oh, right. Sorry, Gina. Forgot to tell you. I thought that guy was a stalker, but it turns out he just wanted to offer me a job. People in this town never do anything straightforward."

"From what you told me, that guy was creepy to the max."

"I already got it done. I won't be seeing him again. He promised."

"Pardon me if I don't sound ecstatic."

"Pay her no mind, Bill," the loudmouth at the table behind them said. "She just doesn't like seeing the customers get hurt. Especially the handsome ones. Right, Gina?"

"Oh, shut up," she said, her cheeks reddening. "All I'm saying is be careful, Billy. This town is full of monsters."

"Thank you, Gina. I get what you mean."

Gina stormed from the bar. The raucous table that had sent jokes her way got an earful from the woman who could stop the world with one word. Chambers was only glad to not be on the receiving end for once.

He smiled. Never before did he realize how much he enjoyed it here. It wasn't much, but it felt like home. That was an odd feeling he hadn't had for years.

"You're looking well, Billy."

An older-looking bushy beard man with wavy white hair sat beside Chambers on the stool. His flannel shirt and jeans made him look like he had just hopped off the truck. That might have been the case, since Chambers hadn't seen him before. However, his identity was clear.

"Your eyes still bleeding?" Chambers asked. He couldn't see The Seeker's real face, but his presence was difficult to mistake. "I can't tell."

"They're fine." His voice didn't even sound the same in his disguise. "You went through worse than I did. A rest would do you well."

"I'm not tired. Just the opposite, actually." Chambers thought a moment. "I found this blog all about you online. I was unaware you had such a dedicated base."

"Julia is good people, don't worry about her. Arlen's been arrested. Since the Commissioner fingered him, he's up the creek. *They'll* be after him to cover their trail, too. Things are about to get exciting around here."

"So? I don't need to know this. I did my part."

"You did. Here's your payment." The old man removed a wad of bills from his pocket and slid it into Chambers' hands. No one noticed as they kept shouting about the game coming on later. "It's legit, if that concerns you. You won't get in hot water over this. Also, it won't hurt you to touch my skin. My power doesn't work without direct contact, and if I will it."

"Thanks," Chambers said. He placed the wad into his jacket pocket and took a sip from his glass. "Anything else?"

"I've had my sights on you for some time."

Chambers rolled his eyes. "What don't you have your sights on in this city?"

"Have you ever heard of Lucky Spider? You remind me of him. A gangster who supposedly disappeared after his gang fell apart. Though, he was smart enough to stay out of the fray after putting his old days behind him."

"What's your point? I'm not him."

"You're right. That's why I'm offering you

a full time position."

Chambers scoffed. "You need a hired gun? You?"

"I'm not hiring you for that. You might have forgotten the low death count of this mission. I need someone who can see everything as it is. Most people know this city is broken, but there's nothing they can do for one reason or another. As you can tell from the last twenty-four hours, things can spin out of control quick. I need a right-hand man who is used to seeing the dark side. Besides, competition is getting fiercer. There's this Flatline character with electricity that shows much promise . . ."

"Give me a break. I've done enough."

"There is no better choice than you, Billy."

Unfortunately, he had a point. Arlen was only a low level player—a patsy for stirring up trouble. Worse things crawled in Summerside's shade.

Chambers sighed. This decision would change everything for him. Retirement sounded good and easy, but easy wasn't always the way to go. Every now and then, it paid to be uncomfortable.

Chambers lifted his glass and downed

what little he had left. He wiped his mouth and pounded the glass down.

"I would have said no a few months ago. Still considering it. But Arlen had something wrong with him—so did those guys in the graveyard. It was beyond what I've seen before, and I've dealt with the worst sort. I can't just turn away if there are more of them out there. But what do you want me for?"

"I need a bird in the sky to help bring justice to this city of hidden evil."

"My codename was a bird once. Most of us were."

"Condor," The Seeker said. "Would you like to give it a new meaning and start over?"

Death or rebirth were his two choices. Unfortunately he couldn't choose the former—not again, and not after what he had seen from Jamie and Rose. He couldn't face them as a coward.

Chambers took a few bills off the wad and slammed them down. "Rounds for everyone!"

"What's that for?" Gina asked. She inspected the bills as if they were going to melt.

"To the future," he said with a grin.

The Seeker stood up from the stool and

slowly strode to the exit. Apparently, he already knew Chambers' choice. He knew him too well already. That was a quality too few bosses had.

Chambers didn't even know The Seeker's real name, or if he had ever seen his face. It didn't matter. He'd taken the position and that was that. He wouldn't regret it. This was the first time he had finished a job with a feeling resembling gratitude for taking it.

And maybe he could feel that again. Jamie and Rose thought he deserved it. At least, he could give them that, and make a few bucks at the same time. Man's gotta eat.

Gina shuffled through the cash she had been given, and Chambers put up a hand.

"Keep the change, Gina. Relax a bit. For now, let's all just have a good time. Who knows what tomorrow will bring?"

"You're looking bright-eyed again," she said.

"I got a bit of spark tonight, I suppose."

Tomorrow, Condor would fly again. Tonight, Billy Chambers would party.

Just for tonight.

Hopefully the boss let him sleep in. Chambers had seen enough sunsets and sunrises to last a lifetime.

About the Author

JD Cowan is a writer with an obsession for stories and Truth. He takes pleasure in looking for Light in the places where darkness grips the tightest.

His works include "Grey Cat Blues", "Gemini Warrior" for Silver Empire, and short stories in Storyhack, the PulpRev Sampler, and the Planetary Anthology Series.

He blogs at wastelandandsky.blogspot.ca and can be found on Twitter @wastelandJD for those interested.

JD's Works

Knights of the End
Grey Cat Blues
Gemini Warrior
Someone is Aiming for You &
Other Adventures
Gemini Drifter [Coming Soon!]
Brutal Dreams [Coming Soon!]